I0659390

THE LAST WAR:
BOOK TWO

SON OF THE EMPEROR

Sylvie Grayson

Excerpt from THE LAST WAR, Book Three, Truth and Treachery, copyright ©2016 by Sylvie Grayson

For information write to
Great Western Publishing at
sylviegraysonauthor@gmail.com

ISBN: 978-0-9947345-4-9

Great Western Publishing is a trademark of Sylvie Grayson.

Cover art by Steven Novak   novakillustration@gmail.com

DEDICATION

I am blessed with wonderful support that has enabled me to write. To my husband, who gives me the freedom to work but is always ready to listen, read and lend a hand with difficult passages. To my children who had faith in me and helped with their support and practical suggestions, the choosing of titles and cover art. To Lara and Nicole, who both inspired me in choosing the cover design, to Nicole for drawing the maps and creating my author photo.

To my critique group:
Anna Markland
Reggi Allder
Jacquie Biggar, who all supported me to polish the words for publication, my many thanks.

Any errors or omissions are mine alone.

Sylvie Grayson

www.sylviegrayson.com

.

SON OF THE EMPEROR

THE LAST WAR: BOOK TWO

Sylvie Grayson

CHAPTER ONE

Along a genteel Khandarken street, the City was quiet. Dusk was just settling on the small ceremonial gardens cultivated at the front of each imposing formal residence.

Julianne Adjudicator heard thundering on the heavy front door of her father's respectable home and ran swiftly down the hall from the parlour at the unexpected noise. Beverly, their housekeeper, had already rushed to answer the summons. Two Constables stood in the doorway, the first with an ominous-looking official sheaf of papers in his hand.

"Is Little Harry Adjudicator in?" he demanded officiously. "We have information for him." He stood ramrod straight, the colour high in his cheeks.

The Old Empire had finally crumbled in upon itself after years of war, rebellion and corruption. New entities had unsteadily risen from the ashes.

Khandarken was the most stable new country in an uneasy alliance of states that for the moment held its own against the Emperor's exiled troops.

The City was the seat of national government, and most of the country's officials resided in this sedate section of the metropolis. Adjudicators, Advisors, even the Leader of the Board of Representatives were established in the elite sections of the largest sprawling borough in the country.

"He's not here," Beverly said, anxiously glancing sideways at Julianne standing in the shadows. "Can I relay a message to him?"

"When do you expect him, Ms?" The man looked even more determined.

"I'm not sure. He hasn't been home for a couple of days, and I'm afraid we've not heard from him."

He passed the papers forward. "We have a warrant to search the house, Ms, to look for Mr Adjudicator."

Beverly went pale and faltered back a step. Julianne moved forward into the doorway. "May I see, please?"

The Constable handed her the warrant and stood silent while she tried to read it. She'd seen many legal documents in her young years, as the only daughter of the Chief Adjudicator of the Supreme Court of Khandarken. But the sense of alarm she felt was overpowering her ability to even decipher the words, let alone understand them. He leaned forward and pointed helpfully to a line low on the page. "Right there, Ms. It gives us the right under the authority of the Chief Constable to search your premises."

She stepped back in a panic as the police entered. *The Chief Constable of Khandarken?* He was the most powerful man in the police, asserting law and order across the country. Why was he searching for Father? Two more men followed them in, and they spread out, several going upstairs, others down the hall toward the kitchens.

Beverly took her arm and pulled her aside to close the door. "Don't need to have the neighbours watching," she muttered. "It's bad enough with those big military transports parked out front for everyone to see." They stood together silently, listening to the thud of boots on the floor above their heads.

After a fruitless search, the men reassembled at the front door and the Constable handed her a second paper from his pocket. "This warrant says that you're bound by law to report to the Chief Constable if your father should appear here again."

And then they were gone.

~ * * * ~

That night, as Julianne lay sleepless in her bed, wondering fearfully where Father had gone and if he'd ever return, she heard her stepmother arrive home. Little Harry hadn't been a great father, but he loved his daughter and tried to protect her after his wife died. Yet when he married Zanata, he'd been infatuated by that witch of a woman, imagining he was getting a new mother for his child.

3

Julianne had loathed her from the start. The biggest passion of her young life was hatred for her stepmother. As an Adjudicator in the Supreme Court of Khandarken, Little Harry had risen to Chief Judge since the Last War ended. But recently he'd contracted a deadly disease from his philandering second wife and Julianne knew, even before he disappeared, that he was ill.

She heard her stepmother enter her own suite of rooms and presently became aware of Zanata's voice droning on behind her closed door. She must be on the voicelink. Julianne crept down the hall and into the attic space where her father had installed his listening post. She'd stumbled on it by accident one day, secretly discovering her father eavesdropping on Zanata's voicelink conversations. Since Harry had disappeared, she'd started her own listening practice, trying to piece together what had happened to her family.

Tonight Zanata was speaking to another judge adjudicator from the Supreme Court, a colleague of her father's. She recognized his raspy tone.

"So, do we have a deal?" Zanata's voice was low and warm, enticing over the voicelink.

"Yes, my dear. I think we do. Your case will come before me in a couple of days. I'm sure I can find a way around the charges. You'll be a free woman again."

Julianne was astonished. He would dismiss the charges against Zanata? *How?* What the charges claimed were true. Zanata had contracted mangohrea, a venereal disease that had no cure, and she'd infected the General's eldest son, Virgil. Virgil Regiment had died of the dread illness, not more than a few weeks ago. It was his father, General Paulo Regiment of the Khandarken military who'd insisted the charges be laid.

Zanata's sexy laugh flowed soothingly along the sound waves. "That's lovely. I'm very grateful, as you well know." She should be, it was astounding that he was willing to do this for her.

"Yah, I do. And I think the exchange is more than fair." *The exchange?* What did Zanata have that would pay for such a huge favour from a powerful figure like this judge adjudicator? Surely no man would want a liaison with her, she was the carrier of a deadly disease.

"I'll bring her to you tomorrow night after the charge is dismissed. She's a lovely girl, untouched and innocent. She'll be yours for the week. Not forever mind," and she laughed softly. *Bring whom?* Julianne felt her blood run cold. What was this bargain? Who was being traded?

"Her name is Julianne," Zanata continued, "And she's beautiful."

The rasping voice came back. "You don't have to tell me. I've seen her with Little Harry many times. I know exactly what she looks like."

Julianne didn't hear the rest. Her numb fingers dropped the listen aid and she sat back in shock.

She'd been traded to a colleague of her father in exchange for charges to be dropped against Zanata.

Alarm shot through her, zapping shock into action. She turned to run for her room, but stopped herself before she took the first step. She had to think clearly and not make a foolish move. Zanata was smart and she'd be watching.

CHAPTER TWO

Julianne Adjudicator slogged down the trail through mud that came up to her ankles. Her dark, curly hair hung in a tangled mass around her face, having broken free of the lace she'd used this morning to tie it back. Her boots were filthy, as was the hem of her dress. The tall evergreen trees pressed in on either side of her, branches reaching across to make the road dim and shadowed.

It was close to nightfall and she needed a place to rest. The trail was deserted, everyone else having the good sense to find a safe haven before dark. It could be dangerous in the Northern Territories on the roads at night. She startled at a sound behind her, but when she turned there was no one there. Her nerves were playing tricks on her. If only she could find a safe dry spot to bed down. She was very tired and her energy was low. She hadn't eaten since early morning.

Last night a good-natured farmer had taken her in, and his wife had washed her dress and hung it to dry while she slept on the bench before the fire. Now the hem of her dress was clotted with half dried mud. Her boots were covered in it, wet right through, her socks squishing inside. She shivered under her cloak.

Walking on, she scanned the landscape ahead. Through the brush at the side of the road there rose a dim shape half-hidden in the foliage. Could she be so lucky? Squinting in the gloom, she moved to the side of the track. Yes, there was something there. Gazing around carefully to make sure she wasn't followed, she broke through the bushes toward the hide roof of a hunter's hovel. Thorns dragged at her dress and hooked into the wool of her outer garment. She tore herself free and pressed closer. The hut was old and windowless, the roof sagging on one side. The door seemed to be stuck, and she tugged with all her might before it opened partway with a low groan. There was a scurrying rustle from inside, and she stepped back in alarm as a small dignified family of olinguitos, two parents and a baby, tore out through the opening. They hustled across her path and disappeared into the night.

It was pitch black inside the hut and smelled of animal droppings and rot, but she scuffed around with her feet, kicking straw into a pile. Exhausted, she sank down onto it. She'd been running for days and still hadn't found safety. Closing her eyes, she relaxed and thought of her father. Was he still alive?

The night she fled the City, she'd gathered some things together along with all the money she could scrounge, as alarm raced down her spine. It had been easy to leave. Her ident was good and the maxibuses ran throughout the night into the territories, although less frequently than during the day. She'd caught the transit to the northern hub city of Wymark, where the Governor of the Northern Territory had his office. It had taken three days to reach there.

At the station she'd noticed an ad for a rooming house. When she knocked at the door, a plump matronly woman, face flushed, welcomed her in.

"Yes, Ms. I have a room ready. How many nights will you be staying?"

"I'm not entirely sure," Julianne said. "One or two."

"That's fine." The woman dried her fingers on her apron and reached to shake Julianne's hand. "Come this way."

She led Julianne up the narrow stairs and down a gloomy hallway. "I only take two roomers at a time, otherwise it's more work than I can handle. The bathrobe is through there and there's plenty of hot water."

"Do you mind if I have a bath?"

The woman waved her in. "Be my guest," she said, then laughed heartily. "But I guess you are, aren't you? Dinner is at six."

Julianne felt herself relax as she settled into the warm water of the small tub and leaned back to soap her hair. It felt so good. If only things could be this easy. Where was she going to go? Should she stay two nights here? She'd had no plan in mind when she fled, just a pressing need to get out of the City and head toward a place where she'd be anonymous. But what could she do? The little money she had wouldn't allow her to stay at a boarding house for long.

After a luxurious nap, she joined the woman and her husband in the crowded kitchen, feeling much revived. The other roomer was an older man who worked at the transit station downtown. Dinner was basic but tasty and she ate her fill. The matron hustled her house guests into the great room and turned on the infolink.

"Nothing like a little news to make you appreciate what you have." She bustled around serving bowls of tea and stale biscuits on a plate. Julianne was daydreaming, sipping her tea and trying to imagine a future for herself, when a programme on the infolink caught her attention. A series of pictures flashed onto the holograph screen with numbers listed below.

Startled, she glanced at the other boarder.

"It's the rewards," he said. "These people have a price on their head. If you know where to find one of them, you'll make yourself a tidy bit of money."

Her whole body stiffened. That was her face she'd seen, Zanata must have posted it. And the reward was substantial. Did the other boarder not recognize it? Maybe she'd distracted him at just the right moment or maybe she looked totally different now, lost and terrified.

The next day, after a good breakfast, she'd set off to walk north out of town. Because she wasn't safe yet.

Now she sighed and rolled over in the straw to get more comfortable. Zanata had spoiled everything. *Julianne* was to marry the General's son, Virgil Regiment. It wasn't a formal arrangement but there had been an understanding between the families. He was supposed to be *her* husband and now he was dead because of an affair with her stepmother. Everything Zanata touched turned to ashes.

Julianne shuddered in the darkness.

CHAPTER THREE

Morning crept slowly into the hut, with small light seeping in around the warped door. She'd slept late. No wonder, she'd been very tired. And hungry. Rummaging around she found the last stale crumbs of pané in her pocket and put them to her dry lips. It couldn't be much further to the Sanctuary. From the rumours she'd heard about the place, she would find safety there.

Heaving herself to a sitting position, she heard mice scamper out of the straw around her feet. As a City bred girl, the sound should have been alarming, but with little energy left, her mind simply turned to how to cook a mouse. If she were to catch one, that is.

Struggling onto her hands and knees, Julianne managed to lean on the wall for stability as she pushed herself upright. The Sanctuary. She couldn't stop now. She was so close. When she got there, all would be well. She'd heard about it once on the infolink back home. It's where women went to escape their circumstances, to get away from men who beat and abused them, a place where they were safe from the outside world.

She staggered back through the bush to the muddy trail, branches snapping under her still damp boots. In a moment of weakness she stood weaving in the muck as her sight dimmed. Then she placed one foot in front of the other, heading north. She just needed to keep moving.

Around noon a mule and cart overtook her, a small family on board. As they passed, she staggered to the edge of the trail to get out of the way. Instead of continuing by, the wagon stopped. The wife peered over the side of the cart at her. "Where are you headed, girl?"

Julianne glanced up at her in surprise and tried to smile, but the woman's face was a blur. "To the Sanctuary," she whispered. "It's not far now."

"No dearie. Not far, but you could use a lift I'm thinking. You won't get there today walking like that. We're going in that direction. Help her up here," she said to her husband.

Julianne stared at the big man as he approached, unsure what his intentions were. He waved toward the wagon, and as she turned her head to follow his gesture, he simply grabbed her and tossed her into the back.

The wife scrambled across the boards. "Don't worry. We mean you no harm. Here you are, dearie." She held out a crust of bread.

Julianne watched her own hand slowly reach for the food as the woman moved to set it on her palm. "Oh, thank you. So much." She took a tentative bite.

The woman passed a bottle of watered ale and she drank greedily, nearly emptying the thing.

"You poor lass," the wife murmured, handing her a lump of cheese. "We've picked up more than one girl on her way to the Sanctuary. I hope they take good care of you." Her expression seemed doubtful.

Julianne slept. When she woke the sun was low in the sky and the wagon had slowed. The wife laid a hand on her shoulder and shook her gently. "We're here, dearie. You have to go the rest of the way yourself. They don't let the likes of us in there."

She sat up in a daze and slid down the boards to the back of the wagon. "Thank you. Thank you, Ms," she called.

The woman's mouth was flat. "Good luck. I hope they treat you well."

Jumping weakly down into the mud of the trail, she stared up at the sign hanging in a tree. *Women's Sanctuary. Caution.*

Caution? That seemed odd. Two men stood guard on either side of the path leading through the forest. They wore identical heavy wool shirts, banners across their chests with letters spelling out 'Sanctuary'. They looked rough but seemed disciplined, armed with rayguns. One approached her, looking her over with great care before turning to grin at his partner. It was such a personal scrutiny of her face and body, the hairs rose on the back of her neck. "Come through," he finally said, waving her on. "They'll be waiting for you."

She nodded and walked unsteadily between the guards. The path was paved with stones, the grass clipped short on either side. Gradually the high stone walls of a compound came into view, the tall gates tightly closed. But a small door set in the sidewall opened as she approached.

A young woman stepped out. "There you are," she called. "Come right in." She wore a grey robe of some heavy fabric that moulded to her body as she swayed on the path. Her long brown hair was brushed back on her shoulders, covered by a short shawl fastened under her pointed chin.

"How did you know I was here?" Julianne's voice shook. She felt light headed and sweat rolled down her back under the grimy dress.

"The guards sent a beltlink message," she answered cheerfully. "My name is Ailene. Welcome to the Sanctuary. You must be tired. Come through." She led the way, closing the heavy door and bolting it carefully behind them. Julianne could barely stand. She'd made it to safety and her reserves were exhausted.

"I think I have to sit down." She wavered on her feet.

"Of course. Come with me." The young woman took her arm and led her into the first low building. The entry was a small welcoming area with cushioned benches arranged down one wall, light blankets folded in a stack at the end. "Lay down right here. You can rest …"

CHAPTER FOUR

When Julianne woke she heard singing in the distance, like a choir of angels. She felt so much better, not nearly as tired. And she wasn't alone. The same young woman was seated on a bench nearby reading a thin booklet, her robe neatly tucked beneath her legs.

She tried to remember the elements of her plan. *Get to the Sanctuary, find safety, then try to find her father.* But people were looking for her and she had to keep her guard up.

"Oh, you're awake. Wonderful." Ailene beamed, the knot on her head scarf bobbing as she talked. "Now you can have a bath and get cleaned up. What's your name?

Julianne felt a shot of alarm rush through her body. This was why she had to remember her plan. "Sasha," she said. "My name is Sasha."

"Come with me, Sasha. The baths are this way." Ailene led her through a series of doorways into a beautiful bathhouse with green tiled floors and wash stations placed around the perimeter.

"You begin here." She pointed to a stand with basin and sponges. "Take all your clothes off. We'll have them cleaned and pressed for you. Don't worry, you'll get everything back. Meanwhile there's a robe to wear once you've washed." She laughed merrily. "This is just the best place. Use the basin to wet yourself down, the soap is there. Then after you've scrubbed, use the basin to rinse. Once you are *very* clean," and she chuckled, "you can relax in the warm bath over there."

Julianne looked where she pointed to see wisps of steam rising from the farthest pool.

"If you find it's too hot, use the other one. But I like that one myself. Sooo relaxing." Her smile was contagious. "I'll come back for you when you're finished. It will be time for evening sup soon. You'll be ready for something to eat by then."

Julianne was floating in the hot pool, more than half asleep when the girl returned for her. "Come along, slowpoke," she called merrily. "Evening sup is being served. Here's your robe." Julianne quickly climbed out of the pool and rubbed the water off, drying her hair hastily on another towel. She picked up the robe, which was surprisingly heavy and had a large S embroidered in yellow down the back. Awkwardly, she tugged it over her head and clipped it at the throat. Her hair was still wet when Ailene gave her a shawl to cover her head and led her down another corridor into the narrow dining hall.

A long table in the middle of the room was set for a meal, with benches lined up on each side. An older woman stood from the armchair placed at the head of the table to welcome them. She was tall with broad shoulders and a stern but kind face. Her robe was of a finer material, more decorative in design, and her hair was uncovered, dark brown with streaks of white twisted into a bun on the back of her head.

Ailene introduced her. "Sasha, this is Sister Three. Sister, Sasha has just joined us today. These other ladies have been here a bit longer than I have. I'm quite new, too." Two young women near Julianne's age with short mousy brown hair, wearing the same robe and hair shawl as Ailene, were seated at the other side of the table.

Sister Three pointed to the bench. "Please sit down, Sasha. These are Yvette and Yvonne." Julianne noticed their distinct similarity, perhaps they were twins. Someone placed a dish in front of her and she inhaled sharply. She couldn't remember ever being this hungry. It appeared to be stew. "Is it lamb?" she inquired.

Sister Three frowned. "I think it's mutton, but we never question our good fortune here."

Julian felt the reproof like a knife, suddenly not as sure of her welcome. "Of course. I'm sorry, Sister."

Sister put her hands together. "Let us pray in thanks." The others did the same and Sister Three began. "We thank you, Maa, for your bounty. We thank you, Maa, for your generosity. We thank you, Maa for your kind heart …"

By the time Sister was finished, the meal had cooled but Julianne didn't care. Her stomach growled as she began to eat. Yet after only a few mouthfuls it became difficult to swallow, her appetite had fled. She'd gone days without regular meals. Still, she struggled to force down as much as she could. She was going to need her strength.

When the others were finished, Sister Three stood and the girls leaped to their feet, Julianne the last to belatedly rise. "Ailene will show you where you sleep. Good night, ladies."

The girls immediately sat down again and smiled at Julianne. She smiled tentatively back. "The Sanctuary is quite small," she said. "I had imagined it would be larger."

Ailene threw back her head and laughed merrily. "This is just the entry. You'll see it all, I promise. It's huge. There are several buildings for sleeping rooms, a gathering pavilion and private apartments. Once you see it, you'll be amazed. The gardens are endless, with flowers, vegetables and fruit trees. Then there are the animal pens. Just immense."

She frowned. "You can't stay there, of course. At least, not at first. First you take your turn here in the entry. Right, girls?"

"Right," Yvette said as Yvonne nodded. "What brought you here?"

"Well, some people in a wagon dropped me off at the entry path."

Yvette smiled. "But why did you come, Sasha?"

Julianne flushed. "My stepmother was selling me."

"Ahh," the girls nodded in unison.

"Our father decided we should be his wife," said Yvette. Yvonne nodded again.

"Oh, my goodness. My father would never do something like that." Julianne was shocked. She wasn't running from her father, it was her stepmother who was the threat.

Ailene put her head to the side. "My uncle thought I should marry his son, a big bully who already wore out two wives."

"So most of the women in here …"

The girls shrugged. "That's right."

"Is Maa still alive? I know she's the leader of the Sanctuary, but the way Sister Three prayed to her it sounded like …" She stopped at the alarm on their faces.

Yvette replied, her voice low. "Don't talk about Maa. The walls may have ears. Maa is very much alive. You'll meet her soon enough."

Yvonne touched her arm and spoke for the first time. "It's not all fun. The time in the entry is difficult. I've finished my turn, and it's over now."

Yvette nodded. "Yes, we both have. But there must always be three women in the entry who know the system, so we have stayed here until someone else came. Now that you've arrived I can join the Inner Sanctuary as soon as you're trained."

"I see. What do I have to do?"

The girls exchanged looks. Yvonne made a motion with her hand and Yvette continued. "The entry is for anyone seeking aid from the Sanctuary. If it's a woman who arrives, you'll do for her what Ailene did for you today. Help her into the women's entry, let her rest, assist her to get clean and wash her clothes. Bring the doctor if needed. The woman may just leave again when she is feeling better, or she may decide to stay and join the Sanctuary.

"If a man comes seeking aid, it's usually because he's sick or injured. They're welcomed as well, of course, but never get to the Inner Sanctuary. They're bathed in the men's chamber, the doctor will assist them and when they're able, they leave."

Yvonne made another motion, and Yvette frowned. "Not tonight."

"Yes, tonight. She deserves to know."

"Know what?" Julianne's gaze moved from face to face as her chest got tight.

"There's more to the story." Yvonne spoke low. "You have to earn your way into the Inner Sanctuary."

Ailene shrugged. "We have guards."

"Yes, I saw two on the path when I entered."

"They're posted around the entire compound. They keep the gangs of dispossessed from storming us and taking over. And they need to be paid. We feed them two meals a day and provide them with clothes." Ailene halted in sudden confusion.

Julianne nodded. "That makes sense."

Yvonne added, "And they get to sleep with a woman."

There was silence.

"All of them? All of them sleep with a woman?"

The three girls nodded. "Not all at once of course, they take turns, but it's part of their compensation."

"What woman?" Julianne's voice sounded faint even to her own ears.

"The latest recruit," Yvonne said. "I've finished that duty and Yvette has as well. The next time it's Ailene's turn." She glanced at Julianne. "You're the newest woman here, so you'll be after her."

Julianne felt sick. The blood must have left her head, because her thinking became fuzzy and disoriented. Yvonne seemed to be saying she'd have to sleep with the guards if she wanted to enter the safety of the Inner Sanctuary. That couldn't be right, because that was what she'd run away to escape, being traded to a man for payment.

CHAPTER FIVE

Abram Farmer was dreaming of home, the warm fires, the comfortable rugs on the floor, the sensation of space and light he always felt at the manorhouse. Farmer Holdings lay in an expansive swath of land in the Southern Territory of Khandarken up against the Adar Silva border. In the dream, his sister Bethlehem had settled beside him on the sofa in the office, teasing him and talking about the day, speculating about what Hannan would serve for dinner.

As he came awake, he felt the sharp pang of loss, of being a long way from home and not knowing when or if he would see it again.

The stabbing pain in his side forced him to roll onto his back on the wool stuffed mattress to ease the pressure. Weeks ago, he and his bodyguard Kerr had been ambushed on the remote trail to Krimen in the

Collaros Territory, and he'd barely escaped with his life. He was almost mended now, but only because these tribesmen had taken them in and cared for them so selflessly. And because of Kerr, of course. His guard had spirited Abe out of the middle of the ambush in the black of night and brought him here to the tribesmen's village, barely alive. They had welcomed them and offered shelter

His wound was slowly healing, and he had Ventuzzo's wife to thank for that. Ada was a little woman, no higher than his chest, quite the opposite of her strapping tribesman husband with his long black hair braided with coloured threads and the fur boots with bells tied to the band at the top. She had nursed and bullied him back to health over the long weeks they'd been here.

It was still dark in the round little hut, but the sun would be up soon. Suddenly he heard the pounding of hooves, shouts and shots in the darkness. Heart leaping in his chest, he started upright on his pallet. He punched Kerr in the shoulder and they rolled to their feet on a surge of adrenaline. Abe felt for his boots in the blackness and grabbed the plasmagun stored at the foot of the bed. Crawling across the hard-packed dirt floor to the entry, he peered outside through the hide flap. It looked like a battleground in the near dawn light.

Two mounted mules galloped past, their hooves inches from his head and three men, by appearance they were dispossessed, ran behind. A couple of the tribesmen's herd dogs barked and jumped at the mules' legs. Between the huts, he saw through to the centre of the compound where Ventuzzo knelt by the elder's home, his ancient weapon levelled at the intruders.

Abe fired off a shot, and one man fell from the back of a mule. Immediately another dispossessed runner leaped into the saddle and swung the animal around to face him. "Abe Farmer," the rider cried in sudden recognition, pointing at him with his crude spear. A second mounted raider pulled his mule to the side to look back in surprise at the call. "Farmer?"

Abe fired again. More men ran past. He heard the shuffle of movement as Kerr crawled out through the doorway behind him, and saw Grainger, the young tribesman interpreter, and his father coming around the back of the hut across from them, crossbows firing. Another man went down.

Kerr leaped to his feet and ran to pick up a raygun that lay abandoned in the road. He settled it in his arms and rolled in the dirt path, firing as he went. He brought down a mule and his rider, and Abe hit a second runner. The rest of the men turned and fled, leaping between the huts and into the forest on the far side of the encampment.

Abe shook his head to clear it and caught his breath at the shaft of pain through the still raw wound in his side. He staggered unsteadily to his feet. *That man knew him?* Impossible. Yet he'd shouted his name. Someone was looking for him, he'd heard there was a reward posted on his head.

Kerr still lay in the path, breathing heavily. Abe walked over and squatted beside him. "Did you hear that? Someone shouted my name."

"Yah, I heard. We can't stay here."

"That's right." He extended his hand. Kerr grabbed it and struggled awkwardly to his feet.

"Are you hit?" Abe felt his stomach tighten. If Kerr was injured and they had to flee, what chance did they have? Abe's leg wound had healed fairly well, but the bullet in his side had to be removed with a set of tongs and the wound drained. He was still remarkably weak.

"I figure so." Kerr gazed down at the hole in his pant leg and the blood leaking onto his boot.

"Get in here, let's have a look."

The tribesmen crowded round in excitement, shouting and pointing as they relived the attack. The elder poked his head out of his hut now that the shooting had stopped, then withdrew again. Ventuzzo came over to help prop Kerr up and drag him into his hut. His wife Ada would tend him as she'd tended Abe.

They managed to get Kerr onto a low stool and Ventuzzo lit the lamp. "Ada," he called and turned toward the bed. Then he let out a cry of shock and anguish, throwing himself on the animal hides, pawing at them and dragging at the body of his wife.

She lay motionless, her face dark with her own blood. There was a small hole in the hide wall above her head. A wail went up, and Ventuzzo tore at his hair.

Abe gazed in shock at the small, loving woman lying dead on the handmade woolen mattress, a gaping wound of anguish opening in his own chest. *Do I bring disaster wherever I go?*

Grainger's wife soon arrived and took over the care of Kerr's leg. The bullet had gone through the muscle, and the hole bled heavily. She bound it for him, plastering it with a poultice of leaves and mud. As the news about Ada spread throughout the camp, the rest of the women arrived in ones and twos, ducking through the doorway and approaching the bed where she lay.

Ventuzzo had stopped talking altogether. Grainger led him away as the women began to clean and dress their friend.

Abe ducked outside through the low doorway and stood tall in the early morning light, watching as the tribesmen bullied one of the captured dispossessed. He wandered over and took the man by the arm. "Do you want to live?" he asked.

The man glanced at him gratefully. "Ah, I can understand you. I can't understand these mountain men."

Abe nodded and waved the men back. "Do you want to live?" he said again.

The man dropped to his knees. "Yah. What do you want?"

"I want to know why you're here."

The prisoner gazed at him blankly for a moment. "Well," he shrugged. "Why we always come. We get a sheep to feed ourselves. Now and then, we even get a woman." He grinned eagerly.

"Do you know who Abe Farmer is?"

He shrugged again and nodded his head. "I know the name. There's a reward posted for information on him."

"What else is going on with your men?"

He glanced around apprehensively, then bowed his head. "We're being recruited," he said low. "The Young Emperor is hiring men just across the border in Legitamia. He wants his kingdom back, I guess." He squinted up at Abe. "I only hear rumours, but three of our fellows have left to join him. Don't know what the plan is. I doubt if he's paying wages."

"What about his father? Doesn't Emperor Aqatain lead his own men?"

"He's dead." The prisoner gave Abe a skeptical glance, obviously reassessing his value as a protector. "Aqatain died about a month ago."

Abe had been out of touch for longer than that. He was surprised how much things could change in such a short time.

"I want your word you'll never come raiding this village again."

The prisoner gaped at him, then a heavy flush rose up his neck. He nodded, then nodded again more firmly as resolution seemed to set in "You have it." His mouth straightened in grim determination.

Abe gave the man back to the herders. "Don't kill him."

He and Kerr made their way over to the elder's hut, where they knew the men would be convening. Grainger saw them enter and waved them to a couple of stools. They sat silently as the men spoke in turn in their tribal language. "I think they're saying it was the dispossessed searching for food," Abe whispered to Kerr.

Kerr nodded but wobbled on his stool.

Abe put out a hand to steady his friend and motioned to Grainger. "We have to leave," he said. "I don't know if we were the cause of this attack, but one of the men recognized me. There will be more men coming, we have to go."

Grainger nodded and spoke for a long time to the elder in the tribal language. After much discussion, he looked back at Abe. "We don't think you were the cause, Mr. Farmer. The dispossessed attack because they want our women and our sheep. We've had to fight them off before. You take the mule you came with, and any weapons you have. We'll give you food for your journey. May the gods go with you."

Abe stood and bowed to the elder and to Ventuzzo. "I thank you for your kindness to us, for your care. Ventuzzo, your wife saved my life. My heart bleeds for your loss. She was a good woman."

Remembering Ventuzzo's son worked for him as a herdsman at Farmer Holdings in the Southern Territory, he continued, "I will give greetings to your son, and the sad news of his mother when I arrive home." *If I arrive home.*

CHAPTER SIX

Abe packed the mule carefully, rifling the clothing and belongings of the men who had died in the raid. There was the plasmagun that he and Kerr had arrived with, and the raygun Kerr had grabbed during the fight. There was ammunition for both weapons and a small cloth bag of polished gem-stones that had fallen out of some raider's pocket. Grainger's wife packed sheets of pané and dried meat for their journey.

They set out heading north, he walked and Kerr rode unsteadily in the saddle.

As Abe gazed back at the village of round huts, surprisingly peaceful now in the morning sunlight, there was little to remind him of the battle just a few hours ago. Flocks of sheep released from the night pens wandered the fields under the watchful eyes of the young herders who stood guard. The boys ran to bid the men farewell, reaching to touch fingertips as they rode away.

He wouldn't be alive today without the aid these northern tribesmen had offered. And the children were beautiful, innocent and well meaning. He wondered deep in his heart if one day he might be blessed with children like this. It seemed a far off dream. First he had to survive the assaults against Farmer Holdings, the assaults against himself.

The trail was rough, pitted and wet. The mud slowed them, both Abe and the mule tiring early each day as they made their way across the plains toward the forest and mountains of the border lands. The wound in his thigh would begin to ache about mid-afternoon so he knew he was getting better, but the pain in his side never quit. It was dangerous to stay out on the road after dark, and they sought shelter where they could, in barns or shanties or with groups of other travellers.

Three days along the trail, Kerr was feverish, his silver hair clinging damply to his scalp. His leg was swollen, the skin an angry red around the wound. He groaned when it was touched. Abe pried the bandages off, heated water and washed the area. Kerr writhed beneath his hands, the lines in his face deep and white from pain.

"I don't know what to do. I'd like to soak it in hot salt water, but there's no salt. No one we've talked to has had anything to offer so far in the way of help."

Kerr lay on the saddle blanket panting for breath, his face flushed. "We need to get to the Sanctuary."

"Yah, I've heard of that. But I don't know much about it."

"The Sanctuary. It's a place where they'll take you in and find a doctor. They have medicine."

"Do you know where it is?" He poured out the wash water.

"It's east of Wymark, along the perimeter road to Discovery. We might have to ask."

"Don't worry, we'll find it." Abe's mouth tightened with determination as he ripped his undershirt into strips to form a bandage. He had nothing to use, no salve or cream. He simply wrapped the leg and sat back.

"Meanwhile, I'll see what I can do about dinner." He pulled a wire trap out of the saddlebag. Ventuzzo had given it to him, but it was the small tribal boys who showed him how to identify a rabbit trail. He had no need to trap rabbits at Farmer Holdings. They raised everything they ate in the vast pastures and garden.

He set the snare, then joined Kerr in a nap before he returned to the rabbit run. There was a good sized animal in the noose. Resetting the trap, he used his knife to skin and gut the carcass before taking it back to their camp. Kerr was still sleeping, breathing raggedly.

He lit a fire, put the rabbit meat over it to roast then went back to the trap. Another rabbit. In all he caught three and cooked every bit of meat. He needed provisions so they could move faster on the trail. From the look of things, they didn't have a lot of time.

He woke Kerr, forced a few mouthfuls into him, and ate the rest of one rabbit. Then he damped the fire. Dusk was gathering and they didn't need to make themselves a target for those who wandered at night.

He hobbled the mule to graze, settled down beside Kerr, pulled their coats closed and slept.

CHAPTER SEVEN

J ust as dawn broke Abe rose. He wrestled Kerr onto the mule and set out for the perimeter road. It was slow going. The road was deep in mud, the mule could not carry two men, and Kerr was losing consciousness. Abe trudged on. Now and then a wagon and team of mules or horses rattled by. Once an official transport thundered past, spewing huge mud clots from the deep tread of its tall wheels.

A small family went by in the opposite direction, a man, his wife and a young boy, all covered to their knees with mud. The husband carried a sack on his back "Is your father hurt?" the woman asked.

Abe felt a ghost of a smile for the first time in days. "Yes, he's wounded in the leg."

"Ah." She was still staring as they passed.

Toward mid-afternoon, Abe saw a signpost – *Discovery 5 miles*. Hadn't Kerr mentioned the Sanctuary was near here? They must be getting close.

Discovery was a small well-built village, no more than some shops and a few dozen neat houses. He tied the mule to a post and checked his passenger. Kerr trembled in the saddle, hanging onto the horn unsteadily with both hands. He could tell the leg was worse, the inflammation clearly visible above the edge of the bandage. His face was flushed with fever and sweat ran down his cheeks.

Abe moved quickly into the ale shop in the middle of the street. There was no one there. He glanced around, then hammered on the table that served as a bar. A man stuck his head through the door at the back.

"I'll just be a moment."

He heard muttering and things banging in the back room, then the barkeep emerged and straightened his vest, tying an apron behind his back. "Sorry, sir," he began before he caught sight of Abe in his dirty and worn tribesmen's clothes. Then his eyes narrowed. "What do you want? I'll see your money before I serve you, *sir*." He laid heavy emphasis on the last word.

Abe smiled, a simple baring of teeth. "Don't worry. I don't have time for service." He looked longingly at the barrels of ale stacked against the wall but drew his attention back to the barkeep.

"I need information. Is the Sanctuary near here?"

The man seemed startled. "The Sanctuary? Are you a mercenary, then?"

Abe blinked. "No, sir. My friend is injured and I'm seeking help."

His mouth straightened. "Well, they do give help. Yet, someone here could help you."

"I need a doctor."

"Hmm." The barkeep wiped the table as he considered. "You've missed the turnoff. If you retrace your steps a few miles, there's a trail heading north that will take you there. It's about an hour, maybe two. There's a sign at the entrance to their track, hard to miss."

Abe bowed his head in acknowledgement and stepped back outside. The mule was moving nervously at the side of the street and Kerr had collapsed forward over the beast's neck. He gentled the animal, tying it more securely to the post. His guard was boneless in the saddle. Taking the laces out of Kerr's boots, he tied his feet to the stirrups. Then he took off his belt and secured his hands to the saddle horn. They'd get to the Sanctuary as fast as he could get them there.

At the edge of the village, Abe heard someone call out to him. He glanced over to see a cripple at the side of the street. The injured man knelt on all fours, using his hands and the stubs of his legs, both his feet missing. "Alms for the poor," he called. "Alms for the poor."

Abe stopped, stunned. He didn't see beggars any more at Farmerville or even Deep Creek. Since the end of the Last War, they'd put together ways to feed people who needed help in the Southern Territory.

Feeling around, he came up with a gem from the small bag in his pocket and offered it to the fellow. "I'm sorry I have no money to give you, but this is worth something."

"Thank you, sir." The beggar became excited as he examined the stone glinting on his palm. "May the gods be with you."

"What are you talking about? There is only one God. May He bless you, sir."

The cripple sat with his mouth open as Abe continued on past, leading the mule.

As Abe walked, he contemplated the encounter with the beggar. He'd been raised by his parents to read the Holy Book. He knew there was only one God. Yet why was he wandering the northern territories, still healing from a devastating injury and trying desperately to find help for Kerr, who was on his last legs? Did God not care at all? Abe had been betrayed by those close to him and he was still struggling back from that fateful event.

He walked at a steady pace, the mule slogging behind. After a while, he dug out some meat and ate as he tramped. Kerr didn't move, and he wondered with a clenching in his gut if they would get there in time. He owed his life to this man and wouldn't let him down if he could help it.

It was nearly dusk when a small light became visible through the trees. Abe stopped and checked Kerr's throat for a pulse. It felt fast and thready. This could be their last chance to get help from a doctor. He prayed they had arrived at the Sanctuary.

Scuffing in the brush, he found a natural hollow and used a sturdy branch to dig a shallow trough. He wrapped the weapons and ammunition in a rag and laid them in the hole, kicking the dirt over to cover them, then leaves to hide the mark on the ground. He removed one of Kerr's bootlaces and tied it to the branch of a nearby tree. They'd need to find this spot again when they left.

"Who's there?

As he moved forward leading the mule, someone stepped out of the darkness. The man was wearing dark clothes, a bushy beard and a banner across his chest with lettering on it. Abe couldn't read it in the dim light, but didn't miss the raygun he held in one hand.

"We're searching for the Sanctuary."

"What do you want?"

Abe pointed to the mule. "My friend is ill. We need help, and soon."

The guard walked around his animal and studied Kerr, slumped in the saddle. Then he grunted and waved them forward. "They'll be expecting you."

More lights ahead. Abe stopped before a set of tall gates as the tension in his body began to ease. They'd made it, Kerr would get help. He hoped it wasn't too late. A small door in the stone wall opened and a young woman dressed in a heavy drab robe stepped out into the gloom.

"Welcome, sir. Come this way."

Thus they entered the guarded grounds of the Sanctuary. Abe prayed they'd come in time.

CHAPTER EIGHT

S able Maude crouched in the dark corner of his prison cell, away from the heavy metal bars of the door. He wore all the clothes he had with him, even his coat. It was probably going to get very messy in here and the clothes might help protect him. And when the time came, he wanted to be ready.

He braced his hands against the stone wall, feeling the damp run beneath his fingers. This prison was the oldest in Khandarken, built miles outside the City walls and now used only for men serving a life sentence or condemned to death.

The smell was fearful in this hell hole. Mildew coated the walls and floor, and the many lives that had expired here had left a permanent odour in the underground bunker. The pee hole was right under his left boot where he squatted. He hardly noticed it anymore. He'd been in here for weeks, waiting and planning. Finally, something was about to happen. He'd received word this morning along with his breakfast porridge, a folded parchment under his bowl. Tonight was the night.

The news was a little unexpected. He'd managed to contact his men from inside, but there'd been little they could do. Now this. He'd take it as the gift it was and see where it led and who was behind it, because the only place this prison cell led was his own death.

A warden strolled past his door. "All's fine in the south quadrant, aisle B," he reported. Sable watched him through the bars as he talked low on a wristlink.

Suddenly there was a thunderous roar, so deep the earth shook, and he felt the rumbling beneath his feet. Sable crouched lower into the corner in his heavy boots, hoping the walls would hold. Stone ground against stone with a sickening scream, pebbles and rocks tumbled about him, hitting his shoulders and bouncing on the floor. The ceiling heaved above his head, and he lifted his arms to try to protect himself. Rocks shot through the air, thudding against the walls and cracking the door on its hinges.

Voices cried out in terror. A cluster of guards ran past down the corridor, quickly followed by a group of filthy men newly released from confinement. As the trembling in the ground slowly ceased, plaster fell from the ceiling like snowflakes in the dim light. A strange odour permeated the dust filled air - mold, explosives, fear. There was silence.

Sable stood and straightened his clothes. Part of the ceiling had collapsed in one corner but most of it still held. The walls had shattered in places, the corridor outside his cell choked with rubble.

He gathered his books under one arm and walked out the cell door. Glancing back, he took in the slippery blackened floor and dingy narrow wooden slat of a bed. He swore that never again would he see the inside of a prison.

A hounding horde of convicts had cornered a couple of guards at the far end of the corridor. A shot sounded above the shouting, then three more in quick succession followed by the sound of flesh hitting flesh, grunts and screams. He turned and clambered over the debris in the direction of the exit, along with a hundred others.

Joining the stream of desperate men running to escape the confines of the jail, Sable Maude walked out. His shoulders were squared, his back straight, his dirty hair combed. He was free and he fully intended to remain free. The gang of dispossessed that had obviously provided the muscle for the prison break charged through the entrance from the other direction, anxious to ransack the place and claim anything they could lay their hands on in exchange for payment.

"Maude!"

He turned his head at the sound. His men were waiting near the wall, hovering in the gloom. Sprinter stood in the shadows just outside the shattered gates, his eyes gleaming in the darkness. He grabbed Sable's arm and steered him toward a battered hydro truck pulled up under the trees in the yard. They heard the faint roar of official transports approaching in the distance and saw beams of light raking the ground from overhead military aircarts swiftly closing in. It was obvious the alarm had already gone out.

"Let's get out of here." Sable leaped into the front seat of the truck.

"Where to, sir?" It was Mateo, his driver.

Sprinter climbed into the back and leaned forward to pass a note to Sable. "This came for you."

Sable took the onion skin in his blackened hand and tore the seal open. He read the missive twice, then smiled as he sat back. It was a message from Duncan, Assistant Chief Constable of Khandarken. Duncan would like to meet with him. What could Duncan possibly want with Sable Maude? They'd never met, and as far as Sable knew, Duncan was the model of rectitude, a police officer and administrator of integrity. On the other hand, he might have arranged the prison break. How else could his message be delivered the minute Sable emerged from the shattered jail?

"To the City, Mateo, through the back entrance. I have some business to attend."

There was hushed silence in the hydro truck, but no one questioned his decision. They knew better.

Sable relaxed for the first time since he'd been caught and arrested for capturing and selling female slaves. He'd been sentenced to death and his appeal was even now grinding its way through the courts, but meanwhile he had languished in an underground Khandarken prison.

Now he was free and today he had a bone to pick with Little Harry Adjudicator. Then he'd talk to Duncan.

The back entrance into the City was a system of tunnels that Sable Maude had discovered years ago as a young boy. His father was Governor of the Southern Territory now, but before the Last War began, Francis Maude had been a Colonel in the army of the Old Emperor. He and Paulo Regiment, also of the military, were often invited to the General's estate for social events. Their sons had tagged along.

Paulo's eldest son Virgil Regiment had been no friend of Sable Maude. But Dante, the second son, had led a small band of boys into all kinds of escapades that terrorized the General's gardeners, and Sable sometimes managed to tag along. It was Dante who first discovered how to open the access door to the spring house, which became their secret headquarters at the bottom of the vast gardens. Behind the spring itself they had found a tunnel leading into the ground.

The day young Dante decided to investigate further, he'd banished the smaller boys from the vicinity and taken a few trusted friends down the yawning hole. It led underground and outside the walls of the City. There had been high excitement amongst them at the discovery.

Sable came back later on his own to explore. He clearly remembered the first time he entered the tunnel, a handlight to guide the way. He still remembered the panic that hit about halfway along the passage when he realized he was beneath tons of earth and didn't know what was at the other end of the hole, or if he'd even be able to get out. When he emerged within the walls of the old hunter's shed outside the City walls, he'd been elated. He'd done it, something Dante Regiment thought he was too young to manage. The knowledge never left him.

He was strong, he was indomitable. And he was underestimated.

CHAPTER NINE

Nettles drove the transport as far as he could along the barely visible track. They walked the rest of the way through the bush to the now collapsed hunter's shed. Sable lifted some rotting boards from the rubble of the hut and carefully set them aside. "Mateo comes with me, Sprinter waits here." They descended into the tunnel.

As an adult, Sable had used the tunnel many times. The City walls were high and well patrolled. The entrances were heavily guarded, and each person leaving or entering had their ident scrutinized and documented. He didn't need the authorities aware of how often he came and went from the City.

Since the time the boys had found the tunnel, the gardeners had installed a door in the spring house which blocked the tunnel entrance. But it was locked from the spring side to prevent children wandering down the hole. Sable easily opened it from the tunnel side, leaving a brick to block it ajar until his return. He'd be back long before some errant worker went in to inspect the premises.

Harry Adjudicator lived on one of the upscale streets of the City, his townhouse painted a classic wine colour as befitted a member of the bench of the Supreme Court of Khandarken. Harry had something to answer for, and Sable was looking for that answer.

When he'd gone to Harry for help in having his man Waite acquitted on smuggling charges, the Adjudicator had complied and that day in his courtroom he'd found a way to dismiss the charges against Waite.

But right after that, things went terribly wrong, and Maude had been caught red handed with a delivery of Oriental women and young boys from beyond Jiran to the west. The line of betrayal led directly back to the Adjudicator. Sable didn't like to act under the impetus of emotion, he liked his revenge served cold. He was looking forward to this encounter.

"Here we are, Mateo. I'm in no condition to knock on the door. I'm filthy. You go, tell Harry I'm here to talk to him." He settled down in the shrubbery at the side of the house to wait.

When his driver rang the house bell, he saw a young maid appear at the entry. They spoke for a moment and he watched as she waved Mateo in. He was gone a long time.

He had dozed off when he finally heard someone approaching. He started awake from a prison nightmare of shouting and shots, guards running and the stink of the cell. He drew a deep breath, took in the blue sky and the flowers in Harry's garden, listened to the birds singing. He was free and he'd never be in prison again. A fierce determination filled his gut.

Mateo slid through the branches and settled beside him in the grass.

"Well, is he coming?"

"He's not there."

"What do you mean, he's not there? You were gone a long time."

"Harry's wife had tea with me."

Sable was silent. *Had tea with Mateo?* This didn't sound right. "What did she say?"

"She took me to bed." The young driver blushed fiercely, hiding his grin with his fist.

Sable sat back and stared at him dispassionately. The stupid little shit. "Zanata, Little Harry's wife, took you to her bed?" It was an effort to keep his voice even.

Mateo nodded, his face beet red.

His voice was low when he finally spoke. "You fool."

"Fool? When was the last time a pretty woman like that invited you to bed?" Mateo was astonished.

"She has venereal disease, mangohrea. Zanata Adjudicator is a one-woman plague."

"Mangohrea?" His driver had gone pale, sweat stood out on his forehead. "Oh, by the graves! There's no cure. I'm going to die!"

Sable settled a hand on his shoulder to steady him. The kid was an idiot, but he needed him right now. "We don't know if you caught it. Now, listen. What did she say about Harry?"

Mateo wiped the sweat from his forehead with a shaky hand. "Harry left. He took off when the General sent men around to arrest him. She doesn't know where he is."

"As I let you live!" he swore. "I don't believe this." He thought for a moment as his anger cooled. "Okay, I have another plan." He crawled along the line of ornamental shrubs to the street, stood and brushed himself off. Not that it made much difference. His clothes were dark with grime.

He looked back at Mateo where he sagged dejectedly on the ground. "Come on, we have work to do."

CHAPTER TEN

Old Towne, in the centre of the City, was ragged and rundown in the bright light of day. The buildings, designed with once-fine architecture that had since gone out of style, now seemed shabby and old fashioned.

The square had a fountain in the centre with walkways and small gardens built around it. Lanes led off from the square like the spokes of a wheel led from the hub. An old man in a very proper but dated pinstriped wool suit perched on the low wall at the edge of the fountain, scattering crumbs to a flock of pigeons leaping and flitting about him.

Sable waded through the pigeons, his boots scattering birds like confetti as he read the signposts for each lane.

"Can I help you young fellows?" the man called. "Are you looking for an address?"

Sable ignored him and pointed past Mateo. "This one." He moved off down Bookseller Lane, his driver at his side. When he heard footsteps behind, he turned and snarled, "What do you want?"

The old man narrowed his eyes. "Nothing from you. This is my shop." He took a set of keys out of his pocket, fitting the largest one into the lock on a door with a sign reading 'Holmes Books and Documents.' He went in and the door swung closed.

Sable allowed himself to calm. He didn't need to be sidetracked by this old fellow, a nobody in his once fine suit. At the end of the lane the last building had been converted into apartments. Sable climbed the steps to the third level and knocked on the door. He waited but no one answered. He banged again, lifting his face toward the window so he could be seen by the occupants, should they be looking out. Then came the rattle of keys.

"Open the door," he called. "It's Sable Maude."

The door opened a couple of inches. Little Harry stood in the shadow of the entry, glancing anxiously up the lane. "How did you know where I was?"

"Let us in." Sable hid his grin. He shouldn't have been surprised, but things were falling together rather nicely. This was Duncan's apartment and here was Little Harry Adjudicator, hiding out from the authorities.

Harry moved back, waving him through. "Hurry. I don't want anyone to see me."

The men stepped inside a tiny residence consisting of not much more than a kitchen with counter and stools, and a half bed sit. Harry hurriedly closed the door and locked it. He seemed different, smaller than when Sable saw him last at the high table in his court robes. His normally chubby cheeks were almost gaunt, the skin hung slack on his neck. His complexion was waxy and his hands shook steadily. "What are you doing here? Did they let you out of jail?"

Sable smiled in sudden ferocious amusement and watched Harry back up a step. "Not exactly. I heard General Regiment sent his men to arrest you. Why was he after you?"

Harry gazed down at his toes. "He found out about our plan with the talc mine at Farmer Holdings. Dr Wessex talked. He's being held even now, along with his assistant, Dr. Beeton. Everything went wrong."

"Tell me." Sable took the best seat at the counter and noticed a bottle of clouded ale in front of him, the cap still sealed. He opened and downed it in long swallows before wiping his mouth and looking his question at Harry. Harry might have been useful to him as an adjudicator in Khandarken courts, but he was obviously less than helpful now as a man on the run.

Harry flushed a dull red. "Dr Wessex from the hospital and I were trying to get control of the talc mine at Farmer Holdings in the Southern Territory.

He'd been doing research on viruses and discovered that talc kills some viruses altogether, stops them from growing. Not all viruses, but the severe high temp virus that came through this year, plus several other illnesses. And not any talc, just Farmer talc. We thought it would be a good investment."

Sable's chest shook with laughter at the folly of such an effort. "So then?"

Harry's face went darker. "Well, someone was working with us from the Constables and…"

"You mean, Duncan. Duncan was working with you."

Harry stalled, his mouth open. "How do you know?"

"Come on, Harry. Whose apartment are we in? Where is Duncan?"

"He's at work, had a meeting with the Chief Constable this morning."

"Ah, the Chief Constable. With someone like Duncan on your side, you can't go wrong, can you? Assistant to the Chief, he has access to a lot of information. What's your plan, Little Harry?"

Harry looked into his eyes, a desperate expression on his face. "I don't know."

Sable nodded. "Tell me how Dante Regiment knew to capture me with a shipment of smuggled women."

Harry's mouth opened in surprise. "Smuggled women? How would I know that?"

"Well, you see, Harry," Sable said, and rose slowly to his feet. "It all went wrong right after I talked to you about my man Waite. What did you tell Regiment?"

Harry had backed up against the door, looking cornered like a rat. "Nothing. I told him nothing. I didn't even talk to him, other than to hear his testimony in my courtroom that day."

Sable nodded, a feeling of finality settling in his gut. He was right, Harry was of no use to him now.

CHAPTER ELEVEN

"Maa wants to see you, Sasha." Ailene appeared in the doorway of the medicine room where Julianne was rolling bandages fresh from the laundry. Her dark blue eyes twinkled excitedly as she leaned around the doorframe. "Better come right away. You don't want to keep her waiting."

Julianne's first reaction was surprise. Although she'd changed her name, she still wasn't used to it. Then she felt her stomach hit her slippers, alarm tightening her muscles. She just wanted to be left alone without attention from anyone, especially Maa.

Everything she'd heard about the woman prior to coming here pointed to a paragon of mercy, who held out a helping hand to those in need. Women running from abusive husbands or family members, homeless and orphaned children, all were welcomed here.

And although the Sanctuary was for women, to protect them in a rough and uncaring world dominated by men, she didn't turn the men away either. That's why this medicine room was so well stocked with pills and patches, emulsions and salves, creams and bandages.

Yet, she'd found those rumours were not quite true. Yvette and Yvonne had both taken their turns with the guard at the end of the week. Maa had used their bodies as payment to the men who did patrol duty here. They were now friendly but silent creatures. They'd been injured, not by life in the rough world outside but by the Sanctuary itself.

The day after Julianne arrived here, all the new women, the acolytes, had been summoned into Maa's presence. There were about a dozen females of various ages, the oldest being more than sixty years with several teeth missing. Julianne was shocked to see the evidence of how much more quickly the women aged in the territories compared to the towns or the City.

Yvette and Yvonne stayed to work the entry while Ailene and Julianne hurried to the open chamber inside the Inner Sanctuary where Maa awaited. It was a lovely airy room, with floors of highly polished rose-coloured tile, walls draped with beautiful tapestries depicting gardens and dancing ladies. At one end was a small platform with two steps leading up to it covered by a beautiful piece of sky-blue rug. In the centre of the platform sat an imposing, intricately carved chair stained dark brown. Julianne couldn't help thinking it had the appearance of a throne.

Maa sat tall in the chair, her fine robes heavily embroidered, the collar at her throat encrusted with pearls. Two women stood behind her like guards or wardens. Maa's snow white hair was cut short and stood straight up, as if she'd been administered a shock. Her features were plain, even ugly, a big jaw, long narrow nose and small eyes seated close together under heavy brows.

Julianne had to stifle a giggle as a phrase her father always used flitted through her mind. *You can dress her up but you can't take her out.* She snorted, and Ailene's head shot around as she glared at her. "Sasha!"

"Sorry, I know. It's just nerves." Julianne ducked her head to avoid others noticing. Even so, Maa's eyes seemed to burn into her.

Maa stood and a hush fell over the room. "Sit," she said.

Julianne glanced around for a chair, but the others took a place on the floor and she followed suit. Maa began to speak. Her voice was deep and melodic, easy to listen to, soothing.

"Welcome to the Sanctuary. We are very pleased to receive you amongst us. We welcome all new acolytes to our retreat, our place of safety and refuge."

Her eyes scanned the faces, pausing on each as she seemed to make a connection with them. Julianne felt her gaze as the brush of a hand on her cheek. It was amazing.

Maa continued, "You are safe here. You may have been in a difficult place when you thought to look to the Sanctuary. It may have been a forced decision, perhaps leaving behind those you love or those who love you. But you made the right decision. We will protect you, we will take care of you."

As she spoke Julianne began to feel drowsy. Before her eyes closed, she noticed other heads nodding.

She woke with a start. She was lying on the tile floor, other women collapsed around her. She heard the snap of fingers, then Maa's voice said, "You are now awake. You will remember all I've told you and be thankful."

Bodies began to stir and Julianne sat up. What had Maa said? She couldn't remember, but was much more at ease with her position in the Sanctuary. As they wandered back to the entry, she realized her dread of taking her turn with the guards had disappeared. It would be all right. She might not enjoy it, but it would be okay and she'd be thankful that she could contribute in some way to the safety and security of this wonderful group of women.

But the euphoric feeling didn't persist. Doubts began to creep in as she learned more about the operations here. Soon she had returned to the fears that first assailed her. Now, Ailene said Maa wanted to see her.

"Just me?"

"Sasha, how would I know? I'm just the messenger. Come on!" Ailene giggled.

Julianne dropped the bandage on the table and took the side of her gown in hand. She hurried after the other girl, down the corridor and through the great door into the body of the Sanctuary. Sister One, a stern looking older woman, stood waiting to escort her to Maa's study. She knocked on the door, which stood ajar.

"Come in." Maa's deep soothing voice was unmistakable.

Sister pushed the door open, waving Julianne in.

"Thank you, Sister One. That will be all." The woman bowed and left.

Maa sat in a cushioned chair in front of a small fireheat, a booklet in her hand. She'd been reading.

"Sit." Maa gave a graceful wave toward the chair opposite.

Julianne adjusted her scarf over her hair and hurried across the floor to perch on the edge of the seat.

"Welcome, Julianne Adjudicator. I hear you call yourself Sasha."

Julianne felt the blood leave her head. "How did you know?"

"I read your ident when you first arrived, while you were recuperating from your journey." Maa's eyes laughed quietly at her, a sharp glint in their depths.

"Yes. That is, Sasha's a nickname."

"Really? That's not what your father says."

"My father?" Julianne glanced around the room in alarm, as if he might be there. "Where is he?"

"Now, that I don't know."

"Oh." She was flustered. "I called myself Sasha because I didn't want anyone to know who I was," she admitted.

"Ah. Well, that makes sense. Clever girl. Your secret is safe with me."

Maa's deep voice was so soothing, Julianne felt herself begin to relax.

"You've come to the right place. I know you have some doubts, but all the women soon discover that they're safe here. We have a good life. Without men in the compound it's soothing and quiet. We don't have the ups and downs, the turmoil caused by too much testosterone." She thought she detected laughter in Maa's voice.

Julianne felt herself getting sleepy. Her head nodded and she jerked upright, shifting in the chair uncomfortably. "Thank you, Maa. I'm very grateful."

"Don't worry, Julianne. Your father will be fine, you will be ..."

CHAPTER TWELVE

When Julianne woke she was in the women's room at the entry. She rolled over on her mattress, then stared at the ceiling. She'd fallen asleep while talking to Maa! How rude! What must she think?

She lay back against the blanket, much more relaxed. She'd been having doubts about being here, and now those doubts were gone. This was a good place, and Maa had said Father would be fine, so she needn't worry.

When she arrived back in the medicine room, the bandage was right where she'd dropped it an hour ago. She read the time keeper with surprise. Much more than an hour ago. She'd missed evening sup.

The others were reading in the break room. They greeted her with smiles as she entered with her booklet in hand. It was Book One of the Maa Series.

63

All the girls here were still on Book One, but she knew there were many more books to read and study as she grew in her knowledge of the Sanctuary

She opened the booklet and read the first sentence. 'You have made the right decision, coming to a place of fairness and peace'.

But she couldn't concentrate tonight. Why did she keep falling asleep when Maa talked to her? And why was her mind changed when she woke? She gave a mental shrug. It was good that she was at ease.

She fingered the page of the booklet longingly. It had been ages since she'd been able to practice her origami and she missed it terribly. She taught at the small school in the City twice a week and took great delight in the excitement the children showed at each new piece they created. There was no spare paper here to work with, and besides, they were here to work.

Just then the beltlink beeped, and she glanced at the device attached to the lapel of her robe. Two men were arriving. She'd need help dealing with them.

"Yvette," she said quietly. "Some men are here, one is injured."

The others closed their booklets and rose.

"You bring them in, Sasha. I'll get the doctor," said Yvette. "The others can prepare the medicine room and the men's bath."

Julianne picked up her handlight and went down the dark path to the perimeter wall. She struggled with the deadbolt and managed to unlock the door, swinging it wide as she stepped out into the gloom. Her light showed a tall, rough looking man standing in the darkness holding the reins of a mule. There was a body strapped to the saddle. *Was his companion already dead?*

"Come in," she said. "This way." They walked through the door and she locked and bolted it behind them.

"We'll take the mule into the barn, then we can carry your man from there." She led the way along the path to the small corral and lean-to that served as a stable for the animals of the transient men who came to the Sanctuary for help.

"There's feed for your mule." She pointed to the covered container. "But perhaps you'll come back to take care of that later." The man barely glanced at her as he unbuckled a belt that was holding the rider in the saddle. The body slowly tumbled off and he caught it, hoisting it onto his shoulder.

"I can help," she offered.

"No need. Where are we going?" His voice was brusque, sharp.

Julianne turned and hurriedly led the way directly to the men's quarters, equipped with a table and benches, a bathing alcove and sleeping pallets on the floor against one wall. "Right here. Lay him on this mattress."

The man leaned and gently laid his friend down. He sighed and straightened. "I hope you can help. He's near death."

For the first time, Julianne got a look at him. His eyes were a light blue, so pale and fierce that they pierced her to her soul and made her breath catch. The face was tanned and stern, sharp lines marked the corners of his mouth beneath the blond beard.

"We will do our best, sir. My name is Sasha." She bowed.

"I'm Abe," he said, and laid a hand on the patient's grey head. "This is Kerr. He's a good man."

She hurried from the room to find the doctor, her mind whirling. *Abe?* His face and bearing were striking, with those pale eyes and white blond hair. Even in his tribesmen clothes he looked like he would take command of the place from sheer force of will. She found the doctor, a middle aged pudgy woman with a keen gaze, in the medicine room packing a basket with supplies.

"He's here, Doctor, waiting. They're tribesmen from the hills."

"Take me to him," she replied and hefted her basket.

Abe helped remove Kerr's clothing, the pants already slit to the knee on one side. A bloody bandage sagged over a dark red feverish-looking wound. Doctor neatly cut the rag off to reveal a hole in the leg that appeared black and rotten in the core. A foul smell arose from the injury. Doctor took a shallow breath and looked at Abe. "Your friend is in very poor shape."

"Yah, I know. We got here as fast as we could."

Doctor nodded and probed the wound with a rubber-plastic instrument. The injured man moaned deep in his chest and twitched on the mattress. "Fetch a solution basin," she instructed Julianne as she took a sharp knife from the basket and began to cut into the tissue. Julianne covered her mouth with her hand and fled.

CHAPTER THIRTEEN

Abe Farmer poured more water over his back and grabbed the handle of the sponge. He soaped and scrubbed himself vigorously. He'd never felt so dirty. As the soapy brown water ran into the drain, he began work on his head. He probably hadn't washed his hair thoroughly since the attack on the road to Krimen with Uncle Jade Hawker weeks ago. His scalp itched from dirt and sweat.

What had Uncle Jade to do with that attack? He had rolled the thought around inside his brain so many times it almost had a sheen on it. Abe had travelled with Jade Hawker on a selling trip to the northern territories. Their last stop had been at the home of a rubber-plastics manufacturer near the town of Krimen where the owner, Mr Laboucaine, had invited them to stay for dinner. But later Jade insisted they leave and set out on the track back to town. It had been nearing midnight. Alarmed, Laboucaine tried to have them stay, told them no one used that road at night, not even his own men.

Yet Jade insisted. He said they had to be on the road to Krimenreh first thing in the morning, and it was important they leave. The attack had happened several hours into the trek, when they were all dozing in their saddles, waiting for the mules to get them to their destination.

The wound in Abe's thigh was almost healed, the skin pink and shiny. It was tender to the touch, but he could walk without a problem. His side was a different matter. He soaped gingerly around the torn flesh. The scar was going to be significant, but it was mending well. It didn't need bandaging any more, thin new skin was beginning to cover the once gaping hole. But it was sore and raw, and he still felt a stab of pain when he tried to lift anything.

Here at the Sanctuary, they could rest for a few days, recuperate. They'd even get fed. Kerr was out cold on the pallet right now. The doctor had dug out rotten flesh from the wound in his leg and packed the hole with medicine, then bound it with a cloth. Kerr had passed out long before she finished tending him.

If they stayed here, he'd begin to mend, there'd be time for him to gain some strength. The mule also needed rest, because Kerr couldn't travel yet on his own two feet. For the first time since the raid on Ventuzzo's village, he felt the tension ease in his gut.

Walking over and testing the water in the steaming bath, he gratefully eased his aching body down into the heat. His side burned. He held his breath and waited while he grew accustomed to the temperature, then managed to lower himself fully. He floated. It felt like heaven.

He was almost asleep when he heard the door open. He froze at the sound. Over his shoulder, he watched the woman named Sasha walk softly into the chamber. She was beautiful, her long dark brown hair curled over her shoulders under the head shawl. She'd helped him arrange Kerr on the mattress, and when she'd glanced up to reassure him that the doctor was coming, he'd been struck by her eyes. They were large, a strange blue grey colour with green mixed in, surrounded by long thick lashes. Those eyes reminded him of a stormy sea. They'd held him immobile for a moment before she turned away to arrange bandages.

She picked up his clothes and folded them in a pile on the bench. He watched her profile, the straight nose and pouting lips, before he half rose from the water. She startled at the sight of him.

"Oh, I'm sorry, Mr. Abe. I thought you were done. I just left your robe and I'll take your clothes to be cleaned. I have Mr Kerr's as well, we'll return them to you tomorrow."

"Thank you. Can I empty my pockets before you go?"

Her laugh ran lightly over his body like the caress of a breeze. Abe sank back into the bath, glad to have the cover of water to disguise his reaction. Had it been that long since he'd been with a woman?

"Of course you can. I'm sorry. Shall I just leave them here? You can knock on this door to let me know when you're ready." She smiled and moved out of the room.

He watched that closed door for a moment, wondering what her role was here at the Sanctuary. Was she new, or had she been here a long time? Could she leave if she wanted?

He shook that thought out of his head and rose to grab the towel hanging on the bar. The robe was warm as he shrugged it on. He couldn't remember being so tired. Emptying his pockets on the bench, he sorted the items he'd collected, folding knife and pieces of rope, dried strings of mutton. There was also the small cloth bag of jewels that had fallen out of the pockets of one of the dispossessed during the fight at Ventuzzo's village. His ident was in a hidden pocket.

He pulled it out, piling everything together. Knocking briefly on the door Sasha had indicated, he went back to the corner of the room where Kerr lay. Tucking the items carefully under the corner of the mattress, he lay down beside his bodyguard and sank into a deep sleep.

There was movement in the room during the night. Kerr groaned long and low as someone tended his leg and forced some pills down his throat, but Abe felt they were safe here and sank quickly again into oblivion.

CHAPTER FOURTEEN

Abram rolled over and slowly surfaced. Rays of light coming through the window were from a sun high in the sky. It must be at least mid-day. He glanced over at Kerr beside him. His guard slept like a dead man, but his skin looked healthier, not as flushed and heated.

Lifting the covering, he examined the uncovered wound in his leg. The colour was much better around the injury. The hole was raw and red, still weeping, but the dark colour of infection had faded. He sighed and sank back on the mattress. They'd just made it. He was convinced Kerr wouldn't have lasted another day.

Yawning, he scrubbed his fingers through the beard covering his jaw. Would he manage another bath before they had to leave? He'd forgotten how it felt to be clean, the ripe smell of sweat had become ingrained until he barely noticed it. He scratched his head. Even his scalp felt better. He grinned and pushed himself to a sitting position.

Better tend to the mule. He'd fed it last night, but the animal would be hungry again. He tugged the strange robe over his head and buttoned it at the throat. It felt odd to wear the thing, with the large S worked into the fabric down the back. Still, he'd get used to it. They were only going to be here a short time, till Kerr was on the mend.

Outside the sun was bright, the sky cloudless. As he emerged from the doorway he saw the girl, Sasha, disappear into the lean-to where his mule was tethered. Curious, he walked closer and bent to peer through the opening. She wore the same garment as last night, a heavy robe of muted grey material. Her long hair shone in the dim light, the head shawl tugged tight under that determined chin.

She poured a bucket of mash into the feeder and stroked the mule's neck as she crooned to him. The mule snorted and dove into the feed, now and then raising his head to butt her arm. She laughed and pushed back, rubbing him between the ears.

"What are you doing to my mule?"

Sasha jumped back in alarm. "Oh, my goodness. You surprised me."

Abe laughed. He couldn't help it. She looked so cute backed up against the animal's neck, her mouth open in astonishment. He wanted to close those pouting lips with a kiss. "You're spoiling that animal. He'll expect me to pet him every time I turn around."

Her laugh was infectious, and he grinned back at her. "You were still sleeping," she said. "You and Mr Kerr. Both exhausted, I expect. Most people are when they arrive here. I thought I'd make sure the mule was okay. You'll want him nice and strong for when you leave."

"When is that?"

"Pardon?"

"When do we have to leave?"

She sobered quickly. "I'm not sure, I'm new here. But I think you have to go once your man is well enough to travel. Now, there's a meal waiting for you. You must be hungry."

Just then, Abe's stomach growled and she must have heard it too, because she giggled and hurried off to the entry door of the men's quarters. "This way."

He followed her into the men's room, watching her hips sway under the loose cloth. A table at the side had been set with two dishes. One plate was piled high with food, and he suddenly felt faint with hunger. He barely restrained from gorging it down in front of her.

As he lowered himself to the bench, she took the second dish, a small bowl of what looked like stew, and turned toward the mattress. "I'll feed your friend if he's able to eat," she said and set it down on the stool beside him.

"Mr Kerr, how do you feel?"

75

Abe watched as he ate. She lifted Kerr's head and propped him up with a roll of blankets, then carefully spooned a few bites into him. She smiled and spoke encouragingly as she held each small morsel to his mouth.

Kerr managed to get some down, but the old man's face was flushed a fiery red by the time he was finished. Abe thought it was the effect of the woman feeding him, rather than any infection. He grinned to himself. Kerr must be on the mend.

Sasha left with the dishes and he lay down again, suddenly exhausted. He slept.

~ * * * ~

At dusk the next evening, three men came into the men's entry, guards from the look of them. They wore full, bushy beards but their hair was clipped short. Their shirts were dark brown wool, nicely stitched. And the banners they wore all said the same thing --*Sanctuary*-- in even letters down the front.

The first man pointed the other two to the bench and proceeded to give himself a thorough wash. He shook himself off and sat in the hot bath for a few minutes. There was the sound of movement behind the door to the women's quarters, then it opened and Sasha appeared. She gazed nervously at the three men staring back at her, then focussed on the one in the bath.

"We're ready for you, Captain," she said. Her expression was sober with apprehension and Abe got to his feet, wondering what was going on. The other men stood as well and faced him, as the captain grabbed a towel and Sasha disappeared back through the door.

"Just mind your own business, man. This is Sanctuary business, Maa set it up herself."

"Okay, fine." Abe sat, his gaze pinned to the door as the Captain went in and closed it behind him. The next man rose and began to wash himself down. Abe heard the echo of voices behind the women's door, then silence for a long time. He'd relaxed on the bench, and the second guard was lowering himself into the hot bath to soak when they heard a high pitched scream that was quickly muffled, followed by the sound of more voices then silence. The guards froze, then quickly looked at each other.

Abe sat with his hands clenched, trying to imagine what was going on. Was Sasha in trouble? She hadn't given him any indication of that, but then she wouldn't know that he'd come to her aid if she needed him. He couldn't bear the stillness and rose to pace.

The last guard watched him pass a few times before he offered in a low voice, "He's just getting his satisfaction. That's all. We all get satisfaction with one of the women when it's our turn. It's part of our pay." He laughed harshly, showing a broken tooth in the front of his mouth. "The best part of our pay if you ask me, apart from the food." The men finished bathing and left, sending two more guards in.

Much later the door opened, and Abe spun around.

Sasha stood in the entry as the captain emerged. The colour was high in his cheeks, a sleepy expression of contentment on his face as he headed straight outside.

She turned back into the women's quarters, her face now white and still. Her hand shook where it rested on the door handle.

CHAPTER FIFTEEN

In the bathrobe of Duncan's apartment, Sable Maude stepped out of the tiny shower and towelled dry. Even in the short time in prison, he'd lost weight. But not muscle. He examined himself critically in the foggy mirror. He still looked good, strong and powerful, just thin. He'd remedy that, given a bit of time. He combed his shoulder length hair back from his face and checked his image in the mirror. He wasn't a vain man but knew he was handsome, with strong features and a wide mouth, his eyes large and persuasive.

Ignoring Little Harry, he donned the clean clothes he'd appropriated from Duncan's drawer. There'd be time to get a haircut and buy himself something else to wear when he left here, another set of garments that would be worthy of a territory monarch. Because that's what he intended to become.

He'd change his name, something from Adar Silva, perhaps. That's where the Old Emperor had had his palace, so there was some logic to it. He imagined his new house, large, imposing, just outside the Khandarken border so the military and the Constables couldn't touch him.

Smuggling had been profitable, not to mention that it kept him supplied with young boys for his bed. His loins tightened. It had been a long time, and he was hungry for some young male flesh. But not yet. There was a lot to accomplish first.

He dismissed Little Harry from his mind. He was of no use to him and would be dead soon anyway. He had mangohrea, caught from his lovely wife, Zanata. He didn't seem to know anything about Sable's arrest, and so he'd lost interest in him.

But what did Duncan want? He was intrigued. Duncan was a force to reckon with. He'd had no notion the Assistant Chief Constable, clever man, wasn't totally dedicated to his job. Perhaps he wanted to make a deal of some kind.

There was a small commotion in the main room of the apartment, and Sable yanked the bathrobe door open. Duncan had arrived. He was a medium height older man, a little shorter than Sable, with dark red hair turning grey at the temples, cut short like fuzz on his head, and long sideburns. He wore the constable's uniform with his rank visible on the shoulder, but had removed the flat hat. "What have we here?" he quipped. "A circus? Some of you will have to go."

Little Harry shivered and shook his head. "I'm not going," he announced petulantly. "I have nowhere to go."

"I'm not staying," Sable replied quietly. "I have plenty of places to go."

Duncan looked at him curiously. "So, you're Maude."

Sable nodded.

"Who's this?" He pointed to Mateo, snoring on the small couch.

"My driver."

"I didn't see a vehicle outside."

Sable felt his face go red at the hint of a cynical smile on the older man's face. It infuriated him. He refused to blush because nothing embarrassed him, but even so he felt colour climb his neck. It was intolerable. "It's outside the City walls," he gritted, glaring fire at Duncan's stupid grin.

"I see. Well, can we talk?"

"Depends."

"On what?"

"The topic."

"Well, that's confidential." Duncan shot a glance at Harry. "Let's step outside."

Sable gave a short nod and walked to the door, Duncan on his heels.

On the landing, Duncan took his elbow and pulled him to the side, away from the windows of his apartment. Sable yanked his arm out of the man's grasp, just managing to refrain from belting him across the face. No one touched him, not without permission, not if he wasn't in jail.

Duncan seemed surprised, but waved him away from the entry. "We just have to keep our voices down," he commented. "No need for Little Harry to hear."

He scrutinised Sable's outfit and snorted softly. "My suit seems large on you, but you're welcome to it."

"My own clothes need burning," Sable gritted.

"Of course, I understand completely," Duncan began. "Now, I have a little something going with Harry."

"The talc mine at Farmer Holdings."

He looked surprised. "He told you?"

Sable nodded.

"I see." Duncan rubbed his chin. "We've had a bit of trouble."

"Such as?"

"We tried an all-out assault and were repelled."

"Is Farmer Holdings that well protected?" Sable sneered. "It's just a farm with some labourers and a few dispossessed living at Farmerville. It couldn't have been much of an assault."

Duncan watched Sable's smile and replied with one of his own. "You've been in jail. What do you know?"

Sable could feel the anger rising once more. *Who did this man think he was?* He was talking to the Monarch of the Territories.

"The daughter married Major Dante Regiment," Duncan continued. "There are all kinds of military out there guarding every access point."

"She did?" Sable felt surprise flood through his brain. *I'm betrothed to her, she was supposed to marry me!* The wedding was to have taken place the day he was arrested. How had she married Dante Regiment within weeks of the date of their own marriage?

He'd been looking forward to that wedding. Not that he fancied women, he didn't. But Farmer Holdings controlled a vast swath of land in the Southern Territory that reached the Adar Silva border and included the market town of Farmerville, the fishing village of Coronation and the talc mines, not to mention acres of gardens and large herds of farm animals. He'd be marrying down in social status, but gaining a lot of collateral. And he'd have a secure and permanent position on the border of Khandarken. What more could a smuggler ask for?

The brother wouldn't have proved much opposition. Abram Farmer was an easy going fellow, from what he'd observed. He ran the place like his father had, with courtesy and inclusiveness but little iron authority. Sable didn't think he'd have been any kind of barrier to gaining control of the operation.

But Dante Regiment was a different story. Dante was the General's only son now that Virgil was dead, and the second son was in line to take the position of General of the Khandarken military when his father retired.

Sable felt this news like a blast against the foundations of his empire. He'd lost his position in the Southern Territory, lost his control of that part of the border lands. He'd have to visit his father to find out what had happened. At least the Farmers wouldn't have the support of their Governor. His father, Francis Maude, must have strongly opposed the match when his son was the original intended bridegroom.

"What is it you want from me?" Sable stood straighter and looked the man in the eye. He smelt the faint stench of sewer rising from the pipes beneath the streets of Old Towne. Amazing that he could identify the odour, given where he'd been living just hours ago.

Duncan shifted his feet. "I thought we could work out a partnership. You seem to have a few good men and a knowledge of the hinterlands."

Sable snorted. Why would he make any information available to this man? On the other hand, he'd broken him out of jail, he might have something to offer. He bent a piercing gaze on the Assistant Chief Constable. "What did you have in mind?"

"Ah, that's better. I think we can do business together."

"Without Little Harry."

Duncan regarded him for a moment. "Yes, without Harry."

"He's dying anyway."

Duncan frowned. "I had something else in mind. I think the talc mine is a lost cause. You can't capture a mine. I know Harry hasn't given up and I'll help him any way I can." He glared down the lane, watching a rat dig in the trash at the back door of a building across the cobblestones.

Then he brightened. "But I like your enterprise on the Jiran borders. There's more money to be made there. I'm setting up some locations for entertainment houses near the territory capitals, and women are impossible to find. If they're captured from within Khandarken, the constables never stop looking for them. We need women like the ones you bring in, from Jiran and beyond. I heard you sometimes get Orientals, they'd go for a premium."

Sable gave him a cold glance. "I already have markets for the women I bring in."

Duncan rubbed his chin. "But the market could be so much bigger. I have some highly trained, disciplined men who are at my command. We'd be partners."

"How long do you think you can remain Assistant Chief with this kind of activity?"

"This is my exit strategy. Think about it."

Sable snorted.

CHAPTER SIXTEEN

Sable made it back down the tunnel under the City walls and out the hole before dawn. Sprinter was waiting, the hydro truck camouflaged by broken branches piled around it, so it wasn't recognizable from the track or the air. He pulled boards aside as Sable emerged from the cavity in the earth, Mateo hard on his heels.

"We need to get to Deep Creek, but I imagine there's a lot of activity on the roads since the prison break."

"I've heard some static over the military waves," said Sprinter. "We can take the back way. But it's longer."

"That's fine. I need some sleep."

By nightfall, Sprinter drove cautiously down the back streets of Deep Creek, and parked near the local market at the transit terminal. Sable yawned and stretched as he sat up. "This is good. Loan me your coat, Mateo. I've got a meeting."

Sable stepped down from the truck and blended with the crowd. His hair was still too long but he fit right in with the farmers who were packing up their produce for the night and loading it into wagons. He took an indirect route, posing as a day worker heading home, head down after a long day. He ended up at the rear door of the offices of the Governor of the Southern Territory. He'd sent a wristlink message to Francis Maude earlier and knew someone would meet him.

When he tested the door, it was unlocked. Easing it open, he stepped soundlessly into the hallway. The only noise was from the street out front, where vehicles passed and pedestrians strolled by. The office was silent.

As he gently closed the door, he heard the click of a pistol being cocked. Ah, Father was here and he was angry. Sable walked into the front room.

Francis Maude lounged in the chair beside his secretary's desk, one leg lifted, the ankle resting on the other knee. He held the pistol down by his side.

"Come in, Sable." He waved the barrel of the gun toward the chairs in front of him. "Take a seat."

He sat, his back straight, head held high.

"What can I do for you?" His father's tone was strained.

"I thought we should catch up," Sable replied in a mild voice. It was dim in the room, weak light leaking in from the streetlamps outside. But he caught the gleam of his father's good eye as he swung his chair around to face him. The black patch over his other eye became invisible in the gloom.

"Good idea. Tell me what you've been doing." There was now a dangerous note to his father's voice. Sable had irritated and angered Maude many times over the years, but he sounded different tonight, iron hard and determined. "Did you organize the jail break?"

"No, I didn't."

"I see. Interesting that it happened just before the verdict was to come down on your appeal."

He remained silent.

Francis shifted in his chair. "What do you want, Sable?"

"I want to know what happened at the Farmer wedding."

His father paused, his single eye pinned to Sable's face. "Bethlehem Farmer married someone else."

"Dante Regiment."

"So, you already know."

"I just found out. How could you let that happen? She was to marry me. She should have waited. A farmer's daughter doesn't just brush off the son of a Territory Governor and marry another man."

Francis snorted. "You are nothing now. Nothing. You're an outlaw and a traitor, and you've lost your court appeal. The verdict came down this morning. You're sentenced to death."

Sable gave no reaction. He already knew that would be the verdict, had been planning against that fact since he was first convicted. "So, now what?" He spread his hands. "Why didn't you stop the marriage?"

"I approved it, Sable. I withdrew the betrothal and gave my approval."

Sable sprang to his feet and found himself staring down the barrel of the pistol pointed square at his heart. "How could you do that?" He felt the rage of betrayal climb his throat, and he shook with the power of it.

His father slowly rose to his feet, forcing him backward toward the door. "Because I had just found out you smuggle women and young boys. I disown you, Sable. You're no son of mine. You're nothing to me now. Leave and don't come back. I'll arrest you and turn you over to the Constables myself when next you cross my path."

Sable backed out the door, turned and stalked with fury from the building. It was better this way. His father had nothing to offer him. He was moving on. He'd be the Monarch of the Territories before he was finished.

And his father would turn him over to the Constables? Sable snorted.

He had the Constables in his back pocket.

CHAPTER SEVENTEEN

J ulianne lowered Ailene into the hot water,
carefully bathing her friend's face and throat with
a soft cloth. She couldn't help but notice the fresh
bruises on her skin, her swollen mouth and the marks
round her wrists where they had been rubbed raw
from being restrained by strong male hands.

Ailene lay motionless, but looked away when
Julianne talked to her. "Doesn't this feel good? The
water is so soothing." She dipped the cloth again and
wrung it out in a gentle shower over the girl's
shoulders.

The other day, after the acolytes had listened to
Maa's talk, Ailene had been happy about doing her
duty with the guards. She'd fallen asleep on the tile
floor the same way Julianne and the others had, and
when they woke and met back in the entry, she'd
been her cheerful sunny self. "I know it's my turn

with the guards this time," she'd whispered to Julianne. "And I'm fine with that. We all should do what we can to make this system work. The Sanctuary has offered me refuge, and it's the least I can do for everyone." She'd nodded decisively.

"I was worried about it, at first," she'd added, a small frown marring her forehead. "When I saw Yvonne, she seemed so silent afterward. It frightened me. But look at the two of them. Yvette and Yvonne are moving into the Inner Sanctuary, and I will too. Just as soon as another woman comes in who will replace me. Just think, Sasha. We'll all be together, protected and safe once you pass through."

Julianne had wondered, knowing her own doubts came and went with her thoughts. But Ailene was a different person now from that confident young woman of yesterday.

"Come on, you can do this," Julianne crooned. "You told me it was going to be all right." Her heart quaked in her chest. She had to get through this as well if she was ever going to be allowed into the Inner Sanctuary. Maa had told them all it was their duty but also their choice. She wouldn't make anyone perform this obligation, but the women could choose to serve. Ailene had been given a drink that made her sleepy, and she'd been smiling and ready when the Captain came into the room. Now she was silent and withdrawn.

"I bet they'll bring a nice syllabub for evening sup." Julianne spoke soothingly.

It was already late in the day, but Ailene had been in no condition to rise from her bed until now. And it was only with a great deal of coaxing and cajoling that Julianne had been able to get her into the bath.

"Let me help." She lifted a towel off the warming bar and held it out, wrapping it around the girl's shoulders as she rose. "Your clean robe is hanging right here."

Ailene let her lower the robe over her head, but then staggered and put a hand against the wall for support. "I think I have to return to bed." Her face was pinched.

"Of course." Julianne put an arm around her waist and led her through the corridor. "I'll bring you a bite to eat when evening sup arrives."

"Thank you." Ailene collapsed on the side of her mattress. "It wasn't so bad," she said, desperation in her eyes as she glanced up at Julianne. "It wasn't so bad, Sasha. I'm tired, that's all."

Julianne felt tears start behind her eyes as she urged her friend to lie back against the pillow. Ailene rolled over and faced the wall. "I just want to be alone for a while."

"Yes, of course." Julianne went back to the bath and tidied up the cloths and soap, the sponges, putting everything in its place.

When she got to the dining hall, Sister Three and Yvette were already seated. Yvonne had gone, graduated from the entry the day before and now had her place in the inner rooms of the Sanctuary. Yvette must be hopefully waiting for another woman to appear soon so she could leave to be with her sister. Julianne took a place on the bench.

"Where is Ailene?" Sister Three's face was serene.

"She won't be joining us."

Sister sighed. "You young girls make such a big thing about the duty to service the guards. In the early days, we all took turns. It was months before there were enough new female recruits coming in to relieve us of the burden." Cheerfully, she helped herself to salad and passed the bowl to the girls.

Yvette bit her lip as she served herself, slanting a look at Julianne.

When Sister had finished she rose, acknowledged the bows from the girls and swept from the room. They sat back down.

"How is she, really?" Yvette had hardly touched her meal.

"She's not well. I had to work hard to get her up for a bath, then she went back to bed."

"Yes, that's how I felt. Too tired to handle anything. Too defeated."

Julianne watched her. "Is it always like that?"

"I'm not sure what it is. It hurts the first time of course, but they don't stop. You don't know the man, there is no connection with him. They tell us the second time we service one of the men it isn't so bad, but for me it was the same."

Julianne felt bile climb her throat and pushed away the remains of her dinner. "I'm not sure I can do this."

Yvette just looked at her. "You have to know if you have a choice. Some of us don't. Do you?"

Julianne shrugged. *Do I?* Going back home wasn't an option, especially if her father was still gone. Zanata would use her as fodder for her plans, and she'd have no escape. It would be the same as staying here and servicing the guards.

Her thoughts drifted to Abe and his injured friend in the men's entry. *Could I go with them when they leave?* They might not want her to come along on their journey. *What other choices were there?* She couldn't think of any, except to stay in the entry for the rest of her life. If she didn't service the guards, she wouldn't enter the Inner Sanctuary.

"I'll take her a bite of dinner; maybe I can persuade her to eat something."

Yvette nodded. "I'll clean up in the men's entry tonight and give you a break. By the way, do you know anyone named Abram Farmer?"

Julianne started to shake her head, but then thought of Abe and Kerr and paused. "Why?"

"Well, I overheard a strange conversation. I was cleaning the tiles in the corridor outside Maa's study today, and the door happened to be ajar. I heard Maa talking on her voicelink. I know I shouldn't have listened, but how could I help it?" There was an impish smile on her face. "She was talking about Mr.

Farmer and how if Zanata wanted to see him, now was a good time to come. I wondered if we were going to have a visit from the man."

Julianne's hands suddenly stilled in the process of spooning a small portion of fruit compote into a dish for Ailene. *Zanata? Coming here?* There was probably more than one woman named Zanata in Khandarken. But the fact that one was coming to the Sanctuary, when Julianne had just arrived here made her skin crawl. And what if Abe with his injured friend was really Abram Farmer? Shouldn't she warn him?

Yvette sighed. "We haven't had a visit from a decent man since I came here. They're always the dispossessed or tribesmen like the two we have now. Maybe he'll be handsome and want to find himself a wife."

Julianne attempted a smile. "Do you want a husband, Yvette?"

Yvette gave her a puzzled look. "You wouldn't think so, would you, after what I've been through. Yet, if I met a nice man, someone kind, I'd be willing. I don't suppose I'll ever meet someone like that in here."

~ * * * ~

Later that night, when everything grew quiet, Julianne quietly rolled over on her pallet to check her companions. Ailene and Yvette were both sound asleep as she silently sat up and tucked her feet into her slippers. Closing the door softly, she moved swiftly across the floor to the men's room.

Only the small care light was turned on. In the dimness she could see the two men asleep on pallets on the floor. She hesitated. They would think it strange that she was sneaking around at night, and if this wasn't Abe Farmer, he might mention to Sister Three that he'd had an odd conversation with Sasha in the entry.

Just then, Abe moved restlessly and rolled over. His pale curly hair caught the low light and gleamed. He lifted his head. "Sasha?"

She dropped to her knees beside the pallet and whispered softly. "Abe, I need to talk to you."

"Yah." He scrubbed his hands down his face and ran his fingers back through his hair. He sat up, his chest bare, and arranged the blanket to cover himself. "What is it? Is Kerr sick again?"

"No, not Kerr. I need to ask you something." She gazed into those pale eyes with their penetrating gaze and felt again that connection that she'd felt the first time she saw him. How extraordinary to find a stranger so compelling.

Will he tell me the truth? She wouldn't know until she asked. "Are you Abram Farmer?"

He jerked slightly, then focussed fiercely on her face. His reaction told her what she needed to know even if he didn't say a word. She sat back in resignation.

"Did you search my things?" He put a hand under the corner of the mattress and pulled out a package of items. She saw his ident there.

"No, but someone must have. I'm sure they search everyone who comes in. They knew who I was."

He nodded, waited.

"Someone is coming to find you."

"How do you know that?"

"I was just told by one of the girls, who overheard a conversation that she shouldn't have listened to."

"Who's coming?" His face was tense, his voice tight.

"Someone called Zanata. Does that name mean anything to you?"

He watched her face but didn't answer. Instead he asked, "Do you know when she's coming?"

"Two days. Day after tomorrow."

"Two days. Are you sure?"

"Yah. Will you leave?"

He nodded, looking down at his friend lying silently on the pallet beside him. Kerr had opened his eyes and was watching them. "Two days, Kerr?"

Kerr nodded.

"Ah," Julianne sat back on her heels. "I wondered if you would leave. Will you take me with you?"

Abe grinned. "I'd love nothing more." There was a snort from Kerr, and he glanced down and added teasingly, "I wasn't talking to you. But you must be feeling a whole lot better." He looked back at Julianne and shook his head. "How can we take you?"

She stiffened. "I mean it. I can't stay here. Zanata is my stepmother. She's traded me to a judge adjudicator in the City for a favour on a court case."

Abe hesitated. "We can't take you, Sasha. We have a long way to go, and you're safe here."

"I'm strong, I walked here. And I can help you."

"You can?" His gaze was pinned to her face.

"I can gather the medicine that Kerr needs, we can get feed from the lean-to for your mule."

"I can get the feed myself." He smiled.

"I can drug the guards so they won't stop you leaving, because they want to strip you of any valuables before you depart. And if I stay, I'll be the next woman that the guard sleeps with."

His playful smile disappeared, replaced by grim determination. "Well, that's not how I imagined the Sanctuary would work. You have my complete attention."

CHAPTER EIGHTEEN

Next morning, Julianne brought the men's meals, accompanied by extra bread and ale that they hid to take with them when they left. She managed to fill a small bag with the medicine Kerr would need.

Did other women run off from the Sanctuary when they'd been taken in without question? She didn't think so. All the security here was directed at stopping people from entering, not keeping them from leaving. It seemed wrong to run when she'd been offered shelter, yet the Sanctuary hadn't been quite the safe place she'd expected.

She located her old clothes, cleaned and mended, in a cubby labelled with her name in the main quarters. The dress and cloak she'd arrived in seemed to be the most impractical outfit to travel through the mud and bush of the territories. Nevertheless, she took them and moved other clothes around so the cubby didn't appear empty.

Surely there was something better to wear. She waited for an opportunity, watching till the room was empty. Pawing through the guards' storage she found a smaller suit of men's clothes that might work. They'd be big on her, but the shirt was serviceable, made of heavy wool, probably waterproof. And the pants would stay up with a belt or string to tie them on. Her own boots were still in good shape. With satisfaction, she took everything back to the entry and hid it in a bundle under her pallet.

When the evening meal arrived for the guards, she volunteered to help Yvette carry it out to the men. She managed to sprinkle sedative powder on each plate, although a sudden noise startled her and she dumped an extra bit on one meal. She giggled nervously. One guard might slumber longer than the others. She prayed they all slept at least until Abe, Kerr and she were long gone.

She was jittery when bedtime came, wondering how she'd know when to leave her pallet. Would they go without her? Cleaning up in the men's quarters, she bent to pick up a damp cloth near the bath and felt a hand at her waist. She jumped as Abe whispered in her ear, "Shh."

Turning, she looked up into those pale blue eyes. His hair was a shock of white blonde curls now that he'd scrubbed the stain out of it. It made him look like a river god. A shiver ran down her spine. Was he really going to help her?

"Listen, Sasha." A jolt of alarm hit her midsection. He didn't even know her real name. That was another problem, one she'd have to address later. Now was not the time to divulge it. "We'll leave in two hours. Do you have a time keeper?"

She shook her head. "There's one on the wall in the women's dining hall."

"Come outside, we'll meet in the lean-to and get the mule. Does the gate have a lock or code?"

"No, just a deadbolt on the inside."

"Okay. Two hours." He leaned in and gave her a soft kiss on the mouth that sent shivers down her throat, then grinned and walked away. She stood with her mouth open, watching him leave. *The nerve.* Well, it had been rather nice, intriguing even. She felt goose bumps shiver down her spine and smiled to herself.

Just as she tugged her robe over her head to crawl into bed, the beltlink buzzed. A message from the guard at the front indicated a single woman was approaching the gate. "I'll take care of her," she said to the others. "You go to sleep, Yvette." Ailene still hadn't stirred.

A middle aged woman, plump, well dressed, her face bruised, stood at the gate. Julianne helped her in. "Welcome to the Sanctuary," she said. "My name is Sasha."

"I just made it," the poor woman gasped, collapsing on the bench. "It was such a long trek and I never thought …"

"It's okay, you're here now. You're safe." This unfortunate woman was going to be next to entertain the guards, if Julianne ever managed to escape.

Tonight all she wanted to do was get everyone settled before it was time for her to leave. She glanced at the time keeper in the dining hall. Another half hour to go. She helped the woman onto a pallet, pulled her own bag of supplies from under her mattress and stashed it outside the main door, then crawled into bed.

A few minutes later, Sister Three walked through to check on the woman who'd just arrived and make sure the doors were locked. Julianne held her breath. *What if Abe leaves without me?*

Sister looked through the woman's things, retrieving the ident from an inside pocket and counting the money she found. Then she put it all back and checked the dining room for cleanliness, running her finger across the table and along the shelf against the wall, as Julianne lay tense in her bed. *Would the woman never go?*

Finally, Sister checked her reflection in the mirror and straightened the collar of her robe before going back through the corridor to the main hallway. Julianne heard the door quietly click closed. Slowly, she let her breath out and eased from under the blanket. She'd had a bath earlier and washed herself thoroughly, knowing it could be quite a while before she had another opportunity.

She didn't care. Even if she had to get dirty, walk into danger, take up with strangers, she wouldn't be at Zanata's mercy again. Because there was no mercy to be had there.

Tiptoeing into the dining hall, she saw with alarm she was ten minutes late. Hastily she escaped through the door into the men's entry and peeked at the pallets. They were empty, the men were already gone. Her heart began to pound heavily in her chest. This could all go wrong in a second.

Darting quietly out the door, boots in hand, she grabbed up her sack from the ground. She heard the nicker of the mule and raced down the path toward the sound. Someone grabbed her round the waist. She opened her lips to scream, but a hand was clapped over her mouth. "Sasha, it's me. Kerr's at the gate, we're ready to go." Her breath was coming in great gasps and her body shook with the effects of adrenaline. She lowered her head, trying to muffle her breathing, feeling her legs tremble in fright.

Abe lowered her to the ground, waited as she shakily laced her boots, and felt for her hand in the dark. He tugged her along to where the gate stood open. Kerr waited outside, already mounted. The guards were nowhere to be seen. They stepped through and Abe pulled the gate shut. "Let's go."

CHAPTER NINETEEN

There was no moon yet but the stars were bright in the sky. Abe seemed to be feeling his way, sticking to the stone-paved path that appeared lighter than the ground around it. Julianne walked behind the mule, nervously hoping the guards weren't waiting for them at the road. She heard a rustle and coughing sound in the bushes, as if someone was being sick, and let out a low yelp triggered by her strained nerves. Abe rounded on her. "What? What is it?"

A guard charged out of the bush and up the path toward them, his heavy beard black in the night, his raygun held low. "Where are you going? You can't leave without …"

Abe leaped forward, sending a fierce kick to the chest with the heel of his boot, knocking the guard flat on his back. His head made a soft *thunk* as it hit the stones. Then he leaned down and grabbed the raygun as the man tried to fumble it into position. When he struggled to sit, Abe hit him again, this time with his closed fist, and the guard's head turned to the side as he sagged into unconsciousness.

Abe slung the gun across his back, picked up the mule's reins and calmly carried on down the trail.

Julianne couldn't stop shaking. As she walked, she stumbled, her breath coming fast. The violent, decisive assault on the guard had caught her entirely by surprise. She didn't know this man Abram Farmer or his friend Kerr. That he could take out that man with his foot, finishing him off with one punch of his fist was so alarming she couldn't get her mind around it. *What have I gotten myself into? Where will I be safe?*

Sometime later, Abe pulled the mule to the side of the track, murmuring something to Kerr in a low voice. When she caught up on wobbly legs, he was digging in the dirt with a tree branch. "What are you doing? They could be coming after us!" A kind of panic rose up her throat. She was in a nightmare, and it could only end in disaster.

"I left something here. We need it." He scuffed with his boot as she watched the dark path behind them in horror.

Julianne tried to see the ground, but there little light. She got on her hands and knees and scrabbled around in the leaves. Her hand slid into a hole and she felt something dig into her palm. "Is this it?"

Abe came over and searched around. "Yah, good girl." He extended a hand to help her up, then pulled a long parcel out of the hole, brushed the dirt off and handed it up to Kerr in the saddle. "Hang onto this, we'll probably need it sooner than later."

They walked on through the black night.

~ * * * ~

A few hours later, despondency had set in. Julianne was so tired and afraid, she began to feel it almost didn't matter if they were caught. She had no strength left to fight. The last thing she wanted was for Abe to be sorry he'd let her come with them, but they'd been walking for a long time and she was afraid of him as well.

She caught up to him, one hand holding the hem of her robe out of the way to avoid tripping on it. "Do you know where we are?" Her voice came out weaker than she'd intended.

He peered down into her face. "We're just outside Discovery. There's a farm near here, if I can find it, with an abandoned barn. We could settle down in the barn for a day, catch our breath."

She let out a sigh. "That would be nice."

Abe reached to take her hand. "Yah, it would. Don't worry, we'll get there."

A sudden rushing sound, accompanied by the pounding of many hooves on the track came at them from behind. Abe dragged at her hand as he ran, tugging the mule off the road into the woods. She stumbled in the brush and fallen logs at the side, the mule huffing in fright just above her head as guards from the Sanctuary galloped past.

CHAPTER TWENTY

Emperor Carlton tugged at the collar of his robe. He liked how it draped around his big frame, but the sapphires that studded the material dug into the flesh at his neck. Perhaps the collar was too tight for him now. He'd put on some muscle in the months since his father died.

He and his men had gathered midday on a small plain in the south of Legitamia, the wild grasses yellow and brown bowing before a light breeze across the rough ground. There was a forest to the back of him, the conifers dark green and stunted from the altitude. A horde of men spread out before him, waiting for his words.

Just inside Legitamia's border, the province the Emperor occupied was a hotbed of planning and conspiracy to reconquer their old lands from the illegal control of others. He was now the undisputed leader of all that activity. The Old Emperor Aqatain was no longer here to deride his ideas, sneer at his attempts at leadership or show contempt for his son. Carlton was free to lead as he decided, not hold back out of a false respect for the old ruler.

General Barrington was Legitamia's dictator. He might be a despot, but he had allowed most of the towns and cities to elect their own government save for the capital, Gilsigg, where he maintained tight control. In the same slightly hedonistic fashion, although he controlled his country with an iron fist, he had allowed Emperor Aqatain to rule his own small and isolated province in the southern mountains, where Legitamia butted up against Khandarken. Maybe he felt they could be allies if it came to war again among the rebels.

Now that Aqatain was dead from a sudden heart attack some weeks ago, Emperor Carlton continued in his footsteps. He'd had a platform built here on a slope above where the troops were gathered, with a tent erected to shelter him from the sun. It gave him a good view of the platoon of soldiers lined up before him. More importantly, it gave the men a good view of him.

His counsellors stood at his elbow dressed in their best garments, twitching nervously. He could feel their anxiety, it seemed to leak out of them like shit from a goose. *What was wrong with these people?* They had no nerve. How could he reclaim an empire without going to war? *Ask for it back?* These scholars and historians, students of the past, they were well read but had no determination. He grunted impatiently as the men gathered before him.

General Elkon had positioned the section leaders below in the first line, many of them veterans who'd served under the Old Emperor during the Last War. *How would Father like that, being relegated to the title of Old Emperor?* During his lifetime it had been Emperor Aqatain, said with great deference by everyone from the boot black boy to the Generals who met with him.

The rank and file were in ordered lines behind them. There were only enough uniforms for the leaders. He'd remedy that soon enough, right after their first victories. But for now it would have to do. He could easily pick out the dispossessed among his troops. They may not have uniforms, but they were all ex-military and knew how to stand, how to organize themselves. They arranged in orderly rows, one pace apart, at attention with bodies in perfect alignment.

The others, mostly farmers, who were still loyal to the Old Empire were armed with axes, crossbows and handmade swords. They milled at the rear with no visible discipline. Every army needed cannon fodder. They would fill an important role.

When Carlton stood, a low sound swept through the men like the passing of a winter wind across the valley. When he raised his hands, there was sudden silence.

"Gentlemen of the Empire." A cheer went up, rising and flowing over the crowd. He waited as it swelled, then lifted his hands again. Eventually they fell silent.

"Gentlemen of the Empire! Thank you for coming to hear my plea. I am blessed to have the presence of my Advisor and esteemed Counsellors." He gestured to the men standing behind him. "Men of utmost loyalties, men of improbable strategies. Men of improbable strategies!"

He especially liked that last phrase. These men did sometimes come up with something that seemed so outrageous it just might work.

He pointed to the Generals at the foot of the platform. "The leaders of my army are here before us, with their hearts dedicated to the Empire. Dedicated to reclaiming our rightful position, our own justified lands. They have remained loyal and trustworthy, even through unctuous actions by the new, unlawful countries that have taken our place. Down with Khandarken! Down with Adar Silva!"

A roar rose from the hordes, and his pleased smile soon morphed into a delighted laugh. "Yah," he shouted, "we will succeed because of your loyalty, because of our determination, because of our triumph over the criminal element. Because of our right to sovereignty!"

Another roar erupted. He bowed his head but the cheers continued. He motioned the Generals forward, and they came one by one and knelt at his feet. He had a vial of his personal incense with him. It smelled of something wild, herbal and powerful. It reminded him of home, that place at the centre of the Old Empire that the infidels now called Adar Silva. He used it to sprinkle each in turn and prepare them for the coming battle.

CHAPTER TWENTY ONE

General Elkon rose from his place at the Emperor's feet and locked eyes with Advisor Judson, standing to the side of the Counsellors on the platform. The Advisor gave him a pointed look and jerked his head toward the back of the tent. Elkon nodded and stepped down to stand with the ranks as the ceremony continued.

Emperor Carlton sprinkled the last General and motioned the tribunes forward to receive his blessing. Elkon was pleased to see the men were in good rank, honoured by the ceremony and acknowledgement of their position. It boded well for the commitment and battle readiness of the troops. They'd been working for months with these men, training and planning. It would be good to get started. There was a time to train and there was a time to fight. The time to fight had come, before they began to lose men to other endeavours out of a lack of confidence or just plain boredom.

He watched as the Emperor spoke to each tribune before he sprinkled the incense. Carlton didn't know their names or their place in the ranks. But he understood the value of recognition, of making a personal connection with his men, maybe more than his father had. The Old Emperor had had little respect for his son, thinking him weak and not of a military mind.

Nor was Carlton a military man by physical makeup. He'd put on more weight since his father's death, fat that showed in a roll at his waist and around his neck. The Old Emperor had been hard in body as well as mind.

But Elkon believed he was smarter than Aqatain in some ways. Aqatain had been a tough man, fierce and ruthless. He could remember more than one occasion where he'd cut a man's throat for interrupting him when he was giving orders. But the Old Empire had been so mismanaged and corrupt at the end, that it was no wonder the constant fighting had finally succeeded in breaking it apart. The lands had been consumed by years of rebellion against Aqatain that eventually transformed and degenerated into battles between the different rebel forces, as well as between the rebels and the Empire.

The result was this mishmash of countries that had formed out of the Old Empire. Khandarken, with Adar Silva to the south as an ally, Jiran isolated to the west and at odds with all its neighbours, and Legitamia with its own replacement dictator. It was a hodgepodge of loyalties, compromises and long held anger amongst its people. It would be good to pull it together again, make it work as a unit under the rightful ruler.

Emperor Carlton was clever about people and not ashamed to let his emotions show. That speech was a good example. *Men of improbable strategies?* What did that mean to anyone when they were engaged in a firefight on the field of battle? But it was a phrase that had clearly tickled Carlton. And he showed it with his laughter. The men standing around Elkon had grinned at the repetition. It touched them.

He walked to the back of the platform in the hustle of bodies milling about. Judson Lanser was waiting for him.

"Elkon, are the men ready for this?"

Elkon nodded. "As ready as they'll ever be. You can't train forever, it becomes pointless and the men get bored."

"I know. But what's the backup plan? We only have two transports and the Emperor will be in one. How do you get to the battlefield?"

Elkon wondered where he was going with this line of thought. "There is no transportation going through the border. It's mountain ranges and trade roads. You know that."

Judson pursed his lips, his long sideburns quivering as he moved restlessly. "I don't think we're ready."

"How so?" The General felt something roil in his gut. If the Emperor didn't have the support of his Advisor, how would the troops fare?

"We need aircarts, transports and troop movers. Khandarken military has all those things, and more."

Elkon snorted, then tried to cover it with a cough, putting his hand over his mouth. "We don't have the budget of that country. And those transports will be useless in the hills at the border where we'll be crossing. All we need is a foothold. A village. If we can get to Discovery, we can take it. It's small, but has the facilities needed to serve as headquarters for the army. We can move on from there. We've been over this before."

He bent a fierce gaze on the Advisor. "We don't need to third guess the decision. It's been made and is now set in motion. What we need is your backing. Do we have it?" His hard tone indicated it was not a question.

Judson flushed darkly. "We've been over it before because it's a major issue." His jaw bulged as he clamped it shut.

"Do we have your backing?" Elkon demanded, his voice rising, and Judson glanced uncomfortably around.

"Yes. I just don't think we're ready."

"Well, the Emperor disagrees. Perhaps that's all we need to know."

CHAPTER TWENTY TWO

The dilapidated barn stood deep in an overgrown field just beyond the outskirts of the village of Discovery, right where he remembered it. Abe was glad the moon rose later in the evening. They would have missed the ruins entirely without the extra light to illuminate the landscape.

He led the mule through the high grass and thistles. Julianne, walking beside him, held tight to his hand. He could tell her energy was spent, and now she dragged one foot in front of the other in a desperate attempt to complete the journey. Her hand felt small and defenseless in his big mitt.

What was he thinking, bringing this girl along with them? Kerr told him he'd lost all reasoning. "She doesn't know yet that there's a price on your head," he'd argued. "But she's obviously desperate. What will she do when she finds out? Turning you in for the reward could be the only way she can get money to carry on. Then what? Besides, she's going to slow us down. Bad enough that I can't walk and your side is still mending."

Abe had ignored him and continued packing. But Kerr was right, of course. She was going to slow them down. The mule couldn't carry two, and here she was barely able to walk when they'd only been on the road for half a night.

But it was the threat of the guards that had made up his mind. That guard going into the women's quarters to have one of the girls had turned his stomach.

There had been a woman that he used to visit. She lived in the fishing village of Coronation, a widow from the Last War. She'd asked him over the first time to check her front porch, which she claimed had begun to sag.

Farmer Holdings owned Coronation and the small houses that made up the village. They rented the homes out to the fishermen and their families. Abe was her landlord. He'd gone to see what needed to be done, and was naively surprised to be invited into her bedroom. He'd been young, Father still off at war, and he'd been delighted at the offer. It had been pretty quick, that first encounter. He'd lain there on her bed, chest heaving, totally elated.

She'd been more pragmatic. "Bring me a case of apples next time," she said. "And be prepared to go twice, because you've got a lot to learn." That had hurt, his ego had shrunk for about a minute. The fact that he'd been invited back and would have knowledge of her more than once had eased that pain almost immediately.

He at once understood it was a straightforward arrangement. Her husband was dead and she still had needs. And so did he, by the graves. He liked it. No, he didn't love her, nor did he expect her love. But it worked so well, he'd been shocked a few years later to discover that he wasn't the only one she entertained. That's when he broke it off. He didn't mind a practical arrangement, but he wouldn't share with other men. Yet, she'd taught him a lot and he was grateful.

Watching the captain of the guard enter the women's chamber had raised the hackles on the back of his neck. The silence that ensued from behind the door had calmed him, but the feminine shriek and muffled cries that later erupted had been almost more than he could stomach. The captain didn't emerge for several hours, which told him the girl had been used more than once.

The expression on Sasha's face as she let the man out had said it all. The pale cheeks and shock in her eyes, combined with shaking hands, told their own story.

What if this was his sister? Bethlehem hadn't known a man that way, but if she had run for help to the Sanctuary and been caught in that trap, he'd have had to go back and kill them all. It shouldn't happen, it wasn't how the Sanctuary was supposed to work. That's when he'd decided Sasha would come with them.

Not that he was unhappy about it. When he'd first laid eyes on her, his focus had been solely to get help for Kerr. But almost immediately after the doctor arrived, his attention had swerved to Sasha's pretty face with the great stormy eyes and long lashes. She was slender under her uniform robe, but he was able to see the shape of her body, the firm little breasts and rounded hips. The thought of not seeing her again had been like a thorn in his shoe. He'd been wondering how he'd be able to catch a glimpse of her, and if the women had to stay at the Sanctuary once they were admitted. He didn't want to leave and never see her again.

This way he could help her and himself. She was with him now, and that's all that mattered.

The barn, when they reached it, was obviously rotting and had collapsed at one end but some stalls still stood, with old bales of mouldy hay piled against the wall. Abe helped Kerr from the saddle, not surprised that he sat down rather abruptly on a stack of bales. His own thigh was burning like fire and there was a knife piercing his side where the wound was as yet unhealed. None of them was in great shape.

He unsaddled the mule and slung the saddle blanket on a rail, hearing rodents rustle in the straw at the disturbance. They'd make a bed of some kind to finish the night. The mule walked into the stall and began munching in the feedbag as Abe tied him to a railing.

Sasha rummaged in the saddle bags, pulling out a bit of bread and a bottle of ale. Kerr grabbed his and ate with fierce hunger, taking a slug of ale to wash it down.

"Abe, here's yours."

He took it from her shaking hand, seizing the bottle before she dropped it. Then he scattered a thick layer of hay and spread the blanket. "This is where we spend the rest of the night," he said. "Sasha, you sleep between us, else you'll be cold. We just have the one blanket."

Her look of alarm almost made him smile. "We'll be gentlemen, won't we, Kerr? But we have to stay warm. Button up and let's get some rest."

Abe lay awake for a long while, smelling the damp and stale animal droppings as he felt her body slowly relax beside him. She curled against his back and when, toward morning, she turned to face Kerr, he rolled over as well and put an arm over her waist for comfort and warmth. For whose comfort, he didn't ask.

CHAPTER TWENTY THREE

The sun peeped through a gap in the slanting roof and shone directly into his eyes. The other two were still out cold. He rested up on his elbow, gazing down at Sasha's peaceful face, her fair skin and curly dark hair. She looked like a young girl, innocent in sleep.

Yes, that's what he'd wanted to protect, that innocence that she wore like an invisible cloak.

Rising, he led the mule out the sagging back door, watered him at the creek and tethered him to graze in the field. As he scanned the area, he realized they weren't visible from the road and there were no other dwellings in sight.

How long could they stay here? Kerr was still weak and Sasha had no stamina. He took the rabbit snare out of a saddle bag and set off to find a trail. When he returned a half hour later with a dead rabbit dangling from his fingers, Kerr had staggered outside to relieve himself and leaned weakly against the sagging barn wall in the heat of the morning sun.

"How are you feeling today?"

Kerr's hair shone silver in the sunlight as he shrugged his shoulders. "Not too bad."

"Yah. That's what I figured. I think we should stay over for a spell. You'll only be better with the wait. I've set the rabbit trap and there's a creek in the trees down there where we can get water." He pointed to the edge of the field.

Abe hunkered down beside his friend. "You'll be stronger. The medicine is working, but you need time. A pack of guards from the Sanctuary went by last night, moving pretty fast. I don't know if they were looking for us or on some other mission. It's too early to tell. But we'll keep watch."

Rising, he ducked into the barn to find Sasha sitting up on the blanket, her hair tousled and an expression of alarm on her pretty face. When she saw him, she startled and then relaxed into a little smile that drew his gaze to that pouting mouth. "I thought you might have left."

He crouched down, brushing her hair behind her shoulder. "Without you?"

"Well, you were both gone, and the mule too."

"Hmm. The saddle's still there."

She looked where he pointed and flushed. "I didn't see."

"We're not going to leave without you."

Her eyes searched his face intently. "My name isn't Sasha," she whispered.

Abe stared at her as sudden anger roared up from his stomach. Since Uncle Jade had betrayed them on the road to Krimen, he'd done his best to rationalize what had happened, to find a way to imagine that the attack was just happenstance.

But there was a burning rage in his gut that wouldn't go away. He was sure it was going to erupt like lava when next he saw Jade Hawker. And a feeling of distrust had lodged in his throat that tended to choke him. Had this little girl betrayed him too?

"What's your name, then?" His voice had gone hard.

She got a desperate look. "It's Julianne. Julianne Adjudicator. My father is Little Harry." She seemed to search his face for a reaction. "Zanata's my stepmother."

"Okay." He searched his mind for some connection.

"Do you know her?"

"No, I'd remember if I did."

"Oh. I wondered why she was coming to see you. Now I'm sure she was coming to see me."

"How would she know you were there?"

"That's what I ask myself." She gazed down at her robe and picked at a thread. "If Maa knew you were there, it would be because she had someone search your ident. She must have done the same when

I arrived, because a few days after I got there she called me in and told me she knew my real name."

Abe nodded, watching her face for signs of guilt. "I imagine she needs to know who's come to her place."

"Yes, but why would she pass that information on to Zanata?"

"Maybe they know each other. Maybe they're friends."

"They're a lot alike," she muttered.

He had to smile, and something inside him eased. "I didn't meet Maa. What's she like?"

"Well, not in looks. But in personality, they're the same. They like to control people. I don't know what was happening but every time I heard Maa talk, I'd get really sleepy and wake up later thinking different thoughts than I'd had before I listened to her. It was strange."

Abe narrowed his eyes. "You mean, she'd talk to you and you'd go to sleep?"

"Yes, then she snapped her fingers and …"

"She hypnotized you."

"What?" She seemed shocked.

"She put you in a trance, and when she snapped her fingers you came out of it."

"There were about ten women and we all went to sleep."

"She must be good at it."

She watched his face intently. "Why would she do that? Why put us to sleep?"

Abe sat down and took her hand. "She was getting you to think a different way. I saw someone in a travelling show near Deep Creek once, he hypnotized most of the people in the audience. How did you feel when you woke up?"

She stared at him, her cheeks pale. "I felt better. I thought it wouldn't be too bad to service the guards when it was my turn. The problem was, the feeling didn't last and I began to worry again."

Abe searched her face, such a beautiful face, as a wave of protectiveness rose in his chest. He'd been right to bring her with them. "You're a strong woman, Julianne." He smiled. "I have to get used to calling you that. So, is there a notice of reward out for you?"

She flushed. "Yes, I saw it on infolink on my way to the Sanctuary. My stepmother must have put it out."

"I thought so. Let's not tell anyone your name."

"Are you going to collect the reward?"

She looked so wary, Abe finally laughed.

CHAPTER TWENTY FOUR

Kerr scraped the hay away from a big circle at the back of the barn and started a fire. Abe put two rabbits to cook over the low flames and went back out to check the trap. When he returned, Julianne had found a bent pot in the rubble, scrubbed it out and fetched water from the creek. She put it on to heat. She had some tea to put in it once it boiled. They were out of ale.

The aroma of roasting rabbit filled the air in the drafty barn. Kerr turned the meat and they watched it cook, fat dripping to hiss in the coals.

"Oh, that smells so good. Wait, I have a bit of salt." Julianne rummaged in her cloth bag and dug out a container. "We'll put it on just at the last so it doesn't get wasted."

When the meat was ready, Abe pulled it from the flames. As they munched contentedly, she said, "Mr Kerr, are you married?"

Abe watched his guard's face flush a dull red as he shook his head.

"I just wondered what your wife would be thinking if she hadn't heard from you for so long. She'd be very worried."

Abe smiled to himself, watching the play of the firelight on her face. "Are you married, Julianne?"

"No, of course not." She looked affronted.

"Well, just asking."

She squinted in a gust of smoke and wiped a tear from the corner of her eye. "Are you related to Bethlehem Farmer?"

Abe felt a jolt to his chest. "Yes. She's my sister." His voice was suddenly guarded.

"How was her wedding? Was it a big society affair or a small private function?"

He gaped.

She watched him curiously for a moment. "Were you not there?"

"Not where?" Both men were watching her now, and she looked uncomfortable under the scrutiny.

"What do you know about that?" Kerr barked.

Her hand shook as she gnawed around a bone and threw it into the fire. "I only know what I heard. My father was talking to the bridegroom, the wedding was to take place the next day."

"When?" Abe knew his questions were abrupt, but he was in shock. "When was this?"

"Um." She looked at both of them in turn, then counted on her fingers. "Three or four weeks ago."

"And the groom?"

"What about him?"

"Who was it?"

"Sable Maude. He was getting married the next day to Bethlehem Farmer."

Abe exchanged a relieved glance with Kerr, then leaned back to gaze into the flames, his whole body relaxing. That was very good news. All this time he'd been afraid that his sister was out there at Farmer Holdings on her own, handling the chaos he'd inadvertently left behind. But with marriage to Sable Maude, as planned by their father before the end of the Last War, she'd have the backing of the Governor of the Southern Territory. That could make all the difference for her safety and that of Holdings. Governor Maude was an honest man, upright and trustworthy. With him as father by marriage, Bethlehem was in good hands.

When he got home to the farm, he'd sort things out. But in the meantime, Beth wasn't unprotected. Something long held tight began to ease in his chest, and he suddenly smiled and jumped up.

"It's getting dark. I'll bring the mule in. We'll stay here another day and we'll all be stronger for it. Kerr, get your leg tended. Julianne, can you help him?"

She rose quickly. "I'll fill the pot again. We can wash."

Abe took it from her. "I'll do it." And he walked out into the field before he took her in his arms and kissed her senseless.

CHAPTER TWENTY FIVE

At the manorhouse of Farmer Holdings, Bethlehem finished her painting and laid the brush down on the stand beside her easel. She rotated her stiff shoulders and stretched the muscles in her back. The women's solar was the perfect place to paint. The light from the east facing windows was soft and soothing, not harsh as in the west or too hot to the south.

She'd been tired lately. Her maid, Joan, said it was no wonder with everything that had happened, but Beth couldn't seem to recover her strength. She and her brother, Abe, had come under some kind of oppression before he disappeared. While travelling in the north, he and Uncle Jade were attacked at night on a lonely track outside Krimen, and Abe and his guard Kerr had vanished. A second guard was left dead on the road.

There was still no news. The Constables and her husband continued to look for information, but there was none. She didn't know if she'd ever see her brother again. It was a bitter pill to face every morning. There was no word, and Uncle Jade had been no help.

Jade was dead now. She shuddered at the memory. Jade Hawker died here at Farmer Holdings, the details so gruesome she could barely think of them. But Beth had been rescued. And her husband Dante Regiment was the one who'd rescued her. Her heart warmed at the thought, even as she mourned the loss of her family. Dante would be home tonight.

Just then the front bell rang, and the signal in the solar told her Pickard had opened the great door. She must have special antenna, because she always recognized the moment Dante came through the entry of the manorhouse.

She held her breath, eyes fixed on the door. In a few moments it opened and he stepped inside. She let her breath out slowly as she took him in. What a beautiful man. He'd laugh if she told him that, but he was. Tall and muscular, he moved with ease toward her. His dark intense gaze was pinned to her face, the smile on his wide mouth tender. It made her quake, knowing what he was thinking, what he wanted to do with her when they were alone.

"Bethlehem." Just her name.

She smiled and put her mouth up for his kiss. Oh, my. His lips were warm and firm on hers, and she tingled all the way to her toes. She placed a hand on his chest to feel his heart beating hard under her fingers.

"Dante, I didn't think you'd be here this early."

He put his hands at her waist and turned her to the fading light from the windows. "I came as soon as I could. You seem tired. What have you been doing?"

He looked at the picture on her easel and a grin crossed his face. "Have you been working on Miss Chickadee? She looks like a little brat in this picture."

Miss Chickadee stood on her splayed, spindly legs in the middle of a ragged green lawn, feathers ruffled and wings aloft, her beak clamped stubbornly around a seed that was securely attached to the nutbush where it grew. She was tugging for all her might. The frown on her face was ferocious and her mouth had a definite pout to it.

Beth laughed, that's what she'd been aiming for. She was part way through painting the illustrations for a children's book that she'd begun before she met Dante. She had a friend who was a printer and book seller, Saxby Wordsmith, who would take care of the printing.

"Well, that's good to know. Because she is a brat, and her brother is waiting patiently to teach her a lesson."

His look gentled and he turned back to her. "Is that what happened to you, Bethlehem? Your brother was there to teach you lessons when you needed them?"

His gaze was so kind, the tears welled in her eyes, and she lowered her forehead to rest against his breastbone. He gathered her close, his arms snug around her as he buried his face in her hair.

She sighed and breathed him in. Oh, he smelled good. "I'm okay, Dante."

"I know." He didn't loosen his grip but rocked her against him. "You're wonderful. My Bethlehem."

"I missed you." She lifted her face to kiss his throat, and he took a quick breath.

"Come with me." He took her hand and quickly led her from the room. Down the long hallway, around to the stairwell and up the stairs, she had to run to keep up.

"Are you in a hurry, Dante?" Her voice was light, teasing.

He turned his head and gave her a dark glance, then swung her up into his arms. Taking the rest of the stairs two at a time, he pushed their bedroom door open with his shoulder, breathing hard. "You might say that," he said, his gaze fierce on her mouth. "I've been gone for three nights. That's a damned long time."

She giggled against his neck.

"Take your clothes off." He ripped his uniform shirt over his head and bent to undo the clips on his boots. "Don't just stand there."

"Are we on a schedule?"

"A schedule?" He reached to gently tug the bow free at the throat of her blouse. "If we were on a schedule, I wouldn't be starving all the time."

By the time he wrestled her onto the bed, her clothes were in a heap on the floor and she was breathless under him. "Dante, go slow."

He stilled, watching her face. "Are you sore?"

"No, I just like it slow."

His gaze softened as he watched her eyes, then focussed on her mouth. "I'll go slow." He laid his mouth over hers.

When he finally lifted himself over her and pressed his way in, she was panting for him. She levered her hips upward. He grunted and tried to hold her back with one hand on her hip.

"Hurry, Dante. I can't wait." Her breath was coming fast and she pressed again to bring him all the way inside. Oh, that feeling, that indescribable feeling of fullness and pressure. His hand was firm on her breast, his mouth around her nipple. Then his gaze was on her face as he began to press in and pull out, heavy invasion, slow torture. That steady fierce gaze as he gauged her readiness, her excitement.

"Dante." She plunged upward. He groaned and moved faster, his fingers between them to urge her further, help her climax. The tumult was too much and she clenched around him, long and strong. He grunted once, then again, and slammed himself home, held hard and deep as he came.

He rolled them over and she lay across his heaving chest feeling completely boneless. She must have dozed. When she woke, he was brushing her hair back from her face with tender fingers. "I thought you wanted to go slow," he teased.

A giggle escaped and she pressed her mouth to his chest. "I thought I did, but then you changed my mind." His laughter rumbled under her cheek.

"How is your cousin doing with his work as a travelling peddler?"

Beth settled comfortably against his shoulder. "I'm not used to that term yet. I've never had a cousin before."

Dante chuckled. "It was a surprise when Loyal Hawker just knocked on the door and walked in."

"I know. Why did Uncle Jade keep his wife and son a secret all these years? It would have been exciting to know we had a cousin …" She paused and caught her breath at the stab of pain around her heart. Abe might never know him. "To know that I had a cousin."

"Bethlehem, don't give up hope about your brother."

She froze. *What did that mean?* When she lifted her head he was watching her, his eyes narrowed.

"Have you heard something?"

"I'm not sure. There was a whisper of something, but you have to understand that it isn't conclusive."

"What?" When he hesitated, she slapped her hand on his chest. "Tell me."

He grabbed her hand and held it, then smoothed her fingers. "It's only a rumour, but you deserve to know. There has been a reward posted for information on his whereabouts."

"By whom?" Her eyes were round.

"It looks like by Little Harry Adjudicator, but it's being handled by an agent. I'm not sure what he will gain with this information. But someone sent in a claim."

"To Little Harry?"

He nodded. "To the agent."

"How do you know?"

He gave a short laugh. "It's my job, Bethlehem. Someone reported they saw him in the Northern Territory near Wymark."

She puzzled that for a moment. "When was this?"

"I found out this morning. I'm not keeping anything from you."

She nodded. "Wymark is a long way from Krimen where he disappeared."

"Yes, but its wild country up there. They could have travelled that far in the time they've been missing, and no one would have seen them."

"What was he doing?"

Dante moved uncomfortably. "That's the tough part. This was a dispossessed who said he was doing business with a group of tribesmen, and saw him in their encampment. He described his light hair and beard."

She frowned at him. "He doesn't wear a beard."

"No, but by now he could have one."

The frown lifted. "That's true. Is he there? Did you send someone to find him?"

"I sent one of my men. There was no group of dispossessed doing business with the tribesmen in the last little while."

Her hopes suddenly dashed, she felt tears gather in her eyes and turned her head away.

Dante smoothed a hand down her arm, and took her fingers in his. "The tribesmen said there was a raid on their village. Abe was supposedly in the village, fighting on their side. At first, they said he was there. Then they got cautious and said they didn't understand what we were asking."

She caught her breath on a sob and laid her head on his chest. His hand stroked her hair. "I don't know what to think."

"No, it isn't proof of anything." His soothing voice spoke just above her head. "The tribesmen didn't trust us, so they weren't being completely open. But you have to admit he's noticeable with the colouring you two share, the pale hair and light blue eyes. And there was no one there like that when my men visited the village. Maybe he moved on once he realized he'd been recognized."

"Why hasn't he contacted me? I can't …" She felt her voice wobble and Dante pulled her closer.

"There could be a lot of reasons. Maybe he was too injured to get to a place where he could contact you. There's certainly no way to send a message from the tribesmen's camp. They live on the open plain with no services anywhere nearby. Maybe he was afraid his call would cause trouble for you, or bring someone down on him. I couldn't keep the information from you, but I'm not sure what it means."

She sighed and sat up. Brushing her hair off her face, she slid to the edge of the bed.

"Where are you going?" His voice seemed to rumble in his chest.

She turned to him. "I was going to get dressed."

He smiled, that slow smile that got her heart pounding harder every time. "What's your hurry? It's not dinner time yet, is it?"

CHAPTER TWENTY SIX

There's more rabbit." Abe smothered a laugh at the quickly suppressed expression of dismay on Julianne's face. They'd been eating rabbit all day.

"I have carrots," she offered.

"Ah, that's a good combination. I'll check the snare again." When he returned to the barn, Julianne was dressing Kerr's wound. He stepped closer. "It looks pretty good."

"Does it? I can't tell." Her glance at him was so innocent he caught his breath. Innocent and concerned. She cared how Kerr was doing. A pinch of jealousy hit him in the stomach, and he tightened his lips. That was ridiculous. Kerr was more than twice her age.

"It doesn't look as angry as before." She finished tying the cloth bandage and pulled down the pant leg to cover it. "And it doesn't weep as much. It must be healing. That's good news, isn't it, Mr Kerr?"

"Just Kerr," he muttered.

"Oh. Well, there you are. I'll do it again in the morning. Are we leaving then?"

Abe squatted down beside her. "Yah, we're leaving. You can't wear that robe, it speaks too loudly of the Sanctuary."

"I know. I thought of that." Her face was eager as she glanced up at him. "I have my dress but I also took a set of men's clothing because it will be easier to travel in. Look." She jumped up and opened her sack, pulling out the shirt and trousers.

"Hmm. that's better. Those shirts speak of the Sanctuary too."

"I know, but I thought once we're away from here, people won't be aware of what a guard's shirt looks like. And I'll look like a man in it, so it might be safer for me."

Kerr gave a short laugh.

"What?" Her cheeks went pink.

"Not a man," he said. "Maybe a boy. You might look like a boy."

She smiled, nodding. "Okay. Yes, a boy."

Kerr blushed under her laughter.

She hesitated a moment, then turned to Abe. "Where are we going?"

"Where do you want to go?"

Her look was measuring. "I'm from the City."

"Yah, I gathered that."

"Now that Zanata is here, I can go back there. I'm trying to find my father, and that's where he was when he disappeared."

"Do you think it's safe?" Abe tried to control his frown. She could go where she wanted as far as he was concerned, yet the idea of leaving her in the City didn't sit well with him.

Her mouth turned down. "I don't have anywhere else to go, and it's not safe out here for a girl alone. I think I have to go back."

The men exchanged a look. "We're going south, back to Farmer Holdings," Abe offered. "We're heading to the coast, hoping to find a boat. You can always come with us."

"I see." She gazed doubtfully at him. "That's very kind of you."

"Is that a 'yes'?" He grinned suddenly.

Her smile was uncertain. "I don't know. Can I decide later?"

Abe stood. "Don't see why not. If we go by boat, we'll be travelling right past the City harbour so you could decide then. Let's eat."

She laid out the cooked rabbit meat and found some limp carrots in her sack. Kerr propped himself against the wall of the stall, resting his injured leg on a mound of hay.

"Is Farmer Holdings near the fishing village of Coronation?" Julianne asked as she chewed.

Kerr snorted, and she glanced uncertainly at him. "It is Coronation," he said. "It's Farmerville, the farm, the mine. All of that."

"On the Southern Highway?" she asked. "I've never been out there."

Abe snapped off a bite of carrot "Yah, near there. Where have you been?"

"Not many places. Father was always working, and he didn't travel much. I've been all over the City, of course, not just the new parts with the high rise buildings, but Old Towne as well. But when I was young, we did make a trip to Adar Silva by boat after the end of the Last War. It was really quite lovely. Sommerset, the capital city, is built around one of the Emperor's palaces. It was beautiful."

Abe nodded and wiped his hands in the hay. "I've seen it. I was there when the Emperor lived in Sommerset, actually. I was only about ten but my father went with a group of farmers who were asking for help in the middle of a long drought. Remember the drought, Kerr?"

"Yah. Nearly finished us."

"Right. The Emperor didn't see us, of course, but his Administrator heard the petition from the farmers. I think they did something. I don't remember."

"They cut the tax in half that year." Kerr threw a bone into the bucket.

"You met the Emperor?" Julianne's eyes were wide. "What was he like?"

"I didn't actually meet him. I was ten." Abe grinned and watched her cheeks go pink. "I doubt Father met him either. I saw him, though. He was quite a sight. Not a tall man, but he stood tall, heavy with muscle, right Kerr? Thick in the chest and arms. And his clothes were striking. Adar Silva belted jacket with the short standing collar encrusted with jewels. I remember his boots, they were really something to see, designs carved into the leather and jet black with polish. My father hadn't had a new pair of boots in years, his were clean but worn and patched at the toe."

"Was he a nice man?" Her eyes shone as she listened to the tale.

"A nice man? No, far from it."

"Oh." She shrugged in disappointment.

"I guess if he was a nice man, there wouldn't have been a war."

Her cheeks darkened. "Of course."

Abe reached and lifted her chin with a finger. "He was bad, Julianne. I watched him have a man killed because he spoke out of turn. He wasn't nice. Just an Emperor." He heaved himself up. "I'll fetch the rest of the rabbits. We should get the fire going again, we can cook everything tonight. Then we'll be able to leave first thing in the morning."

When Abe left to make his rounds, the mule was tethered in the stall for the night, munching on his feedbag and Julianne was heating water on the dying fire.

Ducking under the fallen doorway at the back of the barn, he stood tall to stretch in the darkness. He was pleased to realize he was feeling better. As his eyes adjusted to the night, he could see the canopy of stars scattered in familiar patterns across the sky. The trees on the skyline were barely visible and the air was colder. There was a bank of heavy cloud moving down from across the Legitamia border.

He breathed deeply, then walked around the barn on a circuit. Going as far as the road, he tramped back across the field to where the water ran fast in a small rivulet. There was no one out here.

On his return, he heard the creak of equipment and the sound of hooves striking the trail. He glanced at the barn but there was nothing to see, no flicker of light to give them away. From here it appeared to be a farmer's cart on the road, a couple of men on the seat and three horses pulling. The wagon bed was loaded with cargo, piled high and tied down.

They went slowly past, a low murmur of voices audible from where he stood in the grass, the muffled clip clop of hooves eventually fading in the distance. He let out a breath. This had been a good place for them. He was glad he'd remembered the barn.

Kerr was in better shape, his leg healing nicely. Julianne was rested. They'd head off again tomorrow morning, and all going well, they'd get to the coast without mishap. He was hoping for a cargo vessel, the jewels in that sack should buy them each a space onboard.

Walking around to the back of the barn, he checked for light escaping and bent to glance through the low doorway. Kerr was already asleep on the blanket, his back to the door. Julianne stood on the other side of the fire, out of Kerr's sight if he should wake. She had stripped bare, her Sanctuary robe hanging on a rail of the stall as she bathed with the warmed water in the pot. She lifted her arm to wash, and her breasts swung with the movement as the firelight flickered over her milky skin. Abe caught his breath. She was beautiful.

His whole body responded.

Her hips flared from a slender waist. Her breasts were round and high, the nipples dark and tight in the cold air of the drafty barn. She bent and rinsed the cloth, and he fought for air. When she straightened, she paused and glanced toward the doorway as if she could feel the weight of his gaze. He froze where he stood in the darkness.

Then she looked back down and leaned to pass the cloth between her thighs. Abe faded back into the night and headed straight out into the field. His member was straining against the front of his trousers, making walking uncomfortable. He stopped and stared into the distance, breathing heavily until his heart slowed.

Before, he'd only imagined what she would look like, but now he knew. It was worse than he thought, because she looked so much better then he'd imagined.

Lying beside her that night was torture. She shifted and sighed, and he wanted her to shift and sigh while straddling him. When she rolled against him in her sleep, he wrapped an arm around her and breathed her in, smoky, sweet woman.

CHAPTER TWENTY SEVEN

General Elkon brought his horse to a standstill, calling for a halt, and his sergeant bellowed the order. He heard it echo down the long line of men marching ahead of him into the spreading field of dead grass. They straggled to a stop and some sat down. Those were the seasoned ones, the men who knew to rest where they could. They'd been walking for two days, but had finally managed to cross the border sometime around noon. They were now inside the boundaries of Khandarken.

It had been tough going. The trails were narrow, at times cut deep into the rock on the side of the mountains. The men walked single file then, the mules tied nose to tail bringing them all through. There was nowhere to stop with an assembly this size, and it had made for many hours on the move. But they had come a long way.

The rain had started last night, a continuous, persistent deluge. It was pouring now, water running along the trail under their feet. Small streams had developed overnight and were shooting off the side of the mountain above their heads, straight down into the gorge below. Everyone was soaked. Most of the men didn't bother wiping their faces or buttoning their jackets tighter. The mules in the train stood heads down, water dripping off their hides, their tails straggling against their legs.

"We'll set the Emperor's tent here. Have the men make camp." The space was big enough for the whole troop to bed down, with the Emperor's tents against the mountain at the back and spreading chestnut trees providing some shelter on the far side. Elkon swung down from the saddle and approached the Emperor's cavalcade coming up from the rear. He waved at Judson and pointed them to the spot he'd selected for the Emperor's and Advisor's camp. They turned off in that direction.

Already men had the tents laid out and were erecting supports. There was a stream nearby, so Carlton would have his bath. The tin tub balanced on top of a stack of supplies on one of the mules entering the field with the second wave of recruits.

They were four sections strong now. Two consisted of long-time veterans loyal to the Emperor. The other sections were more casual men, or newly recruited dispossessed, who were likely here for the steady meals and warm clothing rather than out of any firm belief in the right of Carlton to regain the Empire.

Elkon didn't mix the groups. He didn't want new politics infecting his seasoned men, and he intended to make cohesive units of each of these sections. They weren't full numbers, they didn't have that many bodies, but it made the recruits proud to feel part of such a respected group.

He turned to his adjutant. "Tell the cooks to get busy. We've only got another couple of hours of daylight. Then call the generals together for a meeting."

Elkon headed toward his tent which had been set up nearby, and found his men already unloading the furniture. As the generals straggled in, he spread a map of the border area between Khandarken and Legitamia across the tabletop. There were a few small villages marked here, some houses banded together there, but nothing the size of Discovery. Discovery had shops, a drinking house and eating establishments, livery stables and a couple dozen houses. It was big enough to form their headquarters, and it stood on a swath of flat cleared land with room for the men to set up camp. That was their target.

There was some disagreement among the generals about how to overtake the village. The goal was to take it swiftly, and not give the inhabitants an opportunity to send beltlink or voicelink messages asking for help before they were overcome. The men were still discussing matters when Advisor Judson ducked under the flap. "General Elkon, a word."

Talk halted, then one by one the men left. Judson moved forward and stared at the map. "What's the plan? Are we moving on the village tomorrow? The Emperor wants to know."

"I'd be happy to inform him," Elkon replied. He wasn't totally certain that what he told Judson actually got to the Emperor's ears in the same configuration as he gave it. He suspected the message sometimes got twisted to reflect Judson's negative views.

"Just tell me." He waved at the map and pointed. "This is Discovery?"

"Yah. We leave here early, get there before dawn, as the Emperor wanted. It's the best time to strike. The villagers will just be getting up. We want it to be bloodless if possible, as it will help bring the local people onside if we don't kill their henchmen. We're hoping to finish without firing a shot. The villagers don't have guards, there's no army of dispossessed camped nearby that we know of. It should be very straight forward and will give us our base of operations. We proceed from there. Frankly, the Emperor shouldn't even be here. He should arrive after it's done."

"That's not his view of things." Judson's mouth assumed a bitter twist.

Elkon nodded. He'd been surprised at Carlton's insistence on accompanying them. The trek through the mountains the last few days had been hair-raising enough to give even Elkon pause, but Carlton had continued on, at one point getting off his horse and walking through the upper pass along the narrow shelf of trail, with his Counsellors quaking in their boots as they followed. It was one way to weed out the faint of heart. And Emperor Carlton was never that.

"Will you wake the Emperor tomorrow morning, or wait until we have it done?"

"He's given me instructions to rouse him when you leave. He'll follow shortly." Judson's tone of voice had soured.

CHAPTER TWENTY EIGHT

Rain was still pouring down when Abe saddled the mule. Kerr mounted with difficulty and Julianne, in her new outfit, had bundled their supplies and tied it in the saddlebags. Abe was grumpy from tension and lack of sleep, and had received more than one sharp glance from Kerr. Probably because of the way he couldn't keep his eyes off Julianne.

If only he hadn't seen her bathing. But it wasn't just that. He'd already been attracted to her. It hadn't taken seeing her naked to get his attention. He was just a bit more focussed now than he'd been before. He snorted to himself. This scenario had disaster written all over it. Maybe Kerr was right, he should have left her at the Sanctuary.

"Are we ready? We're just an ordinary family heading to town." Abe hitched the plasmagun over his shoulder and slung it down his back, leaving the raygun from the Sanctuary dangling from the saddle horn within Kerr's reach.

Kerr laughed and kicked the mule into a walk. "With grandpa on the mule, I suppose."

"And the poor woman walking," said Julianne.

Both men turned their heads to peer at her.

"Oh, yes, the boy walking. I remember."

"You'd better not talk if someone stops us," Abe murmured. "You don't sound like any boy that I know."

"What would a boy sound like?"

Kerr glanced down sympathetically. "You sound too educated, he meant."

They were soon soaking wet, although Julianne's shirt seemed to be waterproof. She had tied her hair up and tucked it under a knitted hat, but already wisps of inky black curls were trailing down beside her ear. She wiped a drip from her forehead and slogged along behind the mule.

Abe turned forward again. The track was pure mud, ankle deep. Soon his boots were filled with it, his feet squishing with each step. He glanced back to watch Julianne, knowing her boots must feel the same.

The track led into the hills, where waterfalls shot off the sides of rock cliffs to land around them. They came across a spot where a small landslide had come down, and they scrambled over mud and rocks to the other side.

"Julianne, hold onto the stirrup. You can lean on it when you need to, and it will pull you along." Kerr slipped his boot free and pushed it toward her with his foot. "You won't get so tired."

"Maybe we should rest for a while." Abe turned to look back at them.

"Not yet," she panted. "I'm fine."

"Yah, we'll stop." Abe tugged the mule to the side of the track where there was a log to sit on, and waited while Kerr dismounted.

"We'll rest for a bit. I think that mule can take both of you for a few miles. Julianne, you can get on behind the saddle."

She was wet and uncomfortable but smiled at his comment, her beautiful lips curling upward, causing something to move in his chest. His insides warmed. Kerr coughed loudly and he swung sharply around to dig in the saddle bags for food. More rabbit meat, but also the last of the bread.

"Where will we stop for the night?"

Abe handed her a slice of pané. "I'm not sure. Maybe we'll find a farmer along here who will let us bunk down in his barn."

"That would be nice." She munched on the crust of bread, and Abe watched her mouth as she chewed. It was such a lovely mouth, the lips full and expressive. Kissable. He wanted to taste them. He turned his head to think of something else. "How's the leg, Kerr? When are you going to be able to walk on it?"

"Soon." Kerr flexed his foot and winced.

Julianne's head snapped up. "No, not yet. It's just beginning to heal. And the wound was right in the muscle. Not yet, Kerr. You don't want to permanently injure yourself."

Kerr gazed at her as his craggy face softened. Abe had to smile. Even his guard was susceptible to her charm.

They did find a small farm in the hills and, in exchange for one of the jewels and a few coins in return, they bunked down in the farmer's ramshackle barn. He'd taken the milk cow out of her stall and put her in with the two calves. They tied the mule to a railing, fed it some hay and ate a huge bowl of stew and a bread loaf that the farmer's wife sent out for them.

At dawn, Abe was saddling the mule when he heard a wave of sound approaching, swiftly escalating in volume. Shouts went up from many voices. He peeked out the door and saw what looked like an army of men rolling in droves out of the hills behind them.

"Kerr." He kicked his foot. "Move it. There's something going on. Julianne."

As they stirred, Abe quickly gathered their things. "I don't know whether to leave or stay put. We're out of sight for now …"

He never finished the thought. As they watched, four men rushed the farmer's house, crashing through the front door, and Abe didn't hesitate. Quickly he tossed Kerr into the saddle. "Julianne, follow me."

They left at a flat run, but only got a few yards before more men appeared around the other side of the barn. They were surrounded. All three of them were thrown to the ground. A dispossessed with a pockmarked face stood guard while his partner searched their things. They confiscated the food, then the mule.

"No," Julianne cried, trying to rise. "He can't walk!" Abe wrestled her to the ground, knocking the wind out of her and throwing himself on top as the guard turned at her cry to take a closer look.

"It's okay. Take the mule," Abe growled, his hand over her mouth. She reached to tug her hat lower on her head as he slowly lifted himself away.

"Shut up," he muttered, tucking stray curls under the hat. "You sound too much like a woman."

Soon the farmer and his wife joined them in the muddy yard. The farmer had blood running down his upper lip from a rapidly swelling nose. His wife was crying and holding a hanky to it, trying to staunch the flow.

"Who are these men?" the farmer asked low. "Do you know them?"

"No. Never saw them before. There's no uniform, so it's impossible to tell. There are too many of them to be another band of dispossessed."

The farmer nodded and took his wife's arm. "I just pray the women will be safe." He slid a sideways glance at Julianne in her men's clothing, and she turned her head away.

Abe nodded. The farmer had seen through her disguise. So would these men if they looked more closely. They had to be careful.

They were ordered to march west in the thundering rain. Soon others joined them, until there were fifteen or twenty men and two women, farmer's wives who'd been caught along the road by the travelling horde. By afternoon, Kerr was visibly weaker. Abe propped him up as best he could, and Julianne tried to support him on the other side but she was too short for him to lean on. He finally said, "It's not helping, boy. You look after yourself."

They halted in a camp established on a small field in the foothills, where many more men were working. The dispossessed corralled their captives by a rope enclosure, with the mules tied along one side to hem the prisoners in.

There was a cluster of larger tents erected in a staggered line at the edge of the field, backed up against the mountain behind. The largest one had a flag flying from the top pole, and Abe studied the three cornered pattern with a stag's head centred in the middle. "Kerr, what is that flag? It seems familiar."

Kerr stared for a minute then moved his head away in disgust. "It's the Emperor's pennant. What the hell is going on?"

The men exchanged a look, and Julianne leaned near. "What?" she whispered. "Are we in the Emperor's camp? What is he doing here? Aren't we still in Khandarken?"

Abe gazed down into her stormy eyes. "Yes, we're still in Khandarken. I don't know what he's doing here, but I can guess."

The muttering amongst the captives had increased at the sight of the flag and the few military uniforms with the old formal Adar Silva styling.

There was a sense of organization to the encampment, with cook tents in the centre protected by fly roof or tarp in the continuous rain, and shelters set up in rows along the other side. This was an army on the move.

Abe felt a flutter in his gut, apprehension and something else. The gall of the man, to stage an invasion like this. It foretold an uprising, when they were supposed to have finished with war. The Last War had dragged on for more years than he cared to count, slowly whittling the Old Empire down to smaller and smaller areas, until it had finally collapsed in on itself. The fallout from the constant fighting had been devastating for the whole Empire.

Pieces were slowly being put back together. *Now this?*

CHAPTER TWENTY NINE

Someone approached them through the rain, a General, Abe guessed from his uniform. He looked the captives over carefully, his peaked cap giving him some small relief from the deluge. Then he motioned to the two guards. "Bring them to the Emperor's tent. He wants to talk to them."

Julianne's mouth fell open and Abe stepped in front of her, glaring sternly into her face. "Remember, don't speak. Pretend you're mute if you have to."

The group moved together across the flooded field to the largest tent erected on the edge of the camp, where the pennant flew high. The General called out through the flap and a man of remarkable appearance emerged. He strolled under the awning, surveying his captives.

He was short and stocky, thick in the chest and arms, dark waxed hair combed straight back from a smooth angular face. He sported a bushy dark mustache that drooped over his mouth, concealing his expression. A roll of fat showed around his neck.

His clothes were extraordinary. His shirt had a jewel-encrusted collar and embroidered designs in coloured thread on panels down the front. His boots were decorated in engraved leather, highly polished just like his father before him. Abe recognized that face with its high bridged nose and dark eyes, younger than Emperor Aqatain, softer.

Emperor Carlton held up his hand, and everyone fell silent.

"Who have we here, Elkon?"

"These are our prisoners, My Lord." The General stood to the side near the entry to the tent. "These are people we've picked up along the way. If we left them, they'd be able to warn the authorities, and we can't let that happen."

The Emperor nodded. "I see. But they won't remain prisoners, will they?" His expression was benevolent. "Once we've accomplished our task, everyone will be free to carry on with their lives in a peaceful Empire." His gaze roved over the crowd in front of him, pausing occasionally to give greater scrutiny.

"And who have we here?" He pointed to Julianne, who promptly faded back into the crowd behind Abe.

Abe's temperature shot skyward. Kerr grabbed hold of his dripping coat as if to hold him back. The

Emperor waited, still pointing to where Julianne had been standing.

A guard pushed into the crowd, grabbing her sleeve and dragging her forward. Abe stepped up at the same time.

"Not you." The Emperor pointed to Julianne again. "Just him. Let me see." He put a finger beneath her chin and lifted her face. "What a pretty young man."

When he pointed to her hat, the guard lifted it off her head. Her hair, damp and in ringlets, fell down her back and the men gasped. The Emperor's eyes focussed more sharply, then he nodded and turned. "Bring her to my tent and prepare a bath for us."

As the guard took her arm and dragged her forward, Abe leaped to follow but was thumped in the chest with the butt of a plasmagun. "Not you, soldier. Just her."

"That's my wife," he gritted.

The guard was unrepentant. "Just hold yourself lucky you've had her this long. Because you don't anymore."

"She's my wife!"

At his wild shout, the Emperor glanced back, shrugged and walked away.

Kerr grabbed his shoulder and pulled him back into the crowd. "She's not your wife," he muttered in Abe's ear.

"No, but she will be. And that bastard can't have her."

"Keep your voice down! Keep control or we'll get nowhere."

Abe turned to look into his eyes and saw compassion and resolution there.

"There might be something we can do," Kerr added.

Abe took a sharp breath. They were herded back to the enclosure in the middle of the encampment, the mules munching on feed bags in a long line at their backs.

The rain increased in volume as they waited, and the wind kicked up as time moved on toward mid-afternoon. It was miserable. The farmer's wife had stopped crying and instead stood wringing her hands as her husband patted her back. The men moved restlessly in the corral.

"What do you think, Kerr? Can we escape? The army doesn't need us, and when it gets dark they aren't going to care all that much. They'll want their dinner and some rest." He looked anxiously across the ground at the Emperor's tent backed up against the hill, the water pouring off the roof in frothing funnels.

They would run out of time soon. Julianne must be frantic. He'd watched water being heated over a fire someone had built under a canopy, and they had started taking it into the Emperor's tent with buckets, the bath tub unloaded from the mule a few minutes before and dragged through the flap of the entrance.

The Emperor was in a smaller tent with a group of the army leaders, probably Generals and Lieutenant Generals from the appearance of the uniforms. He heard the murmur of voices and once a shout, then abrupt silence. Perhaps there was revolt in the ranks. What was the Emperor doing here? What did he hope to accomplish?

Everyone knew he lived in Legitamia, held a province of his own under the auspices of the country's Leader, Barrington the Benevolent. That's what Barrington had dubbed himself. He was benevolent in some ways, a self-appointed dictator, although he'd given some concessions to the people and they didn't seem too unhappy.

But for the Emperor to cross from Legitamia into Khandarken with an army was unthinkable. It would start another war, when everyone had sworn they'd never need to fight again. And the Emperor wouldn't win. He couldn't.

Abe brushed that thought aside. It was beyond his control. His concern was for Julianne, he had to get her out of there. The guards were all focussed on the smaller tent where the shout had come from. He eased around the outskirts of the crowd, Kerr limping behind and dogging his footsteps.

"Abe, you can't do this alone, and I can't help you."

"I know that." He turned his head and saw one guard twist around to scan the group, then turn back again as another shout erupted from the General's tent. There was a rumbling sound in the air, and the men froze as it grew louder. Rocks began to thud onto the ground and Abe looked up at the mountain in astonishment. Mud and boulders tumbled down the side of the cliff, foaming and scrubbing the planes of the steep hill. The sound rose like the rush of a mighty wind, and the mud came in a slow smooth slide behind it onto the small field.

He turned and ran, darting between the shifting restless mules and into the open, heading straight for the Emperor's large tent. Leaping gravel and mud, he dove low through the entry curtain as the noise outside rose to a roar. Quickly he scrambled to his feet. He was in the outer room of the structure, where a table and several chairs stood to one side, a trunk against the fabric wall on the other, and a curtain at the back covered the doorway to an inner chamber.

A guard stood in the outer room, unmindful of Abe's presence. His attention was riveted to a gap where the curtain swung loose from the wall. Abe kicked him once behind the knees, and as the guard went down he slammed his hand into the side of the man's neck. He fell like a stone. Abe grabbed the plasmagun from his lax fingers before it could hit the ground.

He dragged the flap open. Julianne stood in the light of a small lamp, naked and smooth with water, towelling herself dry. Her head twisted around, and her face showed a start of terror and then delighted surprise.

"Abe!" She threw herself at him, all damp towel and naked skin. He wrapped his arms around her, holding her close, his heart thumping madly in his chest. He'd gotten here in time, but they had to move fast. "Grab your clothes, hurry."

He reached for her boots and socks as she pulled her shirt over her head and picked up her pants. Jumping on one foot and then the other, she tugged them on.

Abe lifted the side of the tent. "Run."

They scrambled under and ran. Shouting and chaos rose all around them. Mules screamed and lunged, tugging free from their tethers. The rocks from the hillside were more plentiful, bigger and bounding with a thud as they hit the ground. The mud was deep and flowing fast down the steep slope.

Abe grabbed her arm, pulling her through the mêlée. A crew of men struggled to dig out the General's tent, which had collapsed. One side was buried in mud, but he heard shouting coming from within.

The camp was half submerged. They trod knee deep in places, struggling across the field as if through quicksand. Abe got to the other side, dragging Julianne behind, and looked quickly around. He didn't see Kerr but knew he couldn't stop to find him. He headed for the road, half carrying Julianne, her boots still clutched in his other fist.

Peering down at her bare feet as she limped along, he wondered if they'd make it. There was no time to stop and put the footwear on. A few of the captured men ran before them, one had a mule, another had a plasmagun cradled in his arms. They didn't stop.

Julianne winced and staggered. Abe stooped, slung her over his shoulder and ran on. He finally reached the road and headed down it, out of sight of the camp. As he ran, he watched for shelter. By an overhanging tree, he stopped and let her slide down his chest, holding her close with arms shaking from fatigue. He leaned his back against the trunk, chest heaving.

"Give me a minute," he gasped, knowing they were only safe for a moment, that someone would be coming for them as soon as the Emperor discovered they were missing.

Julianne grabbed the boots out of his hand and sat down to put them on. "Where's Kerr?" she asked breathlessly. "We might have to go back for him."

Abe choked out a laugh. "You're not going back," he gasped. "Not a chance. But I might. Just let me get my breath."

He leaned forward and braced his hands on his knees, chest bellowing. As she tied her laces, Julianne gazed past him through the overhanging branches, watching the line of stragglers moving down the road, escaping the Emperor's camp. Then she grabbed his arm. "Abe!"

"Shhh. We don't want anyone to see us."

"But look."

He looked. In the gloom a man rode by on a mule with two more on a string behind him. He seemed so familiar. "Kerr," he called softly.

Kerr turned his head and grinned. "I figured I'd find you," he said.

CHAPTER THIRTY

"Good man." Abe grinned at his bodyguard and lifted Julianne onto one of the mules.

"I don't ride," she muttered.

"No, but you can stay in the saddle. Just hang onto the horn in front. I'll lead."

"We'd better move fast." Kerr nudged his mule into motion. "Those men are already getting organized as we speak."

They kicked the animals into a trot, then a gallop, Abe leading and Kerr coming behind to make certain Julianne stayed in the saddle. By the time the mules were flagging, they'd covered a lot of ground and come to a small village along the Northern Highway.

Military transports were parked in a skewed array on the outskirts of the place, and a troop mover hovered in the sky for a few moments before landing in a nearby field. Men in uniform poured out of the heavy aircraft and took up position in long lines facing the road.

Abe reined in. "That's fast work. It must mean the military knows what's going on at the border."

A transport drove past, then pulled to a stop and backed up. The passenger got out, a tall man, lean and tough looking, wearing a Captain's uniform. He waved them down as they approached. "Which direction did you come from?"

Abe swung out of the saddle and handed his reins to Kerr. "We just arrived from the west."

"Were you near Discovery?"

"Yah, north of there."

"Did you see any troop movement?"

"Troop movement?" Abe laughed low. "We were caught by the Emperor's army, and barely managed to escape. Emperor Carlton is with them. I don't know much about what they're up to, but he had about three hundred men, maybe a few more."

"My name's Ooievaar." The Captain shook Abe's hand. "You've come fast. Your mules have been ridden hard."

"Yah. We didn't know how close they were behind us."

"Tell me what happened."

When Abe finished telling the story, with Kerr adding details as they talked, Ooievaar shook his head. "Sounds like an invasion. Good thing it's been raining so hard."

"Yah, good for some things. Listen, we need a rest."

Ooievaar waved to the tent by the transports. "Come with me. I can get you a meal."

Turning back to the mules, Abe held up his arms and Julianne fell into them. Her face was white and her mouth pinched.

"Pretty tired, eh? That was hard riding."

She nodded weakly and leaned against him as her legs trembled beneath her.

"I'll carry you." Abe took off his hat and hung it on the saddlehorn.

"No." A blush rushed up her cheeks. "I can walk. Just give me a minute."

Suddenly, Ooievaar's attention focussed sharply on Abe's face. "Do you know the Farmers of the Southern Territory?" he asked.

CHAPTER THIRTY ONE

Captain Ooievaar took them to the army tent and had them fed while he grilled them for more information. When he'd asked about the Farmers, Abe knew right away he'd been recognized. He didn't confirm his identity, but getting a message to Bethlehem was so important, he decided to take a risk. The military had to be a good bet in terms of security, or where else could he go for help?

Later that night, Abe tossed and turned on the saddle blanket. They were bunked down in a small village east of the army billets. There'd been no room for anyone else in that little hamlet with tents, transports and hundreds of military men milling about, but they'd found a spot here in the stables of the village carter. They each had their own saddle blanket now, with no need to bunk together the way they had, although they shared the same horse stall. Kerr's snores quietly echoed off the wall.

Julianne shifted beside him, and the straw beneath her blanket rustled softly. Was she awake as well? He didn't think so. She'd more or less passed out when they lay down after eating. Maybe she didn't ride, but she'd hung onto that saddle horn like glue during the long rough race to freedom. Her legs must be aching and her bottom … Well, he shouldn't think about that but he couldn't help it. It was round and enticing, with such a tempting sway when she walked that he always had to turn to catch a glimpse of it as she passed.

At least he'd been able to get a message to Bethlehem. When Ooievaar assigned them to a subordinate, they'd been served some dessert and tea. Then Abe had asked to borrow the young soldier's voicelink, and used it to call Beth's particulars.

She hadn't answered. It was a huge disappointment after all this time. He'd give anything to hear her voice again. Instead he'd left a message, knowing that the call might be traced. And if it was, all they'd find was a soldier in the north. They still wouldn't find him.

But Beth would know he was alive. Up till now, she must have been in mourning, not having heard any word for months whether or not he was captured or dead. Things had been so tense and dangerous, there'd been no way to get that information to her.

With a sense of relief, he realized what a weight had been removed from his shoulders.

He settled down to rest. They had to make it to the coast first, and then they'd get home. And Julianne would come with them to Farmer Holdings, because he'd persuade her it was the right thing to do.

~ * * * ~

Next morning, they shopped. Abe visited the local money lender and sold one of the gems from the bag. They paid for their night's shelter, bought a supply of food for the journey and feed for the mules. Julianne asked if she could get some items at the general store.

"Sure. What do you need?" Abe reached to tie the bags behind the saddle on his mule.

Her face flushed bright red. "Um … just some things for …"

He watched her desperate expression and felt his own neck get hot. "You mean women's supplies."

At her quick nod and averted gaze, he waved toward the street. "Get everything you need. We have credit, so use it."

"Thank you," she whispered and darted through the barn door.

What was he thinking? Of course she'd need supplies. Usually women carried such items in their bag when they went out, but Julianne had nothing that she'd left the Sanctuary with, other than that wretched robe, the hem ripped and letters missing. When they got back, he'd burn that thing. He'd buy her some nice clothes. She'd have a clean place to sleep with a comfortable bed and woven wool comforters.

He thought of his room at the manorhouse and his whole body grew warm, because he couldn't avoid the picture in his mind of her in that bed, dark curls against light sheets, her silky fair skin …

Abe twitched around and watched Kerr struggle to heave the saddle onto his mount. "Let me do that, you wretch. You know I'll do it."

Kerr grinned and shook his head. "I've got it, boy. It's just my leg, not my arms and back that bother me."

The carter came in with his assistant and began to back a horse into the traces of his wagon. "If you're heading east, be careful," he called as he bent to fasten the harness beneath the belly of his lead horse. "There've been sightings of mountain lions. They're big around here and usually stay at high altitudes, but there's one that's been prowling lower down."

Abe nodded and thanked him, then led the string of mules into the street. It was time to move on. He needed to get home.

CHAPTER THIRTY TWO

Heading west toward Wymark, Sable Maude rode hard, keeping his men on the road well past dark. He had a meeting with DuSatoy and wanted to get there on time. He'd done business with this man in the past and hoped to do so again. This would provide his foothold in the northern reaches of Khandarken. This was the start of his new plan, after the southern arrangement failed so spectacularly.

Governor Jukes of the Northern Territory was related to the Maude family, a great uncle by marriage, and had always been friendly when Sable dropped in to visit. But now that he was an escaped convict, with a death sentence on his head and a posted reward for capture, things would likely be different.

He felt confident he could avoid Jukes and his Constables, and if he was caught, he might have a chance of reprieve. But his uncle had always been hard to read. He was easy going, much more so than Sable's father, Francis Maude. Whether he bent the rules was only a guess. Sable wouldn't test that theory unless he had to.

He'd spent some time up here a few years ago, smuggling women through the mountains from the north. But he'd run afoul of the local gangs that held power in the small hamlets of the foothills on both sides of the border. He didn't have the backing then to force a standoff, so he'd shifted his operation south-westward toward the Jirani border.

But now his arrest and conviction had closed that door. Dante Regiment and his military force were too active in the western borders to make it an easy life for Maude. He hoped things would be different with DuSatoy to back him. And Duncan of the Constables was his secret weapon.

They stopped at a wayside inn, taking two rooms for the six of them and bunking down after a big dinner. Next morning, they were back on the road.

He could have taken the transit line from Navoly Station, the central hub of the train system for Khandarken, and saved many days of hard travel. But the transit was heavily monitored. And it led straight to Wymark, where the Governor's office was located.

Sable had been travelling through the north east setting up his networks, his assistant with him. Waite was a good man. He'd only been working with Sable about a year, but he got things done. He was the reason Sable had approached Little Harry in the first place, to have some smuggling charges dropped against him. Now he acted as Sable's right hand.

Waite had stayed behind in the little hamlet they'd just left to organize a handpicked group of men who would move through the mountains on a smuggling route mapped out by the military. Sable had conveniently borrowed the map from one of Dante Regiment's men when he hadn't been paying attention. The women would be funnelled through Assistant Chief Constable Duncan and his network, with DuSatoy's backing.

They were four or five days east of Wymark and had a few more calls to make on the way. Slowing down outside a little village, he pulled abruptly to a halt. There was a small party of riders coming toward them, three men on mules. He recognized the head of hair on the lead rider, would recognize it in the dark if needs be.

He sat his horse patiently, waiting for the mules to approach. The group spotted him and slowed cautiously, moving to the side of the road. Sable took off his hat and saluted the leader of the group.

That man leaned to say something to the others and came forward alone, leaving his two companions stopped a ways back on the trail. His hair was the colour of winter wheat, a pale white blonde that curled tightly when it was long like now. It was a riot of curls all over his head and a blond, curly beard covered his lower face.

"Farmer!" Sable waited.

The man gave a smile and moved closer. "Sable Maude. What are you doing here?"

"I'm here on business. I heard you had disappeared into the hills."

Abe gave him a penetrating stare. "Not exactly."

"Good. Some people fear for your life." He smiled but it wasn't a nice smile. He didn't have such an expression in his repertoire.

"Do they? Are you one of those?"

He shook his head. "No. It doesn't matter to me one way or the other."

Abe frowned. "But we're family now, you're my brother by marriage. How's Bethlehem?"

Sable blinked in surprise, just once because he caught himself in time. "She's fine. I was sorry to leave her so soon after the wedding. But duty calls."

Something relaxed in Abe Farmer's face. "That's good. I'm glad to hear she's okay. How's your father?"

He kept his gaze guileless. "Good. You know the Governor. His eye is never off the ball." He gave a guffaw of laughter.

Abe chuckled, but looked a little uncomfortable at the reference to the Governor's single eye. "Can we share a meal, maybe here in the hamlet? Catch up on news."

"Sorry, Abe. I wish you'd caught me at a better time." He let his eyes twinkle. "I'm in a real hurry."

"How was the wedding?"

"Rushed, as you can imagine. But good, as these things go." Sable tried to seem pleased. He gritted his teeth, sorry now that he'd stopped to talk to the man.

"If you're heading west, you should watch out for the Emperor's men. They've invaded."

Sable narrowed his eyes. "Emperor Carlton?"

"Yah, they're just across the border inside Khandarken."

"Where's the army?"

"They're there too. Be careful, it's chaos. I'm heading back to Farmer Holdings as soon as I can get there." Abe's mouth firmed to a thin line. "Can I take a message to your wife?"

"No, I'll take my own messages. I'll take transit back, probably be there before you. How are you travelling home?"

Abe's expression grew guarded. Sable didn't blame him. He'd be keeping his secrets close, too, if he were in Farmer's shoes. "We're riding, got some business of our own to tend to."

Sable measured him with his gaze. "Yah." He spurred his horse and went by them, his riders coming fast behind.

CHAPTER THIRTY THREE

Abe watched the horses gallop past, and then turned his mule again toward the east.

"What did they want?" Kerr had reined in his mount next to him.

"That was Sable Maude."

Kerr twisted in the saddle to look back at the disappearing horses. "Sable Maude? What's he doing out here?"

"Good question. He just got married to Bethlehem." Abe glanced sideways at Julianne, but she seemed to be drowsing in the saddle. Poor thing. She'd hung in there, done her best not to slow them down. Would he really let her stop at the City instead of coming home with him? He didn't think so.

"So what did he say?" Kerr wouldn't let it go.

"He was surprised that I knew about the wedding, even though he tried to hide it. Said he was on business, couldn't stop for a meal and get caught up on news."

"Seems damned odd if he's your new brother, doesn't it? Do you trust him?"

"Yah, it seems odd. When he asked how we were getting home, I said we were riding, because we had business to tend to. I didn't mention the boats."

They rode on in silence.

~ * * * ~

"Major, we have another reported contact of Abram Farmer. He's been sighted again in the northern territories."

Dante sat in his office in the military headquarters outside the City walls and narrowed his eyes at the window as he listened to his executive assistant on voicelink. "Malahide, it's got to be confirmed before I can do anything with it."

"I know. But this is that contact with the particulars that I've been monitoring out of Cownden Lanser's office."

"By the graves." Dante felt like banging his head on the desk. "Is it Cownden's voicelink or not?"

"No, not his. We know which ones are his and monitor them. But this one is attached to his office. So it's either an extra voicelink that he uses personally, or someone in his office has their own that they've attached to the official system. The encryption makes it damned hard to decipher."

"What did they say?"

"It's cryptic, as usual. Hold on." There was a pause, then Malahide came back on the speaker. "Here it is. *Saw Farmer. Looked good. North by east, pre Wymark.* At least, that's the best we could do, pre Wymark. The other person asked, *Tell LH?* And the first one said, *Why not? Give him something to think about.* And there was a laugh. Then the line went dead."

"You're sure it was a man?"

"Yah, but scrambled. Wouldn't be able to identify him by his voice."

"No, of course not." Dante sighed. "Well, LH could be Little Harry, as he's still missing out there somewhere."

"Hadn't thought of that, but it would make sense."

"I know. This voicelink device is connected to the talc mine and the attacks at Farmer Holdings. And Little Harry has been involved with that. So these people know where Little Harry is. The reference to Farmer… well, it could mean all kinds of things. Maybe he saw a farmer that they both knew. It doesn't have to be Abe Farmer, does it? What does pre Wymark mean?"

"Well, we figured if he was travelling west it could mean before he got to Wymark."

"Right, but it could mean the opposite too, if he was travelling east."

Malahide was silent.

"Okay, keep on it."

Dante hung up. He wouldn't tell Bethlehem about this, it was too vague and probably didn't have anything to do with her brother. She'd been so hopeful and then so full of despair when he told her his last piece of news. He couldn't bear to see her swung around like that. It hurt his heart to see her cry. He rubbed his chest with his fist.

He'd wait. If this brother of hers really was alive, there'd be confirmation of that fact sooner or later. Meanwhile, he'd let his wife have hope and not fill her with false promises. He looked at the time keeper. It was already late, he wouldn't get home tonight.

It was so damned frustrating. She couldn't leave Holdings because she was the only Farmer left and needed to be there. And he was here running the army. When were they going to sort this out? What if a baby were to come? Would she still insist she had to stay there, and he'd be separated from them both?

His thoughts grew dark. He needed to get things settled. He wasn't going to have a part-time marriage. His trips out to the different territories to supervise the troops were bad enough without him and his wife living in two different regions of the country.

He put in a call to Cownden Lanser. The Chief Constable wasn't available, so Dante left a holograph message. *Who owned the voicelink out of Lanser's office?* He doubted he'd hear back, but he'd keep asking.

CHAPTER THIRTY FOUR

A t the end of the day, Abe led them into yet another barn and started to unsaddle the mules. Julianne tried to help, tugging on the strap around the mule's belly with both hands, but it wouldn't give. Maybe the mule had puffed up with air. She'd heard they sometimes did that.

"Leave it," Abe said, his voice sharp. "I'll do it."

Injured, she gazed at him for a moment before dropping the strap and pulling the bags from the back of the animal. His curt tone hurt her feelings, and she couldn't wait to have something to eat and just go to sleep. Then she wouldn't have to feel the hot glare of his eyes on her back, or hear his questioning comments.

Kerr coughed, and Abe turned slightly to catch his eye. He must have given him a glare too, because Kerr shrugged and began to work on the next mule.

They'd been travelling for days. Kerr's leg was still improving, he even managed to walk sometimes to give his mule a rest and exercise his leg.

Julianne pulled the medicine sack out and sat down to sort the supplies. "Kerr, let me do your leg while it's still light. Perhaps we won't need a bandage tonight; we're getting low on medicine." She bent over the wound as Kerr pulled his pant leg higher. "It looks good. How does it feel?"

Kerr smiled and sat in the straw next to her. "It feels much better. You've given me good care."

The colour rushed to her cheeks at the unexpected compliment and she slid a sideways glance at Abe. His mouth had tightened and he jerked the saddle blanket off the back of her mule with more force than was necessary. She sighed and bent to tend the wound. Nothing made him happy. His tanned face was set like stone and he snapped at everything. She was miserable. What had she done wrong?

She set about pulling out the stale bread left in their food supplies, and found a jar of meat.

Abe shook his head. "We'll eat with the farmer. His wife is preparing a meal for us."

Julianne dropped her hands in her lap, the food spread around her. She couldn't do anything right. Kerr reached to help stuff it back in the sack, and she heard Abe's exasperated breath.

The farmer came to get them for dinner and they trooped into the house, kicking their boots off at the door. The smell they gave off must have been pretty ripe, because the wife wrinkled her nose and waved them quickly to a table on the porch. She set bowls of stew and platters of steamed vegetables before them, a loaf of bread cut in rough slices to dip in the broth. It was delicious. Julianne ate until she couldn't force down another bite. Even Abe seemed to relax and she caught a slight smile on his face.

They leaned back and lingered over hot tea and gingerbreads, talking as the wife bustled around them, then left to set the table in the kitchen for her own family.

"How many days to the sea do you think, Abe?" Kerr broke another piece of gingerbread off and popped it into his mouth, then took a sip of tea to soften it.

"Not many. Two or three."

Kerr nodded.

"Then what?" Julianne had eaten half her cookie and pushed the rest toward the men, unable to finish.

Abe turned to look at her with those pale eyes and actually smiled. "Then we hope to find a boat to carry us south. There's a lot of trade up and down the coast. Someone should be able to take us." She felt her chest relax under his gaze.

"What do we do with the mules?" Kerr asked.

"Good question." Abe caught the grin on his guard's face and chuckled at the grilling they were giving him. "We sell them. We can't take them, we don't need more mules at Farmer's. Someone will want them."

"Then we can stop at the City on the way south?"

Abe's grin disappeared as suddenly as it had arrived. He nodded, gazed at her mouth for a long moment and shoved his chair back. "Let's go."

He headed out, stopping to lean in the kitchen doorway. "Thank you for the great meal. We really enjoyed it. One of the best we've had on this trip." The wife blushed under the praise as Abe turned and, smile gone, stalked out the door.

Kerr rose and waited as Julianne scrambled to grab her boots and fumble them onto her feet.

At the barn, the men stopped outside while she got changed in the dim light of the stall. She still wore the Sanctuary robe to sleep in. It allowed her clothes to dry during the night and gave her a change even when she couldn't have a bath. As she slipped it over her head, she heard low voices near the doorway and turned. Kerr and Abe were standing just outside the wide door, staring off into the distance as they talked.

Julianne folded her shirt and pants, laying them on the stall rail to air.

"Why, Abe? You don't have to be so grumpy." Kerr's gravel voice came from outside the entry to the barn.

Abe mumbled something terse in reply. There was a pause. Julianne shifted her blanket and lay down on it, pulling more straw under the end to pillow her head.

"You're just making her miserable."

"I can't seem to help it!" The mules had stopped munching for a moment and the words came through clearly. "I know it's bad. I should know better." He paused and Julianne strained her ears to hear. "I try, but then I see her face and I want to kiss her. And I can't." There was more said, but the animals shifted and muffled the sound. Julianne closed her eyes and pressed her face into the musty blanket.

Was this why he'd been so short with her, because he wanted to kiss her? She wanted to kiss him too. Was that all he wanted? She wasn't sure, and the thoughts she had about the possibilities made her temperature rise and her face get hot. Maybe he wanted her the way she wanted him. He was so attractive, with the pale blue eyes and almost white hair curled all over his head. Even his beard was curly, a slightly darker shade of blond. His smile made her heart flip over in excitement. And when he took her in his arms, he was gentle, firm but tender.

He'd dragged and hauled her all over the place since he'd rescued her from the Sanctuary, even physically carried her out of that dangerous situation with the Emperor's men, but she'd always felt protected. He'd even kissed her, just a quick kiss dropped on her mouth that made the breath catch in her throat.

But he hadn't touched her since they'd escaped the Emperor.

She heard footsteps and peeped to watch Kerr enter the barn. He shifted his blanket and tucked straw beneath till it suited him, then lay down, setting his boots beside him. Abe didn't return for a long time.

When she woke the next morning, the men were just stirring. Abe sat up and pulled his boots on. "Kerr? You awake?"

Kerr grunted.

"I am," Julianne said.

Abe glanced over at her and smiled. She watched him cautiously for a minute in the dim light, then smiled tentatively in return.

He offered his hand. "Are you ready to get up?"

He gave a tug and as she rose, caught her at the waist with his other hand. "There you go." His voice was strained but he didn't turn away.

She searched his face. He hesitated, then leaned in to press his lips to her forehead "Don't look at me like that, Julianne. I'll kiss you if you do."

Hastily she glanced away and reached for her clothes, taking them into the next stall to dress. If he wanted to kiss her, she wouldn't stop him. Why would she? It felt wonderful when he held her in his arms and laid his mouth over hers. Shedding the robe, she pulled her shirt and pants on.

She heard the men readying the mules, and the farmer came out to see that they didn't steal anything. They mounted and rode out.

CHAPTER THIRTY FIVE

Midday, they stopped beside the trail to eat. Abe used his knife to open a jar of elk meat from the Emperor's stores, and watched Julianne quickly school her expression of distaste at the sight of more preserved meat. They spread it on dried bread from the pack and divided it up between them. The mules grazed as they rested.

"I wonder how much the reward is for finding me."

Abe glanced up and caught the girl's gaze. She looked so innocent it was hard to believe there was a reward on her head. "Let's hope we don't find out the hard way. There's one on my head as well."

Julianne gave a start of surprise and stared at him. "There is? What have you done?"

Both men laughed. "He disappeared," said Kerr. "That's his crime. They can't find him, so they're hoping someone will turn him in for the money."

Sudden hoof beats approached at a steady trot from the direction they'd just come. Abe jumped to his feet. "Here, Julianne. Take the mules to water down at the creek bed. Wait for us there." He grabbed one mule and pulled it forward as he seized the tether ropes on the other two. Kerr positioned himself to face the trail, as she turned and led the mules through the trees and down the bank to the edge of the creek.

Abe straightened in time to watch Sable Maude ride into view. He slowed his mount, reining it over to the side of the track. "There you are, Farmer. I've been looking for you."

"Have you now?" Noting the grim set to the man's mouth, Abe stepped back within arm's reach of the plasmagun lying on the blanket. "Why would that be?"

"I have a bone to pick with you." Sable gave him a steady gaze from the back of his horse. Abe returned the stare. He'd met this man a few times while doing business in Farmerville and Deep Creek, but had never spent much time with him. He liked his brother by marriage less and less as he got to know him.

Sable dismounted, throwing his leg over the horn and sliding to the ground. He gathered the reins and tied his horse to the nearest bush where it started grazing the tall grass at the edge of the road.

Maude moved forward a couple of paces, then propped his hands on his hips. Abe saw a pistol shoved into his belt under the flap of his jacket. Kerr obviously saw it too, because he stepped away to give them both room to maneuver if they had to. There was tension in the air. Was this going to be a firefight? He hoped Julianne stayed out of sight.

"What seems to be the problem?" he said impatiently. "Spit it out, Maude."

"You set me up." His eyes narrowed.

"I don't know what you're talking about."

Maude's voice went flat. "The military were waiting for us on the road to Wymark. Half my men were killed and the rest of us fled. You told them where I was." He was clearly furious, although his face was nearly expressionless. His body vibrated with anger.

"Don't be a fool. Why would I do that?"

"Nobody calls me a fool." His lips curled in a snarl. "You told them because there's a reward on my head. You need money."

Abe laughed and Maude went red. "I'm laughing because there's a reward on my head, too. Why would I try to turn you in when I could get caught at the same time?"

Maude's face had gone from flushed to pale. He took a fast step forward as he dragged the pistol from his belt, raised it and with one swift motion levelled it at Kerr's forehead. "I'm nobody's fool. Now, brother by marriage or not, you don't get away with this. Don't reach for the plasmagun, Farmer. My men are right behind me, and I'll shoot your man dead if you move."

Abe froze, his hands held out at his sides, as panic multiplied in his chest. "By the graves, you've got it wrong, Maude. Put the gun down. We haven't spoken to the military since we left the Emperor's camp, which was long before we met you on the trail."

Maude gave a cold smile and moved forward until his gun was pressed hard against the skin at Kerr's temple. "No one, and I mean no one, tells me what to do. I'm the Monarch of the Territories. I'll tell you how it's going to be." He cocked the pistol with a small distinct click.

Abe gaped as Kerr's face went white. The man had gone mad. *The Monarch of the Territories? What was he babbling about?*

"Put the gun down, Maude. This is my man you're threatening, you're related to me, married to my sister. It's wrong. You can't do this."

Maude's face twisted with rage. "I had plans and you ruined them!" He calmly pulled the trigger. Abe heard the hammer hit home as the bullet ratcheted down the barrel and flew out the muzzle of the gun. The sound was deafening. Kerr hung momentarily in the air like a puppet whose strings were cut, then dropped lifeless to the ground.

Deafened by the roar of the shot, Abe bellowed with fury and grappled with clumsy hands for the plasmagun on the ground between them. He felt like he moved in slow motion. He was too far away to reach Maude with a kick or his fist. His brain wouldn't work and his muscles seemed frozen.

Kerr was dead. He lay motionless, his head fallen awkwardly to the side, one half of it blown away, blood and brain matter leaking onto the blanket. The universe was out of kilter. Sable Maude had conjured up an imagined slight and killed Kerr over the manufactured event.

He rose from the ground in a rush, plasmagun gripped in both hands as Maude whirled to face him, the pistol moving at an infinitesimal pace toward a target in the centre of his chest. Then a rumbling growl came from the bush at Maude's back. He paused, and both men turned to gape toward the sound. The roar grew louder and the noise of rushing feet filled the air.

Abe leaped awkwardly backward, as Maude stumbled under the assault of the huge mountain cat. Its small round ears were laid back against the sides of its broad head, tail out parallel to the ground as it moved in low. The cat knocked Sable down, and as he scrambled to get his feet under him, it sank its teeth into the side of his head.

Maude screamed.

Abe heard the sickening crunch of bone beneath its jaws, but the eyes in the fiercely grinning head were pinned to his own face. He backed further away at the horrific sight. The cat let go for a moment and Abe fired. The shot missed by an inch.

The lion moved in a sinuous motion as its tawny coat glowed dully in the light, almost dancing as it positioned itself over Sable for a second bite. It roared, widened its jaws and clamped its fangs on the side of his face.

Bile rose up Abe's throat as he staggered sideways. Maude's horse bucked and reared at the end of its tether, and there was the sudden thunder of hooves pounding on the road behind him. Those would be Maude's men arriving.

Kerr was dead and he had nothing to gain by staying here and much to lose. Turning, plasmagun in hand, he ran for the creek bed through the trees, branches whipping at his face and chest.

At first he couldn't see her as he crashed through the bushes. He swung his head wildly. Staring up the creek, he caught sight of a mule, saddlebags bulging on its back, tail swishing leisurely. Julianne huddled against the wide trunk of the oak, reins gripped in bloodless fingers. Her eyes were huge in her face as she fearfully watched downstream.

He reached her at a run as the sound of hooves and neighing of horses came from the hillside behind him. "Come, but don't talk," he said low.

Grabbing hold, he tossed her up into the saddle of the nearest mule. Seizing the reins, he mounted and led them up the creek bed through the water, moving at a steady, silent pace between the banks of long grass and low trees around a bend in the waterway. He kept going, glancing back now and then to see that they weren't followed. Julianne was motionless in the saddle, her gaze pinned to his back. He felt the hot weight of it between his shoulder blades.

Finally, she urged her animal forward until she was almost even with him, jostling his mule for space in the narrow stream. "What about Kerr? Where is he?" Her whisper was low, hesitant.

"Kerr's dead." Abe's voice was flat, cracking with emotion. He could feel the rage building in his chest, rising like a volcano. He knew he had to deal with their perilous situation before he let anything else escape his lips.

He wanted to bellow and howl, he wanted to rant, to shoot something. He just kept riding, staying in the creek bed, travelling on the gravel and sand for a few more miles to hide their tracks. Then he led them out onto dry ground and headed overland for the sea.

CHAPTER THIRTY SIX

They travelled east at a single-minded steady pace. The rain had stopped, but fog hung in the air like a heavy blanket. Abe felt as if he'd left his body altogether and was looking from above, watching himself ride toward the ocean in a small pack train of three mules. The woman riding behind him said nothing as they rode, seeming to hold onto the saddle by sheer determination.

"If you can keep going a little longer," he said, "We'll be safer the farther we go."

A nod was her only response.

Abe called a halt as the light grew dim, and searched around for a place to make camp. The mules were flagging and needed to be fed. And so did he. Julianne had not said another word but her face was set, her lips pressed determinedly together, small resolute dimples showing in her cheeks.

He led his mule into the bush, the others following. The ground rose slightly as they went and tall trees dominated the landscape, leaving the undergrowth sparse. "We can stop here. We can't be seen from the road and it's on a rise, so if it rains we won't be swamped."

He tied his mule to a tree branch and reached up to help her from the saddle. She collapsed against him. As he tightened his grip, she laid her cheek against his chest and burst into tears. He lowered his head to rest it against hers and stood there, feeling her heaving sobs shudder through him. The sound undid him. It was as if she wept for them both. Tears backed up behind his eyes, and he tried to will them away.

"Why did Kerr have to die? It's not right," she gasped out between sobs. Her voice was so faint he hardly heard her.

"There is no right in this. There's no fairness," he choked.

"How can you say that?" Her eyes were luminous as she looked up at him. He became lost in their stormy depths and lowered his mouth to cover hers and stop the flow of words that he could barely understand.

His sense of connection was instantaneous. She fit perfectly against him, and the feel of her mouth under his was everything he had imagined. She drew him in, her lips clinging to his, her round breasts pressed against his chest. His heart beat hard and his throat seemed to close. He could hardly breathe. He finally lifted his head to get some air.

She gazed up at him with such a sense of wonder on her face, he had to lower his mouth for another kiss. His mule nudged him hard enough to knock him off balance and he stumbled sideways, holding Julianne away from him to avoid stepping on her.

A tide of embarrassment rose up his neck. "I guess we'd better tend to business. These animals need to be fed."

She straightened her shoulders and moved toward the saddlebags. "I can do that."

He let her get started and dove into the other storage bags. These mules had been part of the Emperor's pack train, and there was an interesting array of articles stored in the gear. He pulled out a fly tarp, and began to string it low between two trees to provide some protection from the weather. Then the saddle blankets hit the ground, two on the bottom for cushion, one on top for warmth. They'd sleep together tonight, no more separate pallets in some farmer's stall. Kerr was gone. His heart clenched painfully in his chest. That hard fact was too difficult to swallow.

He didn't light a fire. It was risky, and they had enough food for their dinner. They could cook in the morning, in daylight when others wouldn't see the flames flickering through the trees.

By the time he'd sorted the supplies and repacked the saddlebags, Julianne had arranged the cooked meat and cut vegetables on a chrome plate. "Sit and eat, Julianne. You're tired and we need to rest."

He picked at the food, until he realized she wasn't eating anything at all. "I'll eat two mouthfuls, if you will."

Her gaze was soulful.

"Just two mouthfuls," he encouraged. Her attempt at a smile broke his heart. She picked up the meat and chewed off a bite, munching dutifully on the tough dry texture.

"You, too." She shoved it toward him and he took a bite. In that manner they managed to achieve a small meal, and she tucked the leftovers back into the saddlebags that Abe then hung high in the tree to keep away from predators.

"Come to bed, Julianne."

She eyed him tentatively before crawling under the tent he'd arranged. As she removed her socks, he bent low to peer inside. "You finish and get organized, then I'll come in. There isn't room for us both to be pulling off our boots."

She murmured something when she had settled beneath the top saddle blanket, and Abe shuffled in on his knees, tugging his boots off to set them by the entry. "Let me get my jacket off."

Crawling under the blanket, he curled up against her, cradling her with his body.

"Tell me, Abe. What happened to Kerr?"

Abe felt a lump of rage and loss crawl up his throat and lodge there. He could hardly speak past the blockage. "Sable Maude returned."

"Sable Maude? Whatever for? He said he was heading west on business."

As Abe relayed the story, she began to shake, and he wrapped his long arms around her as she cried. His own tears fell, leaking from the corners of his eyes.

"So they're both dead."

Abe grunted. "I would have killed him where he stood, but the cat got there first. I thought the mountain lion was coming for me, but he just repositioned himself and took a better hold on Maude's head."

She shuddered in his arms.

"Don't cry, Julianne. Don't cry." His voice shook with repressed emotion, his whole body vibrating. "I want to hit something. I want to shoot him over and over again, even though he's already dead."

She ran her hands across his chest and he exploded with need. His mouth came down on hers with fierce concentration, yet she answered him with her own power. The kiss seemed to take her as much by surprise as it did him, but Abe didn't hold back. He'd wanted her and now there were just the two of them. Kerr wasn't here to caution him, remind him he was a decent man. When virgins were thrust into his care, he didn't take them to bed.

He forgot all Kerr's admonitions. Fumbling with the buttons on her shirt, he managed to get several undone and find a way inside. Then he felt her warm flesh under his hand, and his fingers closed around her. Her breast was firm and soft, the nipple a hard nub digging into his palm. His breath came fast, and he heard her panting in his ear as he lowered his mouth to suckle her.

He thought he was a man who was experienced with women. But this was so different from anything he'd known with the widow in Coronation. He was ablaze.

He fought with her clothes and then with his. The saddle blanket shifted to the side and night air swept his bare back as he shoved his trousers down. "Julianne," he gasped. "Tell me if you don't want this. I'll marry you, I promise."

"All right," she said, as if distracted. "Touch me here." She pulled his hand lower and his brain exploded. *Touch her there?* He'd touch her anywhere she asked him to. His fingers smoothed down her belly, the skin silky soft, and threaded through the curls between her legs. This wasn't the way to make love to a woman the first time. It should be satin sheets and a warm fire, a glass of wine together before seducing her.

But his mind was so far from that, he couldn't even contemplate it. His brain shut down and his belly filled with fire, a fire that was consuming the rage in his gut and the fury in his fists. He found her in the dark, his hand searching and discovering her wet and ready, pushing carefully into her with his finger as she took a surprised breath beneath his open mouth.

The urge was so strong he thought he might come before he even got inside. "Are you all right?" he whispered. "I want you. I need to come in you."

She spread her legs and he surged over her. "Julianne, I'll marry you." And he pushed at her entrance.

She was tight and he pressed there, forcing his way inward. When she gave a gasp, he halted, sweat dripping off his shoulders. He wiped his forehead with the sleeve of a shirt he found under his hand.

"Baby, I need to get inside you."

"Yes, I know." Her voice was faint.

He placed his mouth over hers and began a slow sweet kiss that was like a lullaby, soothing and soft. He felt her relax against him, and then he pushed.

She caught her breath, and he pushed harder. Her hands were on his chest, holding him back. But it was too late, he was seated within. She shuddered, the shaking took her whole body in its grip. He wrapped his arms around her and held on, hoping he could wait. The pressure was fierce. He moved out and in again because he had to. His lungs laboured and he heaved again as the heaviness built and crested, moving over him, tightening his muscles, his limbs in spasm, his groin taut and driven to finish.

He all but collapsed on her, sliding to the side at the last moment leaving one arm wrapped possessively across her breasts. His chest bellowed and he couldn't move, as the tight grip of anger slowly released him from its grasp. When he finally settled at her side, he felt peace flow out of him like water.

She was beautiful, lying across his arm. Her face was pale, no wonder after all she'd been through. Her rosy lips pouted softly, the fan of dark lashes against her cheeks, the whole package excited him.

How he wanted to look his fill. He'd seen her in the firelight that night in the barn, and the memory was burned in his brain. The round little breasts with their pointed nipples, the indent of her waist. Making love to her was like magic. He hadn't had nearly enough. Yet he hadn't waited for her either, he'd been too overwrought with the events of the past days to get himself under control.

His chest grew tight. She'd been a virgin, and he'd taken that from her on the ground, on a saddle blanket at the edge of the track. And he was the only one who'd had any pleasure from it. He had to do better. She wouldn't come to Farmer Holdings with him if he didn't give her a reason to be there.

Kerr was dead, but he was alive, vitally alive. And he had her now. Julianne was his.

CHAPTER THIRTY SEVEN

Julianne woke to a breaking dawn. There was a warm body at her back and a weight across her chest. She turned to find Abe snoring softly beside her, his arm heavy across her breasts. Her belly curled in excitement as she realized what they'd done. She'd let him make love to her, with her.

Had he said he'd marry her? She couldn't really remember. The whole experience had been so new, she'd been completely overcome by the feelings it evoked. She'd never been overtaken like that, simply swept away by the physical attentions of a man. His hands had been everywhere, he'd touched her in places she'd never imagined someone would touch her. It had been so intimate, so exciting. A warm flush spread up her throat to suffuse her cheeks.

His hand moved, smoothing her skin, to catch a lock of her hair between his fingers. When she glanced at his face, he was watching her sleepily with those pale blue eyes. He rolled toward her and pressed his mouth to hers. Oh, no. Was he going to do it again?

A mighty thrill rippled over her body just at the thought. What had happened to her? She was such a careful, thoughtful girl. This wasn't careful, not even thoughtful or well planned. It was probably one of the more foolish things she'd done since she ran from her home in the City.

She hesitated for a moment, and then opened her mouth and he plunged in. She was overwhelmed again. Because he was touching her in all those sensitive places that he'd touched last night. His eyes grew darker as he watched his hand move over her skin, then he dipped his head and fastened onto her breast. The sensation took her by surprise, and the pleasure swept downward.

When he finally lifted his head, she thought she'd never breathe again. His gaze was intent on her face, his teeth gleaming white in the shadow of their tent.

She felt a small smile curve her lips upward.

"I want to make love to you again. Are you sore?"

She hadn't even considered that. Was she? He didn't give her time to decide, just tugged on the blanket and rolled it down. She grabbed for it in sudden alarm. "Abe …"

He laughed. "I just want to look at you. I didn't get to see you last night." As he pushed the cover aside, she saw his naked body emerge from the bedding. He was lean and corded with muscle, a wedge of blond hair matting his chest. He was beautiful. The sight of him made her breath catch in her throat.

"I think I went too fast last night."

"Too fast?" she said doubtfully, glancing back at his face.

"Yah. I didn't give you time to come with me."

She blinked. *What was he talking about?* He leaned to kiss her mouth thoroughly, then down her throat while his hand soothed her below. Quickly she grew wet, her excitement mounting. How did he know to do that, how did he know what would feel good? By the time his mouth reached the smooth skin of her belly, she was panting hotly, her fingers tangled in his hair. The sense of anticipation mounted.

He pushed his fingers inside her and she gasped low. Then he rubbed her there on some sensitive spot that sent shafts of excitement straight to her belly. When he lifted himself and pressed into her, the air left her lungs. She caught her breath and tightened her legs around his hips.

"Are you sore?" he choked out. "Do you want me to …"

She didn't know what he was offering, but it didn't matter. She relaxed back onto the blanket as he pushed his way in. He withdrew and drove back in. Each time was better, the excitement wound tighter inside.

"That's a good girl," he whispered. "Good girl, come on. Just relax, enjoy it." She didn't really take in what he said, just that he was talking, his voice low and crooning in her ear.

He placed his hand between them, using his thumb to rub that sensitive spot, that vulnerable place, and the feelings escalated. "Julianne, honey, we're almost there." He kissed her, deep and thorough, and wrapped his forearm under her lower back to hold her tight against him. Her hands ranged across his wide shoulders. She gripped his hips and pushed upward, then stiffened and groaned. It was indescribable, like a long warm wash flowing over her and sweeping her away. She hardly noticed when he collapsed on his side, his arm locked around her. She must have slept.

When she woke, the sun was higher in the sky. She opened her eyes to find him gazing straight into hers. "Hi," she whispered.

A smile bloomed across his face, such an expression of tenderness after all the anger and sorrow. Her heart suddenly didn't have room to function. He looked back at her. "Hi, yourself."

She giggled, and he laughed and gathered her into his arms. "We'll get married," he said, "as soon as we get to Farmer Holdings. Just in case. There might be a baby." He looked at her questioningly but she just smiled. *A baby? Not this quick, surely.* And she had to get back to find her father. She stretched languidly against him and saw his face turn red.

"We'd better get moving." He yanked his gaze away and fumbled for a cloth to offer her.

"I'll get dressed," she said.

As she crawled toward the opening at the end of the tarp, dragging her clothes with her, she felt his hand smooth across her skin and down her buttocks. Startled, she turned toward him. He shook his head and swatted her lightly. "We have to go, don't distract me."

She burst from under the flytarp, giggling, and dragged the shirt over her head. As she struggled into her pants, Abe crawled out behind her. Standing tall, he stretched in the morning light, unconcerned with his nakedness. His limbs gleamed pale in the shadow of the trees, his shoulders broad and thick with muscle, his thighs lean and powerful. As she watched, his male member stirred and stood out from the bush of hair at his groin. Startled, she glanced up at him and caught his fierce gaze on her face. Hastily she looked away.

When he bent to pull his clothes from under their shelter, she caught sight of the injury in his side and her breath caught. He'd almost died from that dreadful wound.

"Abe."

He turned, a questioning look on his face. "What is it?"

She placed her hand over the thin new skin of the still healing injury. Then she leaned into him, pressed her face against his chest and breathed him in.

CHAPTER THIRTY EIGHT

Beth drove down the mine track on her new solar scooter, a cloud of dust following her progress. She had to remember to plug it in when she got back to the manorhouse. The old one had been taken off active duty and put in the shed to be used for parts. Her husband, Dante brought this one home from the City the week before, saying his wife wasn't going to ride around the farm on an unreliable vehicle.

She grinned to herself. The old one was the scooter that she'd ridden the day she met him by the pond, when she was still betrothed to another man. That was also the day she'd learned that Uncle Jade and Abe had been attacked in the north and her brother was missing.

Her smile faded. There'd been no resolution for her. She still didn't know where he was or if he was alive.

There'd been rumours, of course. Dante told her whenever he heard something. But no word from Abe. She didn't know when the time would come that she'd have to face the fact he wasn't coming back. That time was not yet.

She wiped a tear off her cheek and kicked the scooter into low gear as she reached the bottom of the track. Bowcott stepped forward from the small guard shed, lifted the gate and saluted her. It always made her laugh, as if she were army. But now that she was married to a Regiment, all the workers had started saluting. She could see they liked it. It was a sign of affection.

"Your uncle sends his best wishes and asks you to join him for lunch," she said as she pulled to a stop. "Faden's instructed someone else to take the second shift. He's got llama stew up there."

Bowcott grinned as colour washed his cheeks. "Thank you, Ms. That will be welcome. I'm famished."

"Good. I gather you're to become his new assistant." For years Kerr had been Faden's assistant, before he disappeared with Abe in the north.

Bowcott's blush deepened. "Well, I don't know about that."

"Hmm. I do, we just talked about it again. He says you're learning the business fast and Mr Kneebone, our talc agent, has great faith in you."

He blinked, then nodded. "Thank you Ms. I'll take that as a compliment. Uncle Faden is a knowledgeable man."

"Yes. It was meant as a compliment. You'll be good at this, Bowcott. And Faden's the best there is to learn from. His knowledge is deep and long standing. He'll be a great mentor for you." She shook his hand and revved the motor, booting it into high gear as she headed across the plains for home.

The track was dusty, they'd had little rain in the last weeks. The land unrolled ahead of her, fields of pasture, of lentils and vegetable gardens. She kept an eye out for the sheep flock, spotting it off in the fields to the east. She knew the llama herd was even farther away in the low hills. There was still a mountain lion roaming their land. The herders had spotted it several times and she didn't want to encounter it out here by herself.

By the time she got to the yard, she was starving. She parked near the transit shed and plugged in the solar machine. There was no military guard at the manorhouse now. Things had settled down and they weren't under attack anymore. Little Harry had disappeared and perhaps his men as well, because the assaults against Farmer Holdings had stopped.

She opened the back door and left her shoes neatly in the cloak room. As she pushed the kitchen door open, Hannan was just pulling a baking sheet out of the oven.

"There you are, Ms. I was expecting you back earlier."

"We had quite a bit to deal with up there. That smells good. What have you made?"

Hannan beamed. "Gingerbreads, Ms, the Major's favourite. They're for dinner. But I could let you have one after your lunch."

Beth laughed. "You tease. What's for lunch?"

"Grilled rabbit, steamed vegetables, fried lentils. I've got roast mutton for dinner. The Major will be here."

"Oh, so now only the best dishes when Dante's here. What about me?"

Hannan swatted her backside with a drying towel and turned to hang it on a hook. "Don't get sassy," she muttered. "We have to keep the Major nice and strong so we can have some young babes around here soon."

Beth snorted a laugh. "I don't think that's a concern. I'll just wash up." She wandered down the hall to the bathrobe and stepped inside. As she washed her face and hands, she stared into the mirror at her reflection.

Did she look any different? She didn't think so, perhaps there were darker shadows beneath her eyes. But she felt different. She was with child, and the signs were already there. Her breasts were tender, her nipples unusually sensitive. She was tired a lot, had naps on days when Dante wasn't home.

And food was becoming an issue. Grilled rabbit sounded fine, even the steamed vegetables. But fried lentils? Her stomach churned just at the thought, and the smell of them in the kitchen had caused her to silently choke back a gag of revulsion.

Hannan would cook her anything she asked for, but she needed to tell Dante about this first, before anyone else. And he was home tonight. Her heart leaped at the thought.

She went into the office and sat behind her desk. There were a few messages on her infolink that needed attention. As she opened the message account and began to sort through them, her voicelink beeped.

Where was that thing? She should have taken it with her in case Dante phoned. But it didn't get good reception out in the fields, it was the beltlink that kept her in contact with her workers and the manorhouse. She found the device under a sheaf of papers on the side table. It was blinking orange.

The first message was from Dante. He would see her this afternoon, but he could only stay one night. Her mouth turned down at the news. Only one night? He was busy and away a lot. Sometimes it was disheartening.

The second message, from Deloume Renfrew, said he'd scheduled a meeting with Governor Maude for tomorrow afternoon. She should attend. They were going to discuss security at Farmerville. She made a note in her journal.

The third message was from a military particular in the north. "Hello, Beth. It's me." Her breath caught in her throat. She knew who that was. 'Me' was how he'd always identified himself. He used to tell her that if she didn't recognize his voice by now, all hope was lost. They'd laughed at that, it had been a joke between them.

Abe was alive.

The message continued. "I'm heading home from east of Wymark. Circuitous route. Don't want to give any info but I'm well and mobile. See you soon. I send all my love."

Her heart beat hard and she gripped the voicelink with both hands, hugging it to her breast. *Abe was alive. He was coming home.* She skipped a few steps out the office door, then ran full tilt down the hall toward the kitchens.

"Hannan! Listen to this. You won't believe it!"

The cook listened to the message, then hugged her so hard, she all but squeezed the breath right out of her.

"Now, we can't tell anyone," Beth cautioned. "He's obviously being very careful about letting any information out."

"Not even the Major?"

Beth hoped her slight hesitation didn't show. It wouldn't inspire confidence in her new husband if the staff thought he couldn't be trusted. "Yes, of course we'll tell Dante. But no one else. No one here on the farm even. Not till Abe gets home."

CHAPTER THIRTY NINE

Later, Beth was waiting when Dante's military transport pulled up in the gravelled quarter near the wide front steps of the manorhouse. She ran down the stairs to meet him as Samuels climbed out and opened the door of the vehicle.

"Must be nice, having your own chauffeur," she whispered loudly. Samuels laughed and Dante grinned, wrapping an arm around her as he handed a sheaf of papers to his driver.

"Saucy wench. Have you been getting into trouble while I was gone?"

"Of course not." She tried to seem appalled at his suggestion, as Samuels turned away to give them privacy. Dante gave her a fierce kiss, then reached back to grab his case.

She smiled impishly at him. "Come inside, I have news."

"So do I," he said as he took her hand and led her to the verandah. Parker opened the door for them and Beth quickly showed him into the office.

Dante raised his eyebrows. "The office, huh? You must mean business."

She grinned delightedly. "Tell me your news first."

"Okay. Come and sit down." Leading her to the divan under the window, he pulled her onto his knee. "This is straight from the Northern Territory."

Her eyes grew round.

"Ooievaar called me. He's sure he's seen your brother."

She threw back her head and laughed. Dante watched in surprise as she tried to gain control of her giggles.

"Okay, it's good news. I know that." He looked more confused.

"Dante, listen." She pulled the voicelink out of her pocket and scrolled to her messages. "Here it is." She played the message, and Dante's face grew still as he listened.

"Is that him? Is that your brother?"

"Yes. It's him."

"When did you get this?"

"It came in last night. I didn't check my messages this morning, went straight up to the mine to work with Faden. It was here when I got back."

"You're sure that's him. He doesn't give his name."

221

"No, but he doesn't have to. That was a joke between us, about 'this is me.' I recognize his voice."

"Well, by the gods. I can hardly believe it." His head fell back against the cushions.

"You thought he was dead?" Her face was suddenly serious.

"I didn't know what to think, Bethlehem. I didn't want to give up searching for him, but the chances seemed slim that he'd survived." He stroked the backs of his fingers against her cheek. "I'm very glad for you."

Tears started in her eyes, and he wiped them away with his thumb as they fell. "Be glad."

"I am." Her smile was tremulous. "I am. I can't wait for him to get home. See, the particulars are military."

Dante nodded, smiling ironically. "He must have borrowed a voicelink from one of our men. Ooievaar is near Wymark in the north. There's been an attack through the Legitamia border, the new Emperor is on the march. And he saw Abe on the road, got information from him about the dispossessed army that's working with Emperor Carlton. That's why I can't stay longer. I have to get up there as soon as possible."

Her mouth turned down and he kissed her. "We better not waste any time." Laughing, he tugged her toward the stairs.

Later as he lay staring at the ceiling above their bed, chest heaving, she stirred in his grasp. "Dante, I have something to tell you."

The face he turned toward her was suddenly hard and set. "What?"

She paused, wondering why he looked almost angry. "Dante, it's okay. It's just something you should know."

He surged up on one elbow. "Is this about when your brother returns? Am I not welcome anymore?"

"What? No! No, nothing like that." She took his hand and dragged it down her body, pressing it against her abdomen. "We're going to have a baby, Dante."

His face changed in an instant from rigid to tender. His fingers felt her carefully. "You are? We are?" He laughed softly. "Sorry, I just thought …"

"We're married, no matter if Abe was here or not when it happened."

"You were betrothed to another man when he was home last."

"I know, but that's over. It's just us now."

"The three of us." He pressed a deep kiss to her mouth.

"That's why you have to be careful. When you travel north to put down the invaders, you have to keep yourself safe." She ran her fingers over his heavy shoulders, feeling him shiver at her touch. "You're going to be a father."

He regarded her soberly. "And you. I think I'll leave Samuels here while I'm away, he can pull in a few men to support him. He likes Hannan's cooking."

Beth giggled. "She likes him, too."

His gaze dropped to her breast and he enclosed her with his hand. "Can we make love again? What does this mean?"

"Oh, yes. It means we should make sure I'm pregnant. We don't want to leave it to chance." Her smile was tantalizing as she beamed up at him, her gaze open and welcoming.

CHAPTER FORTY

Julianne pulled herself into the saddle. The wool Sanctuary shirt was water repellant and had kept her warm throughout their hectic journey, but the coarse material of the pants chafed between her thighs. Today she was even more sensitive.

Abe had been gentle with her, but she was new to a man's attentions. She sat gingerly, then immediately stood again in the stirrups, feeling the tenderness between her legs. She looked sideways at Abe, who had stopped packing the last mule to watch her. The back of his neck went red.

"Are you sore?"

She carefully eased herself down. "A bit."

His face flushed a brighter colour. "Yah, that's what I thought. Wait a minute." He dug through the saddlebags and pulled something out. "Try this."

It was a square of cushioned material, hemmed neatly at the edges. She examined it curiously, feeling its texture with her fingers. Then she stood in the stirrups, laid it on the saddle and sat down again. That was much more comfortable.

"Thank you." She smiled down at him and he grinned back. His gaze lingered on her mouth, and she turned away in embarrassment.

She hadn't learned yet to interpret his expressions. Although this morning he was especially open with her, watching and anticipating her needs. His smile was relaxed. Maybe he wasn't angry anymore. He seemed different.

Abe swung into the saddle, leading the third mule, and she followed through the trees and out to the track heading east. She watched his back, the muscles bunching and moving under his shirt.

It had been exciting to make love. The feelings he aroused had taken her by surprise. It had been pleasant last night, being close to such a powerful body, having him so focussed on her as he stroked and touched her skin. But this morning had been different. How did he know to touch her there, rub her in such a way that she bloomed? That's what it had felt like, a flower moving from bud to full blossom. Spectacular.

"How far now?" she called.

He turned his head and smiled. "Ride up here so I can talk to you."

A spark of pleasure flowered in her chest, and she reined her mount alongside him. The trail was wide enough for a team and wagon but no more than that. The trees were tall along both sides, keeping the undergrowth to a minimum. They had passed a couple of small cottages here and there, clustered together in a clearing, large gardens planted and animals behind fences.

"I think we should get there today," he remarked. "Tomorrow at the latest. I'm anxious to get home."

She nodded. "So am I. I haven't got any clothes, no money, nothing. And I don't know where my father is."

Abe was watching her closely and seemed about to say something, then closed his mouth in a thin line.

"He might need my help," she explained. "He may be ill, he was ill when he left the house."

"Why did he run?"

"The General was looking for him."

"So you said." Abe appeared determined.

"The General had a warrant for Zanata, because she has a disease that she passed on to his son, Virgil, but I'm not sure what the one for my father was for. Perhaps he thought Father was guilty as well."

"Sounds complicated."

She scrutinized his face. "It must be. I didn't know what was going on until Father left. Then what I learned was from the voicelink, listening to Zanata's plans."

"You might not be safe in the city."

"Why do you say that?"

"We were going to get married," he added, squinting as he scanned the trail ahead of them.

She watched him, astounded. *As if it didn't matter to him one way or the other!* The warm feelings from the morning cooled rapidly, and her temper stirred at his apparent indifference.

She waited until he turned back to her before she replied. "You didn't ask me, you just told me." If he thought she was a silly City girl who didn't know her own mind, he'd soon find out differently.

He went pale. "Of course. Pardon me. Will you marry me, Julianne?"

"I'm not sure. I'll consider it." To her sudden amusement, he flushed a dull red and frowned at the mule's ears.

"We've already made love," he said, as if the final decision was inevitable.

"I realize that. I was there too."

He narrowed his eyes. She tried to smile serenely but thought it probably looked more like a smirk. The man was irritating her no end.

"I see."

He did? She swung her head to look at him, but he just urged his mule forward and set a faster pace. "We should try to reach the shore by tonight. We don't have that much food left."

By the time he pulled to the side of the track for lunch at a grassy spot near a small watering hole, she was ready to get off her mule. Climbing awkwardly down, she hung onto the saddle to steady herself. She felt his hands at her waist and turned to find him standing very close.

He leaned toward her, his face lowering to hers. She raised her mouth for his kiss, but was disappointed when he just asked, "Are you all right?" His eyes were concerned, his hands gentle. "Come and sit over here."

He took her elbow to help her across the uneven ground to a fallen log. Slapping the cushion down, he eased her onto it, then stood back. "How's that? I'll find us something to eat."

She rested while he watered the animals and tethered them to graze, then rifled one of the saddlebags for their remaining supplies.

"We have lunch," he announced. "Adam's ale from the stream, along with meatloaf sliced on pané." Julianne took the chrome plate and balanced it on her lap as she ate.

"We're just country folk out at Farmer Holdings," he said conversationally after a few bites. "The manorhouse isn't like the beautiful houses in the City. The main floor has the great entry hall like most homes. Along one side is a formal parlour, then a rather large office. My sister and I share the office, as we each do different bits of business for Holdings. There's a library. Both my parents must have been committed readers, because we have a lot of very old books as well as tomos and sonic readers.

"Then on the other side, there's a smaller less formal parlour for when friends come to call. There's a formal dining hall and an informal family dining room. My sister's favourite room is the women's solar where she does a lot of her painting. Then the ..."

"Painting? What kind of painting?" she interrupted suspiciously. Why all this information suddenly? He'd been a very private man up till now, only sharing information with Kerr. She felt a sharp pang at the thought of the guard, he'd been such a nice man. He'd been kind to her.

"She does all kinds of painting," Abe said loftily. "Water colour mostly. She gets her paints from a manufacturer in the City who uses our talc for his product. Her latest project before I left was a children's book, she was painting the pictures for the story."

"Oh, how lovely. I'd like to meet her."

"Well, you'd have to come to Holdings to do that. At any rate ..."

"I do origami."

He paused. "Origami?"

"You know, the folding of paper."

"Yes, I know what it is. You do?" He seemed confused.

"You wouldn't understand." She took another bite of meatloaf and watched the mules butt each other for the best patch of grass.

"I won't understand if you can't be bothered to explain it to me." He stared at his sandwich, then took a long swallow of water. "Tell me."

"I fold paper. There are so many levels of expertise that it's hard to imagine. Beginners do designs that have fifteen or twenty folds. Then they progress and move up to several hundred folds, even thousands. The designs get more intricate. You can curve the folds, make them heavy or barely there." She warmed to the subject, as she always did when discussing her passion.

"I started when I was small and studied it growing up. I teach at the young school, the children are so open and creative. We sometimes wet the paper so it takes on a different sheen and quality, and the folds are more deeply engrained." She realized she was rambling and closed her mouth.

He had stopped eating and sat watching her as she talked. "And?"

She shook her head. "And nothing. That's all."

He leaned forward and placed his mouth over hers. It felt so right she opened her lips and he took advantage. When he lifted his head, she was short of breath and leaning into his arm. He propped her back up and went back to his sandwich as if it hadn't meant a thing to him.

"So when you come to Holdings, you can show me. Show Beth too, she'd like to see that."

When she came to Holdings? She felt the irritation niggle again in her throat. "Perhaps," she said, and polished off her last bite. She wouldn't make it easy for him. He'd barely asked her to marry him. Barely.

CHAPTER FORTY ONE

That afternoon, they caught sight of the sea. The trail widened and became more heavily travelled the closer they got to the water. A flurry of carts drawn by mules or horses had passed them going in both directions. A few scooters had whizzed along the track, startling the mules. Two transports came toward them, moving ponderously and taking up most of the width. They moved to the side to let them pass, the dust choking the mules and landing in a thin layer over their clothing.

A cluster of houses appeared in the distance, their thatched roofs gleaming in the bright sunlight. Further toward the water, the buildings became larger, many of the roofs the dull red of clay tiles. Boats dotted the shallow curve of the bay, where small ripples showed white against the dense blue of the water.

"I think we've arrived. This must be Eight Mile. I can see the docks from here."

Julianne pulled up beside him and peered through the gap in the trees. "Oh, I see. Why is it called Eight Mile?"

"I'm not sure, someone once told me it was eight miles from the Legitamia border."

"So that's a new name from when the borders were first settled after the War. They didn't want to be seen as Legitamian."

He shrugged and waved toward the trail. "Let's go down there and get settled. We should be able to find someone who can take us with them on tomorrow's tide."

The road into town was a steep descent, ending at a set of docks that went a long way out into the water. Boats of all types were tied up along the fingers, some of them sunken and hanging in the sea from rotting ropes.

"This doesn't look good." She frowned down at the derelict vessels that cluttered the waterway. "Why do they leave them there?"

Abe grunted. "Times have been tough. And if no one owns the dock, who's going to pay to have them removed?" He thought of Coronation and how many days in the last few years he and his workers had spent pulling wrecks out of their small harbour to put on the burn pile or try to repair for use or sale. "During the War and after, no one had the time or money to deal with such things."

He turned back toward the main street and moved slowly along it. "We'd be better to go to the end. I can see a stables and carter's yard down there." He gave her a quick glance. "We don't have to stay in the stables, but I'll arrange to leave our mules."

By the time Abe made provisions for the animals, dusk was falling. He walked Julianne along the street to what appeared to be a popular restaurant near the docks.

When he opened the door for her, she looked at him aghast. "I can't go in there like this!" She gestured to her clothes. "The shirt is filthy and my pants are held up with a piece of rope. Not to mention …" She gestured at her hair, then peeked wistfully through the door.

"I'm in the same condition," he said encouragingly. "So is everyone else in there. The light's dim, it's mostly dock workers or fishermen, and perhaps we'll meet someone who can give us a ride south."

"Well, all right." Pushing her tangled hair behind her shoulder, she stepped hesitantly through the door that he held open. It felt as if all eyes turned toward her. They were strangers, after all, maybe the only strangers here. She was grateful that Abe moved close beside her and pulled out a chair at a corner table. She sat.

"What will you have?"

235

She saw the barman waving to them from where he waited on a table nearby, and looked at Abe in indecision.

"Two ales," he called, then dropped his voice. "I hope you like ale."

"I'm not sure."

He nodded. "Try it. If you don't like it, we'll order something else."

"How are we going to pay for this?" She tried to keep her voice down, but saw someone at the next table turn to stare at them. Her face got warm.

Sitting beside her at the table, Abe covered her hand with his and leaned in toward her ear. "Don't worry so much. We're fine." She warmed at his touch. He took his hand away, then placed his arm along the back of her chair, not quite touching her as he scanned the crowd.

"Do you see anyone you know?"

"Not yet. I thought I might. Some of the fishermen from Coronation come up this far on their trips."

The ale arrived and she took a sip and smiled. It was good, strong and flavourful.

"Like it, do you?" She glanced up to find him watching her, and had to laugh. "Well, I was thirsty. Does that have anything to do with it?"

The smile on his face was arresting. He seldom smiled, but right now his eyes were alight with laughter. "I'm sure it's just a very good ale." His lips relaxed as he laughed. "What do you want to eat?"

"Hmm." She studied the scratch board. "I wonder what there is. Looks like roast pheasant. What language is that?"

"I think it's hybrid, Legitamia and Khandarken. Don't speak too loudly."

She ducked her head and glanced around. "Sorry. I've forgotten my manners. I've been too long in the wilds of the north."

She watched his face soften at her words. "Not your manners. Just your inhibitions."

He glanced back at the board, his neck suddenly red, and she could imagine why. *Had she lost her inhibitions?* Would she have slept with Abe if they'd met in the City or even out at Deep Creek or on his farm? Not likely.

But everything had been different in the north, life or death. There'd been no alternative but to do whatever they had to in order to survive. And they had survived. She looked at his red face as he pretended to read the menu board. They'd survived and he'd helped her. She loved him for it.

Would he make love to her tonight? She shivered at the thought as Abe rose from his seat. "So is it pheasant you want?"

"Abe." She leaned forward and he sat back down, looking at her curiously. "How are we going to pay for this?"

"It's okay, I still have money left from the sale of some of the gems. We're covered."

"Okay. What else is on the menu? I can't read it."

"Oh, sorry." He pointed as he read. "Roast pheasant with lentils, baked sablefish and tomato onion sauce, fried olinguito." He glanced back at her. "I like olinguito, but prefer pheasant tonight."

"I've never eaten it. Pheasant sounds good, if we can afford it."

He gazed at her, his face softening. "We can afford it, Julianne. I'll order." He rose and made his way over to the counter to speak to the boy waiting for their order. On his way back, he stopped at a table of half a dozen rough looking men quaffing ale and talking loudly.

He asked a question. The group stilled as if caught in a spotlight, then one of the men replied. Abe asked something else, and soon they were all involved in the conversation with much pointing up and down the bay.

When he returned to their table, the food had just arrived. Bowls of a thick vegetable soup, the roasted pheasant and lentils displayed on a second plate swimming in aromatic gravy. The waiter returned with rough sliced bread and buttery garlic cream. It looked wonderful and smelled delicious. Her mouth watered.

When was the last time she'd had a decent meal? It had been fire roasted rabbit, and days of stale bread and canned meat. She picked up her knife and fork.

Abe dipped his bread in the gravy and took a bite. "It's that good. Real meat gravy." He smiled at her. "At the manorhouse we have a cook who's been with the family for years. She started waiting at table in the dining hall when she was young, and began work in the kitchen before our last cook retired."

"What's the best thing she makes?" She watched his eyes get a faraway look as he thought about it.

"Just about everything."

Julianne had to laugh as he grinned and continued. "Biscuits and gingerbreads, Bishop's cake. She's great with lamb and mutton, llama meat. We have our own fowl so she does all that – chicken, duck, turkey, goose. She makes a mean soufflé for Sunday brunch."

"Bishop's cake? I don't know that."

"Ah, well, you'll have to come and try it. I'll get Hannan to make one when we get home." He turned back to his plate and picked up his knife and fork, demolishing half the pheasant while Julianne stared in frustration at his bent woolly head. *When we get home?* She hadn't agreed to go to Farmer Holdings, and it wasn't her home, anyway. Uncomfortable in the silence, she returned to her dinner. The soup was delicious, had a curry ginger flavour to it.

"We don't have to stay at the manorhouse," he continued between bites. "We have a summer place at Coronation on the beach. It's a lovely sandy area, great place for kids to play." His pointed stare burned into hers.

"Well, when I get home I'm going to find my father and secure the help he needs. And I've got my own quarters with a maid and house staff." She folded her lips firmly and glanced at him sideways to gauge his reaction.

"You might be with child." His tone was matter-of-fact.

"What?" She gazed at him in horror. "We only did it once, well twice if you count ..." She felt a fiery blush suffuse her face.

"If we count both times," he finished for her.

"I can't be pregnant from once." His expression was so tender, she felt a wave of heat flood her cheeks. "Can I?"

He nodded. "Of course you can. And," he continued briskly as if it made no difference to him, "we have a place in Deep Creek. So if we have to go to town on business we have somewhere to stay."

Her mouth was still open from his last comment. *With child?* She closed her mouth. Oh, no. Would she *have* to marry him?

CHAPTER FORTY TWO

I t wasn't that she didn't want to marry Abe. It was just that he'd simply assumed she would and hadn't asked for her consent.

He turned toward the bar and waved his hand, two fingers up. He must be ordering more ale. Her glass was still half full, but maybe he could drink more as his was already empty. He was relaxed tonight, his face expressive rather than mask-like. He looked confident, contented and handsome even in his tribesmen's garb and heavy boots.

She wanted to marry him. But she didn't want to be cornered into it. And he had to ask, he couldn't just tell her they were to marry. What kind of life would that be, with a mate who dictated what she was going to do? Not one that she wanted. Her father had had such a life. Zanata directed traffic, told him how it was going to be. They used to fight, she'd heard the shouting from behind their closed doors.

Would that be how Abe acted with her? She didn't really know him. The memory of how he'd dealt with the guard at the Sanctuary popped back into her head. He'd felled the man with one kick, then knocked him out with his fist. It made her nervous, perhaps he was violent. She gazed at him cautiously.

"What did you talk to those men about?" She nodded toward the group of fishermen.

"I was trying to find out where they were from, but they hail north of here, Legitamia. We might have to wait for a southern ship to arrive. Are you finished?"

"I think we should sleep in the stables," Julianne said as she wiped her hands on the napkin and stood. "The mules might get stolen."

Abe's mouth went flat at her comment. "He locks it up at night."

"Do you believe him?"

"Yah. He has his own animals in there."

"Where will we go then?"

"I've rented a place from the stable keeper. He has a boarding house on the next street over. You can have a bath."

"Really?" She felt herself glow with pleasure.

He laughed and took her arm. "Really. This way." They crossed the street and he moved to hold her hand as they walked along the boardwalk.

"Here it is." They stopped before a tall narrow building with a small blue sign above the front door. The woman of the house welcomed them in and pointed to their room down the hall. They had their own private bathrobe. What luxury.

"You go first." He pointed to the bathrobe and moved toward the door. "I'll get our saddlebags from the stable, all right?"

"Yes, thank you."

He examined her face. "You're welcome." He leaned down and pressed a soft kiss to her lips. "You're more than welcome." Pulling the door open, he left.

Well. He was a man of many moods, apparently. She touched her mouth with unsteady fingers. That was a nice kiss. Quick, but promising, a reminder of what it could be like between them. She opened the hot water faucet and got the bath running, shucking her filthy clothes onto the floor. Climbing eagerly in, she leaned against the slanted end and gave a long sigh. This was lovely.

Grabbing a package from the box beside her, she emptied the perfumed salts into the water. This was heaven.

She lathered her hair vigorously, then scrubbed herself all over. Her skin tingled when she was finished. It had been so long since she'd had a good bath. Not since the days at the Sanctuary. She contemplated her clothes on the floor. She could wash them, they might be dry by morning. Climbing out, she dumped everything into the water, then stepped back in to stomp the clothing until it was soaked and soaped.

By the time she had them wrung out and hanging to dry, she heard the outer door open. She looked wildly around. There was nothing to put on! Grabbing a drying cloth off the rack, she wrapped it around just as a knock sounded and the bathrobe door opened.

Abe poked his head in. "Need someone to scrub your back? Oh, you're finished." He seemed vastly disappointed, and she couldn't stop a silly smile from forming on her face.

"Your turn."

She walked past him to find two saddlebags on the divan and her clothes spread on the foot of the bed. "I didn't know what you'd need."

She glanced back at him as a huge yawn overtook her. "Um, I'm sorry."

He laughed and she had to smile. "This is fine. You just crawl in while I have a bath."

Crawl in? This must mean they were sharing the bed. Well, of course they were. He'd rented a room and there was one bed. She felt a thrill of excitement shiver down her spine. Did this mean – Yes, from the expression on his face, it meant they'd make love. Anticipation unfurled in her belly. She wanted him again.

~ * * * ~

When Abe emerged from the bathrobe, he was scrubbed clean and his clothes had been left hanging to dry alongside hers.

Julianne was sleeping soundly. She lay on her side facing him, one hand under her cheek. He lifted the covers to discover her body enveloped in that ugly Sanctuary robe. It's what she'd used for a nightdress during their whole journey. He slid in beside her and lay still for a moment, burning with longing for her.

He shouldn't have been so hard on her the first time they made love. He should have held back and let her heal, because she had to ride the mule. But he couldn't. That driving urge had overcome him. She was so enticing with her stormy grey green eyes and pouting mouth, a mouth that just asked for his kiss.

He flicked off the light and rolled onto his side. She was so close he could smell her sweet scent. He reached to find the mound of her breast beneath the robe. Curling his fingers gently around her, he relaxed against the sheet.

What if she wouldn't marry him? She'd become awfully stubborn all of a sudden. Well, he'd fight for her because he was determined to have her. She belonged to him now.

CHAPTER FORTY THREE

Julianne woke in dim morning light to find Abe's pale gaze pinned to her face. He reached to touch her cheek with his fingertips and she smiled softly.

"You're awake."

She yawned and tried to stretch, the heavy robe tangled about her legs. "Yes. Did you have a good sleep?"

"Mmm." He nodded and shifted his weight over her as he leaned up on one elbow. "But I'm glad you woke up." He settled his mouth on hers. His lips were hot and firm. She warmed inside, his kiss like sweet honey. Lifting his head, he watched her face. "You're beautiful, Julianne. So lovely."

She felt his fingers tug gently on the ribbons at the neck of her robe, and they gave under his hand. Cool air swept over her throat as he spread the lapels. Then his mouth was back on hers, coaxing and inviting. She opened her mouth and his tongue skimmed the edges of her teeth. "Abe," she sighed. "Do that again."

His smile was like a gift, so tender. He kissed her once more, his tongue invading and plundering her mouth. The warm glow inside her grew in intensity, became a hot ember that burned, demanding more. She took his hand and placed it on her breast, and he squeezed.

"Let's get this thing off." Tugging at the robe, he finally dragged it up her body and over her head. Her arms got tangled in the billowing fabric, and he laughed as they struggled to free her.

"Maybe I'll never have to wear this again," she muttered.

"It can't be too soon for me," he exclaimed in frustration.

She burst out laughing and he joined her, wrapping his arms around her and rolling across the bed. She loved the feel of him, the thick muscles of his chest with a mat of springy hair between his rigid nipples. He was hard, pressing against her stomach.

He suddenly grew serious, his gaze focussed and intent on her face. "You're my woman, Julianne. I've made you mine."

His kiss was fierce on her mouth, then her throat as he massaged her breast. He felt so right against her, his hands big and strong, his curly hair tickling her skin. Then his mouth reached her nipple and he fastened on. She lifted against him, sensations pouring through her from breast to belly and lighting a blaze between her legs. He was a conjurer. He practiced magic.

"Let me inside," he said low. "I want to come inside you."

Ah, that heavy invasion began. He must be too big for her. Otherwise she should be used to the size of him after doing this already. She quivered, trying to allow him entry, but pulling back at the same time. "I don't think ..." She tried to hold him off, but he pressed forward.

"It's okay." He had a desperate look in his eyes as he pinned his gaze to her face. "It's all right."

He rubbed his fingers along her opening, slippery fingers that slid inside her. That felt good. She pushed against his hand and he rubbed her again, using his thumb to stroke that hidden spot that sent a flush of pleasure through her. How splendid, wonderful sensations swooped up from her abdomen and centred in her nipples.

He did it again and she moaned low in her throat. He shifted, she pressed against him and he slid inside. Startled, she stared up at his tense face. He moved and she moved with him, enticed along by his low words, the way his hand stroked her, soothed her.

He pulled out to her entrance, then pushed in again and her muscles tightened around him. The sensation was indescribable, a fluttering feeling of joy and anticipation until she could hardly bear it. She lost track of time and where she was, so focussed on his face, his pale blue eyes, and then on the feelings he invoked. There was an almost unbearable pressure and expectation. She gasped for breath, then again. And the pressure splintered, breaking apart in a million pieces and shattering all around her, glittering in the sunlight. She closed her eyes.

Julianne became aware of his fingers on her breast, squeezing gently, playing with her nipple. So sensitive. She placed her hand over his to stop the torture and opened her eyes.

They were lying sideways on the bed, covers strewn around them, the bolsters missing entirely. Abe lay beside her, his gaze on her breast where she'd trapped his fingers.

He glanced up and smiled at her. What a smile, so tender and intimate. She felt tears start behind her eyes and blinked to keep him in focus.

"Will you marry me, Julianne?"

What could she say? "Yes."

The expression on his face was wonderful to see, such joy after all the tough times and sorrow they'd been through. "Thank God." He grabbed her up and hugged her tight against him, wrapping a hand in her hair. "Thank God."

He seemed short of breath, and she put her arms around his neck to snuggle against him. It felt so good, warm and inviting.

"As soon as we can," he said, running a palm down her back and over her buttocks. "As soon as we get home."

His erection pressed against her leg as he leaned forward to place a kiss on her mouth. Oh, my. Excitement expanded in her breast. Was he ready again?

~ * * * ~

"I think if we ride along the sand, we might find someone." Abe turned his mule toward the tow path that lead down to the long beach past the docks.

"Why don't we ask at the dock?"

"I did, while you had another bath." He watched her cheeks turn rosy and grinned to himself at her constant questions. "There are a lot of boats out in the bay, and we might see someone we know."

He turned back to the path and heard her mule clopping behind him. So, she was coming. She queried everything, and he'd learned the hard way that he couldn't just assume what they were going to do next. He shouldn't need that lesson again, it had been a tough one to learn the first time. He still felt the uncertainty riding his gut at her refusal to agree to marry him.

He reached the beach and turned his mount toward the far end, riding near the surf at the edge. There were several boats out in the bay, men barely visible in the fog as they reeled in lines or pulled nets.

Half way down the beach, he pulled his mount to a halt and strained his eyes. "By the graves!" Julianne turned to look at him. "It's Treeline. Hold the reins."

He leapt from the saddle and tossed the reins to her, ripping off his jacket and slinging it to the sand.

As he shucked his trousers and boots, he heard her squeal.

"Abe! What are you doing?"

He hopped on one foot to get his leg free of his pants. "It's Treeline. He seems to be bringing his nets in. I'm going out to see him."

And he dove into the water. On first impact it was freezing cold, always felt that way no matter the time of year, but it never took long to get used to it. As he moved into a smooth stroke, he heard Julianne shouting at him from the beach. He twisted back to look at her and give a wave, then turned and concentrated on reaching the vessel before the fishermen pulled anchor.

Treeline was a long-time tenant of Coronation and Abe had known him for years. He liked to fish in the north, did a lot of diving for abalone and swore the shells were nicer the farther up the coast he went. His boat was at anchor, but Abe could see him raising the dinghy by pulley to sling it on deck. He swam harder.

One of Treeline's men stopped what he was doing and pointed excitedly. Treeline put a hand over his brow and frowned into the fog, searching the waters as Abe waved his arms above his head, then swam on. When he got closer, he could see three men lined up against the railing watching his approach. Treeline pointed at one of the men, and a rope ladder dropped over the side.

Abe reached it and hung on, gasping for breath, his heart pounding heavily in his chest. It had been quite a while since he'd had a swim like that. Glancing up, he saw three woolly heads hanging over the side of the vessel.

"Who goes there?" Treeline's voice was unmistakable, hoarse from smoke and heavy weather.

"It's Abe," he replied, but the words came out weak. He began to pull himself up the rope. When he got near the top, many hands reached to grab him and tip him onto the deck. He lay like a beached whale, breath heaving out of him.

"By the dogs of hell," he heard Treeline exclaim. "Abe?"

Abe looked up at him and grinned. "Naked and alive."

Treeline roared with laughter. "By the gods. Get him a blanket, boys." One of the men ran across the deck, the other grabbed his arm and heaved him to his feet.

"I can't believe it. We didn't think …" Treeline glanced uncomfortably across at his deckhand and changed the topic. "Well, this is wonderful news. Look at you." His observant eye had fallen to the still mending wounds at his side and thigh. "You've had some rough encounters, I see."

Abe laughed and turned to accept the blanket offered to him, wrapping it around his shoulders. Treeline, master of the understatement. "Are you heading south?"

"Yah, we were just pulling anchor. We've got a hull full of fish and abalone, and a few stops to make before we get home."

"Can we get a lift?"

"Well, you know you can. You and who else?"

"A woman. On the beach there." He pointed to the two mules barely visible in the fog. "We need to get to Coronation and Holdings."

"We can take you. What will you do with the mules?"

"If you can give me an hour …"

CHAPTER FORTY FOUR

Two hours later Abe slung a couple of saddlebags over his shoulder and led Julianne down the dock and up the plank to board *The Terra,* Treeline's forty foot fishing vessel. The engine rolled and the boards rattled beneath their feet as they stepped aboard.

The two mates were tying gear down, and Treeline stood ready to welcome her. His gnarled fingers grabbed hers in a gentle grip and guided her up the last step. He touched his forehead in respect.

"Welcome, Ms. Any friend of Abe's …" He glanced at Abe and didn't finish the sentence, but a sly smile appeared on his face. Abe felt himself flush. Good old Treeline, a long-time family friend who liked to take advantage of the fact. "I've given you my cabin. Let me show you."

He led the way across the deck and down a few steps. Sliding the panel open, he gestured inside. There was barely space to turn around in the little room, but it would give them some privacy. Abe watched her face, uncertain if he'd be welcome in here with her but she gave no clue, just smiled at Treeline and thanked him before placing her pack on the bed.

"What can I do to help?" She turned her bright face up at him. "Perhaps I can cook."

Treeline seemed uncertain. "My first mate does the cooking, Ms. We don't want to upset his feelings now, do we?"

"No of course not. Well, I can clean or haul rope."

"No Ms. That's for us to do. Perhaps you can keep me company on the bridge for a bit. Then you might like a nap. I know from what Abe's said, you've been travelling hard for a lot of days in a row."

Julianne lasted half an hour on the bridge before her head began to nod.

Abe helped her down the ladder and back to the cabin. "Have a rest and you'll feel better." He shifted her things off the cot and leaned to kiss her, then lingered over the sweet taste of her mouth. She was the match to his tinder. With reluctance he pulled himself away and left her to sleep.

Treeline nodded as he climbed the ladder to the bridge. "Donk is getting us a cup of tea. Settle down right here." He pointed to the other old cushioned chair and checked the instrument panel.

"What do you do when your system goes down?" Abe looked at the array of instrument faces. "Solar powered, are you?"

"Not anymore," Treeline said, correcting the steering. "Old technology. We do wind/water now, easier and cleaner. But when it goes down, and it has," his brows rose in an expression of amazement, "Then I just use the charts and compass." He pulled out a wide drawer under the desktop and showed him the rubber-plastic charts laid out flat, one atop the other. The bronze compass seemed like an ancient relic mounted on the frontboard.

"We don't go that far from home anyway. One end of Khandarken to the other mostly, no more than a week or ten days. Although I hear the abalone along the Adar Silva coast to the south is starting to pick up, and it has a particularly good blue tint to it."

He grinned wryly. "So, who's the woman? The lady, that is. She's definitely a lady, even with those clothes on. A beauty, that."

"She's to be my wife." Abe clamped his jaw shut and waited for the verbal buffeting he expected from the old fisherman.

Treeline just smiled and nodded. "Thought as much. Classy woman, that. Where'd you meet her?"

"You wouldn't believe it if I told you, Treeline, and I don't have time right now. What's been going on at home?"

"Tell me about the wounds first. The one in your thigh looks like quite a blow, almost mended. But what's that in your side?"

"I nearly died."

Treeline's mouth turned grim. "That's what it looks like. That's what I would have guessed. How'd you get it? I haven't seen wounds like that since the Last War."

"I was on a buying trip with Uncle Jade, and we were attacked on the trail outside Krimen. A raid of some kind. I can't wait to hear what Uncle has to say about it. I was shot. Kerr got me out of there and kept me alive until he found help with the tribesmen."

Treeline shook his head, his face suddenly pale at the mention of Uncle. He said nothing for a long moment, then commented, "Those tribesmen are good people."

"Yah, they are. One of them has a son, Ventuzzo, who works for us at Holdings with the llama."

"Huh. So where did you leave Kerr?"

His heart seemed to contract in his chest. "You wouldn't believe it if I told you, Treeline. But he's dead, and there's no going back."

The old fisherman stared at him in alarm and blinked rapidly. "Dead? Well, I shouldn't be

257

surprised. From the look of your wounds, it's surprising anyone survived the trip."

Abe drew a deep breath and rubbed his fingers together to ease the tension. "Anyway. Is Beth well?"

"She's fine. She's uh – she isn't working right now, because you've been away and she didn't want to leave the farm. But she'll be very glad to see you return home."

"Okay. That's good news." He nodded, tried to smile. "Do you mind if I have a nap? We've been under the gun for weeks. It's been a grueling journey, and my head is spinning."

"Go." Treeline waved him away. "Go. We'll call you for dinner, such as it is. Fish, you know."

Abe slid the panel quietly open and peeked inside. Julianne had moved her things to the small desk tucked in one corner, and taken off most of her clothes. She lay on one side of the bed under the top blanket, a thin shirt covering her to the elbows. Her hand was curled under her cheek as she slept.

He toed the door closed and flipped the latch. His boots ended up just inside the door, everything except his shorts landed on the seat of the chair. He tugged the light blanket up and slid under. His back cracked as he relaxed on the pallet. Then he sniffed. Farmer soap. Treeline must have changed the sheets for them while they disposed of the mules in Eight Mile.

Sliding an arm under her ribcage, he tugged Julianne closer, till her head fit on his shoulder and her hand rested in the centre of his chest. That felt better. He slept.

CHAPTER FORTY FIVE

They'd been travelling on the Catastrophic Ocean for days, and the City was drawing closer. Treeline had made two stops along the coast, where he'd unloaded more than half his cargo of fish and a lot of the abalone that rested in his cold lockers below decks. His last stop before Coronation was the fish market in the City, where he'd sell the rest of his load. Julianne seemed anxious to get home.

They'd had dinner with the crew, but it was crowded in the tiny mess with two extra people so Abe urged her back to the cabin. "He can marry us now," he said casually, arranging two cups of tea on the corner of the little desk.

Her head jerked up. "Who can?"

"Treeline. He's the ship's captain. He can marry us."

"Really?" She squinted at him as if her head hurt. "Why would he do that?"

"If I ask him, he will. It'll keep you safe."

"How?" She gazed cautiously at the cup he handed her, as if it might contain some unknown substance.

Abe laughed at her expression. "If you're married, you're no longer under your father's protection. You're under mine. I'm alive and well, and I have some resources. And your father doesn't. Nor do you know where he is. What if Zanata is back in the City waiting for you?"

"Yes, I've thought of that." She stared doubtfully into the murky liquid, then took a small sip and winced.

"And you might be pregnant."

Her face flushed, her cheeks going a fiery colour under his watchful stare.

"We've done it more than once."

Her gaze skittered around the cabin. She was so volatile, he only had to lay his mouth over hers and she lit up like a candle. It was amazing. Even since their conversation where she doubted she could be pregnant after 'just one time,' she'd immediately succumbed to a third and fourth seduction. Right now he forced himself to casually sip his tea and keep his mind on business, knowing he had to persuade her before he took her to bed.

A soft knock sounded on the door and he leaned to shove it aside. The first mate grinned at him and handed in a plate of biscuits. "Just baked," he said cheerfully. "You left before I had time to serve them."

Abe took the plate, thanked him, and pushed the door closed. "Have a biscuit."

She glanced at him anxiously, then at the plate. "I'm not sure …"

"You have to admit the food's been pretty good. The sablefish was excellent."

She smiled, selected one from the plate and took a bite. "Mmm. You're right. Its cinnamon and allspice. Very nice."

"Let me taste." He reached a long arm to place his hand at the back of her neck and pull her toward him, laying his mouth on hers. She tasted of cinnamon and something else. Her tea cup hit the edge of the desk, and he moved to steady it as he deepened the kiss. By the graves, she fired him pretty fast. He lifted his head, chest heaving as he examined her face. Her pupils were dilated and her mouth was a pretty pink.

"If we got married, you'd be safe," he whispered. "And you'd be with me. Don't you want that?"

"Yes." Her voice was low, he had to strain to hear it. "But I don't want to be married and have a husband who orders me around and tells me everything I have to do." Her mouth firmed into a stubborn line. "I want to have a say in what I do, what we do."

He kissed her again, running his tongue along the edge of her teeth and then easing in to touch the tip of her tongue. It was a while before he remembered what they were discussing. Then he drew back, shifted over to the bed and pulled her beside him.

"I won't order you around. Have I done that?"

"Yes"

He reared back to stare at her. "When did I order you around?"

"When you said we'd get married. You didn't ask me, just said we would."

A flush rose up his neck. "Okay. I was anxious to get it settled. I wanted to make sure we'd marry. I admit I was pushing."

He glanced at her sideways and rubbed his palm up and down her arm. "I love you, Julianne. I want to marry you. And you've said yes, so why don't we get it done? If you go back to the City as a married woman you have different rights."

She leaned her head on his shoulder and he tugged her tighter against him. "Maybe."

He laughed low. She wasn't letting him off the hook that easy. Pushing off the bed, he knelt on the shifting deck, taking her hand in his. "Will you marry me, Julianne Adjudicator?"

Her smile was like sunshine escaping the clouds. "Yes, I will, Abram Farmer."

He kissed the backs of her fingers. "And will you marry me here and now?"

"Yes, sir. I will."

"Good." His breath escaped his chest in a gust of air. He wrapped his arms around her waist and laid his head against her breasts. "Let's consummate the marriage. We can get Treeline to conduct the ceremony later." He pushed and she toppled onto the mattress, erupting in giggles. He had to laugh. He had fun with her, she tickled his funny bone. Tickled him in other places as well.

He flipped her shirt up and dove under to latch his mouth onto her nipple. The giggles stopped and she grabbed his head with both hands, holding him tight against her. "Don't stop," she muttered. "Abe, you make me feel so good."

Blood rushed to his head, he was suddenly deaf from the impact. He lifted his head to look at her and drowned in her gaze, her eyes wide and stormy, her mouth pink and shiny from his kisses. He moved up her body and ground his mouth onto hers while his hands tried to divest her of clothing. They teetered on the edge of the bed, and she scrambled further back to keep from falling to the planks.

He'd forgotten all his techniques of love making, everything he'd learned at his tutor's breast in Coronation. His trousers hit the floor, his shirt tore as he yanked it over his head. When his skin touched hers, he slowed and his mouth fastened on her throat, his fingers wrapping around her breast. That felt better. He calmed a little.

But when he slid his hand around her hip and inward, smoothing the beautiful soft skin, in toward the dark curls between her thighs, and inward again to the sleek wet place, the slippery inner lips, he felt like he went deaf again. But it didn't matter.

Even with his hearing gone, he still understood the small gasps she made, the groans as she held onto his shoulder, arching up against his hand. He was so ready. He rolled to the side and held her facing him, pulling her leg up over his hip. Then he nudged himself in. Just a nudge, the head of his erection right at her entrance. He lay there gasping, then grabbed her hip and eased further inside.

"Don't stop."

He groaned out a laugh. "Don't worry, I won't be stopping any time soon," and he surged forward, impaling her. The sensation must have been inspiring because he did it again.

Desperate, he rolled her onto her back and braced himself above her. She panted lightly, eyes half closed in concentration. "Touch me here." She dragged his hand down her body.

"I know," he whispered. "I know." And he rubbed her there, gently and slow, then faster as he moved within her tight wet sheath. He pressed lightly and then firm with his fingers, his movements steady and powerful. She held him like a fist. He just had to hang on, wanted to hang on.

He dropped his head and kissed her, taking her in with his mouth, absorbing her moans as she came. She milked him dry.

CHAPTER FORTY SIX

Treeline married them that evening on the open deck of the boat, under a midnight blue sky with stars just beginning to peek through the dark curtain above. Julianne had put on her one and only dress, the hem hastily mended and mud brushed out of it. Abe wore his tribesman's shirt, a pair of pants borrowed from the deck hand and his tribal boots with the bells removed.

He held her hand in his, his chest tight with emotion. Marriage. Something that hadn't even been in his peripheral vision a couple of months ago, before he was injured. He'd been doing business as usual, dealing with his father's death and the demands of the farm, the villages and talc mine, never giving a thought to his personal future.

He gazed down at the woman standing beside him. She stood straight with shoulders back and chin held high. Her lashes were lowered and he couldn't see the expression in her eyes. Her nose was small, her full lips in a delightful pout. She was his.

He glanced up as Treeline began reading from his book. With a start he realized it was the Holy Book that his parents had taught him as a young boy. He listened intently, responded where prompted. When Treeline asked Julianne if she allowed him to be her husband, his breath caught in his chest at her hesitation. But she squared her shoulders and her hand tightened involuntarily in his as she said, "Yes."

It was done. Every man on the deck kissed her on the cheek. Her face had a pretty flush to it by the time it was over. Treeline coaxed them all down into the tiny mess where he opened a bottle of single malt whiskey and pulled out assorted bowls and cups. He dropped a dram in each and handed them out.

"To the married couple," he announced. "To Abe and Julianne and happily wedded bliss." Treeline blushed and smiled. He was a confirmed bachelor himself and seemed a little in awe of the situation.

Abe laughed and kissed the bride to the cheers of the three fishermen. Then he lifted his glass and toasted his wife, "To the bride."

He drained the glass. Treeline poured him another.

~***~

Abe peered blearily around the small mess. Julianne had just left to get ready for bed and the men all had a weary, slightly blurred look to them. This single malt was powerful stuff. He hadn't had a drink since before his trip with Uncle Jade. Perhaps he was out of practice. Even with the tribesmen, he'd only had medicinal alcohol that Ada forced down his throat with all kinds of vile tasting ingredients in it.

He surged to his feet, clapping a hand heavily on Treeline's shoulder. "Thank you, my friend." He staggered out the door as the ship rolled beneath his feet.

Wearing a light shirt, Julianne was just climbing under the blanket when he slid the door open. "You should put it on the latch," he said. "Anyone could come in."

"But they wouldn't, would they?" Her look was innocent, and a turmoil of emotion fought in his chest. He was torn between possession – she was his and he didn't want anyone else catching her undressed – and a deep tenderness at her naivety even after all they'd endured.

"Probably not. But we don't want to entice them." He yanked his shirt over his head.

"Entice?"

"Yah." His trousers landed on his shirt, and he lifted the blanket and slid in beside her. "I'm the only one who gets enticed on this boat."

She giggled against his chest as he wrapped an arm around her and dragged her up against him. He kissed her long and deep as he felt her relax under his hand. He fondled her nipples as they hardened to peaks under his attention. *She was his wife. He was a married man.* Shock flashed through his system, and his breath suddenly came harsh and tight.

He lay back and tugged her over him. "Come on top of me, honey." The boat rolled as she lifted herself, and he caught her before she flew off the mattress.

"What do you want – I don't know ..." She thrashed under the blanket.

"Calm down. Hold it, just ride me like one of the mules." She burst out laughing and quickly pressed her mouth to his shoulder to stifle the sound. He chuckled and helped position her above him.

"Oops, careful. That's better." The laughter left him as quickly as it had come. There she was, open and ready for him. He nudged himself inside her welcoming passage. She gasped as he pushed a little further. "That's right. Just let me ..." His voice was hoarse, his chest constricted. And then he was inside.

Gripping her hips, he held himself seated. The urge to come was right there, at the tipping point. She sighed and took his hand to guide it between her legs and he suddenly changed his focus. This wasn't about him any more. It was about her, about them. He began a slow sweet massage as he lifted his head and took her mouth with his. "I love you, Julianne," he muttered. "I love you, honey."

When he felt her tighten around him at last, he gathered himself and surged upward to finish. He was a married man now and it was about both of them.

CHAPTER FORTY SEVEN

When Abe woke, the engines were still rumbling below decks. He grabbed his clothes and eased out the door, silently sliding it closed behind him. Stretching, he walked out on deck to see where they were. The City skyline was receding into the distance behind them.

"What's up?" He caught Donk as he rushed by heading for the plank to secure it to the railing.

"We've just finished unloading our catch. We've got the pay chit and we're making a beeline for Coronation. Can't be too soon, we've been gone longer than usual this trip."

Looking off the stern, he spied boats that had left the City docks after them, moving in a long line heading for the breakwater and open seas. Travel lights glowed on the bow spits.

As Donk darted to tie down the shock absorbers along the side, he glanced up to see Treeline through the window on the bridge. He waved and headed up the ladder.

"That was fast. I didn't even know we'd stopped."

"Yah, never takes long at the City. There are only a couple of reliable fish buyers. I deal with one or the other, that way I'm sure of getting paid. How's the bride?"

Abe glanced at his sly expression and grinned as he felt the heat climb his neck. "She's fine, thank you."

Treeline gave a deep laugh. "Good, good. We'll be home in Coronation by late afternoon. I sent a message to get your summer house ready for you. Must be a bit musty, needs airing, eh?"

"You sent a massage? To whom?"

"To the wharfinger. He's a good man, doesn't talk."

Abe nodded and his gaze shifted to the frontboard. "What kind of communication equipment have you got on here?" He'd been so focussed on getting safely home, he hadn't taken much interest in the ship.

"Voicelink, but it only works when we're close to shore or in dock. Beltlinks between us, for when Donk is out in the dingy fishing for abalone. I used to have a facelink but it got knocked off the desk and broke, and it never worked out on the sea anyway. No reception. But we have a device on the antenna and we can communicate through the military system."

"They let you?"

"They encourage us. It keeps eyes on the water, doesn't it? They're kept informed of what's happening out here."

"Makes sense. How are you paid for the fish?"

"Direct. These guys are reliable and we get the pay chit as a receipt."

"Hmm. Just like the talc mine. It's easier. And no worries about whose account is no good."

Treeline gave him a direct look. "We've all heard about the problems with the talc."

"Well, I don't know what to say about that. I've no idea what's happened since I left, but there was never anything wrong with the talc. I had a good deal laid out in the north before we were attacked, and hopefully it's still there when I can contact the buyer again."

"I imagine so. Farmer talc has a good reputation."

"Not when I left. Rumours were flying that it was contaminated."

"That's all cleared up now." Treeline stood and shouted down to his mate. "A couple of teas up here, Donk. Make that three."

Abe leaned forward in time to see Julianne emerge from the captain's cabin, her hair tousled around her shoulders. He grinned. "We don't have a comb or brush between us."

"She looks good like that." Treeline took his cup of tea, ignoring Abe's narrowed gaze, and took a sip.

"I doubt if a brush can be found amongst any of us, either," he added.

Julianne climbed the short ladder and peeked into the bridge.

"Come in, Ms. Here's tea for you."

Abe moved out of the way to give her a place to sit, and Treeline's face was wreathed in smiles as he handed her a cup.

"When do we arrive in the City?" She took a brave sip of her tea and stifled the shudder as the hot liquid ran across her tongue.

Treeline smiled. "We've been and gone, Ms. We're on our way to Coronation, be there about dinner time."

"Oh." Her startled glance ricocheted off Treeline and landed on Abe. "I thought we were going to stop there."

Abe raised his brows. "They'd already left the City before I got up."

Treeline adjusted the control. "Our stops are short and sweet, Ms. Half an hour, maybe less. Just enough to unload the fish."

Her glance fell on the view behind them, and she turned in the chair to stare at the bank of fog receding from view.

Abe leaned to take her hand. "We can get to the City any time from Holdings, honey. Beth goes to work on the maxibus and we have a petrocar or scooter to take us in whenever we need to go."

"Thank you." She sipped the tea again, obviously having built an immunity to the taste. "Hopefully, I have some time. I don't know where Father is, but when I get back I'll find him."

Coronation was visible on the horizon just before dinner and they had docked before dusk. "We made good time." Treeline threw ropes to the men on the docks and the boat was soon tied up.

Abe helped with the mooring and met Julianne on deck. She carried all their belongings, two saddlebags clutched in her arms.

"Here, I'll take them." He slung them over one shoulder. "Thank you, Treeline, you and your crew. We were praying we'd run into someone we knew who could get us home, and there you were."

"Yah, well." His eyes damp, Treeline shook Abe's hand hard, then shook it again. "Glad to be of service. Nice to meet you, Ms, and congratulations again. The news will spread the moment we alight."

Abe laughed and shuddered. "Let's go."

Taking her hand, he led Julianne down the dock and up the broad foot path to the street. "We have our summer house along here toward the south end of the beach, right on the water. It'll be comfortable there. But perhaps we need something for dinner first."

"I don't know. I'm so tired, I can't think straight."

Abe lifted her hand to his lips and kissed those pretty fingers. "I know. Let's pick something up. We can go right in here." He moved onto the sidewalk and down a couple of shops.

Pushing open the bakery door, he let a waft of delightful aroma escape. "This will do. They have the best meat pies in the south. "

The young blonde girl tending the counter gave him a smile, and then her eyes widened. "Mr Farmer? Mum, it's Mr Farmer!"

There was a bustle of sound in the back and an older woman, also blonde but a little heavier than her daughter, came through the door at a near run. "My word. Oh, my word. It is. It's Mr Farmer. You're alive."

"Ms Kunz, good to see you."

"How are you? Does your sister know? Oh, my word." Within minutes, it seemed there were a dozen people crowded around them in the small shop. Abe pulled Julianne aside. "I want to tell Beth before I tell these people that we're married," he muttered. "Do you mind?"

He signalled to the baker. "Could we get some meat pies ready to go? We're in a hurry."

"Of course, Mr Farmer. Daughter! Four meat pies for Mr Farmer." She hustled behind the counter and pulled out a box to put them in. "Here you go. No charge, Mr Farmer. We're just that glad to have you back with us."

"You're very kind, Ms Kunz. Give my best to your husband. We'll just be on our way."

He dragged Julianne by the arm out the door and down the street before the crowd realized they were leaving. When the door burst open behind them with a small throng looking up and down the way, Abe broke into a jog. "Over here." He pulled her down an alley, and onto the next street.

"Keep your head down. Follow me." They were both breathless by the time they came to the last house on the lane. Abe led her through the gate and onto the porch. Reaching into the bottom of a plant pot, he dug out a key.

Julianne giggled as he brushed the dirt off it. "That's too easy."

He gave her an injured look and walked to the end of the porch where a weather vane was perched on a post, turning slowly in the light breeze off the water. Abe fitted the key into the base of the post and opened a hidden door. Inside was a second key.

"Oh." Her expression was puzzled. "That's tricky. Has no one ever found it?"

"I'm not sure they'd be looking. Everyone in the village knows who owns the house. They take care of it for us, keep an eye out. There aren't many strangers in our own village."

Her eyes widened as he unlocked the door and stood back to let her enter.

CHAPTER FORTY EIGHT

It was a beautiful little cottage, the cosy entry had closets along one side, a bench along another wall. Beyond was a spacious open room that led back to a wide, nicely arranged kitchen and dining area and a relaxed landing. The landing opened onto a long deck overlooking the beach. The Catastrophic Ocean sparkled in the darkness. "How lovely." Dust sheets covered most of the furniture.

"The power should be working." Abe flicked a switch and then turned it off again. "If we turn on lights all over the place, we'll be inundated with visitors. Let's do this." He closed the blinds along the street front windows and down the side. "If we're careful, we can have a low light at the back and use the lights downstairs on the water side. They can't be seen from the street."

He found the voicelink, an old fashioned device tucked in a drawer in the kitchen. Its power was depleted. He plugged it in and turned it on. "We can use that in a bit. It's old, but still worked last time I was here."

"Come outside." He slid a door open onto the deck and led her to the divan. The heavy indoor air flowed out into the mild evening atmosphere. Abe settled her with a pillow behind her back and lifted her feet onto a footstool. "I'll get dinner." He went back for plates and utensils and found fresh lemon water in the cooler, obviously left by the wharfinger Treeline had recruited for them. When he sat, she sighed and leaned against his shoulder as his arm went around her.

"Are you okay? You'll feel better when you eat."

She nodded against his shirt.

"Just a couple of bites. Try it." He cut into the first pie and scooped a bite onto his spoon. "Open up."

She opened, and he placed it carefully on her tongue. She seemed weary. His heart compressed in his chest. What did she think of that mob that had gathered in the bakery? She must imagine it was strange to have everyone crowding them like that, demanding answers. He spooned another bite into her mouth. He wanted to protect her from all that they'd encountered since he met her at the Sanctuary, from the scramble of getting from one place to the next, evading capture, riding mules and running from armies of the dispossessed. No wonder she was exhausted. He offered a sip of lemon water.

When she shook her head at more, he ate the rest of the pie and settled back into the divan to hold her against his chest. "The sea is lovely this time of night."

The water sparkled under the stars that were just making themselves seen against the midnight blue of the sky. The moon was a slim shadow low on the horizon. One boat moved seemingly effortlessly across the water and turned in to pull up against the dock far down the beach. The peaceful scene slowly seeped into his bones and his muscles relaxed.

"Shall we go to bed?"

He peered down at her, but she was already asleep, leaning bonelessly against his shoulder. He should have known. He sat for a few moments more, absorbing the familiar place. He'd grown up with the sea on one side of his life and the farm on the other. He was home. This was home.

After he tucked her into bed, he went back upstairs and checked the voicelink. It was charged and he entered the particulars for Beth's location. She answered after a couple of rings. "Hello?" Her voice sounded puzzled.

"Beth, it's me."

"Oh." There was a moment of silence. "It's you! Abe, you're in Coronation."

"Yes, we just arrived." His voice became hoarse and he coughed to clear it.

Bath gasped out a sob. "I recognized the particulars, but couldn't figure who would be calling from the summer house. Oh, I can't get there tonight."

"No, don't come tonight. We're fine here and we're both bone tired. Come tomorrow, mid-day. We should have rested a bit by then. And bring transport. We've got nothing here."

"How did you get to Coronation?"

He gave a laugh. "I found Treeline's boat. He was fishing up north and gave us a ride."

Her giggle was light, almost giddy, then quickly turned thick with tears. "That's wonderful. I'm so glad. Abe, I can't wait to see you. I'll be there at noon."

He took a deep breath through his nose. "Yah. Have a good sleep, and I'll see you tomorrow." He went back downstairs and climbed into bed, tugging his wife snug against him as he wrapped his arms around her.

CHAPTER FORTY NINE

Dante climbed out of the transport and walked across to the headquarters set up on the field outside the small village. Ooievaar emerged from the tent and saluted. "Major, good to see you. We've got quite a situation here."

"So I heard. Better fill me in."

"Yes, sir. Come look at the map." Ooievaar took him into the tent and pointed to his map table. "It's a bit of a mess. Here's Wymark. The Governor is here, by the way, arrived just before you. He's at the mess tent."

Dante grunted. "I'll see him there in a minute. Show me the layout."

"Right. The territory highway runs right along here. Then the perimeter road takes off in this direction. Here's the border." As he talked he traced lines with a marker on the map.

"This is a village called Discovery. Emperor Carlton arrived through the border here." Ooievaar pointed to a mountainous region north of the village. "From what I gathered from people who were escaping the area, they'd set up a camp here. But we've had heavy rains, and there was a landslide, wiped out half the camp. The emperor's tent collapsed, the generals were in the strategy tent when a mudslide caught them. Several men died, Carlton was there and injured his leg. I guess it was chaos.

"But that didn't stop them. Once they rounded up their mules and got the army fed, they attacked Discovery early the next morning. They're holding it now. We can't lay boms with the villagers there. They've established a camp of their men on a wooded lot right next to the settlement, so we can't get a clear view from the air because of trees. And there's another group of Emperor's men coming through the border a little east of that. We spotted them yesterday, tried strafing, dropped a few detonations. It slowed them down, but I don't think it's stopped them."

"By the dogs of hell." Dante rubbed his chin tiredly. "What have we got here in terms of firepower?" They went over the state of affairs, the number of men, weapons and transportation.

"I'll talk to Governor Jukes. Do you know what he has in the way of Constable numbers?"

"Not a great deal. I'll let him tell you."

"Come with me. I need a meal and we can talk at the same time."

The mess tent was half empty. Jukes sat with an aide at a centre table. He was a short square man, heavily muscled in the arms and chest, thick in the middle. He wore his uniform well, obviously custom made for his stocky frame.

When he spotted Dante, his eyes lit up and he waved him over. "Sit here, Major. We can catch up." Jukes's aide stood, took his mug of ale and exited the tent.

Dante introduced Ooievaar and waved to the server for two dinners.

"Good to see you again, Governor. It's been a while."

Jukes' smile held a hind of irony. "Yah. But if I don't see you on a formal matter, I always feel that's a good thing."

"Right. No problem, no official visit." Dante's smile was rueful. "But lots of problems today."

The governor nodded. "I was glad to see your boys arrive so quickly. My office received one voicelink from Discovery before Carlton took it. Although I don't suppose Carlton is the one who took it. From what I know of him."

"Tell me what you know." Their meals arrived and Dante dug in. He'd been on the go for more than twenty hours, by aircart and transport.

"Most of it I learned from your man here."

Ooievaar nodded to acknowledge the comment.

"But," Jukes continued. "I got a voicelink from a constable who was on vacation near Discovery."

Dante snorted. "People vacation there?"

Jukes laughed. "He hunts with his sons. They saw the second army approach. They heard the first lot, the animals and men marching. It's a noisy business. So they moved east to get away from them and ran up against the second group. They're not as organized, more farmers than dispossessed is my guess. But still about a hundred and fifty strong."

Dante grunted. "So they've been halted right near the border. Is that true, Ooievaar? Or have they managed to progress further?"

Ooievaar consulted his beltlink and nodded. "They're still outside the border, held back by air bombing and a few good men on the ground. Don't know how long they can keep them there."

Dante swung back to face the Governor. "We need more men. I think this is a full scale attack. Is Barrington involved, have you heard anything? We don't know. We can't take action inside Legitamia because we don't want to incite war here in the north."

"I have two thousand Constables at the moment." Jukes slapped his hand on the table. "Half can be at your disposal immediately. And a lot of them were in the military during the Last War. They know what to do and how to do it."

Dante nodded and reached to shake his hand. "Thank you, Governor. That's a big help. I'm going to call up the reserves to help maintain law and order. The borders could turn into a sieve if we don't keep an eye on things. And Jiran is always a powder keg waiting for a light."

"What about Adar Silva?" Jukes gave him a keen eyed look.

"What about it?"

"Will they help? We signed that pact with them."

"Yah, I'll keep that on the back burner. I'm hoping we can handle this ourselves. Carlton can't have that many men."

CHAPTER FIFTY

Abe woke to find he was alone in the bed. He leaped off the mattress before he had time to think, lunging for the bedroom door with his heart hammering in his chest. Then he heard her humming as water splashed in the bathrobe. It was okay, everything was okay. She hadn't left.

His reaction was frightening, the feelings so powerful they'd overwhelmed him. If he didn't show trust in her, it would quickly become apparent, and things would definitely deteriorate between them. He had to trust her. Trust seemed to be in very short supply.

He'd been betrayed by the Constables who first targeted him months ago in a firefight on the Southern Highway. Then by his uncle Jade Hawker on the track near Krimen, and finally by Beth's husband, Sable Maude.

What was he going to tell his sister when she arrived? He hadn't killed her husband because he hadn't been given enough time. But he would have shot him dead if the mountain lion hadn't interfered. He still marvelled at the timing of that.

But Beth was coming to take them home, and he had no answers for her. Just bad news and heart break.

The door of the bathrobe opened and Julianne emerged, appearing scrubbed and wrapped in a cloth, her face rosy and bright. He had to smile.

"Hello, wife."

She dimpled and his heart eased in his chest. "Hello, husband."

"I'll bet that's the first time you've greeted someone that way."

She laughed and laid her hand lightly on his chest. "Don't you have to put some clothes on?"

"Yah, my sister's coming. But not till noon."

"You're sister? Help! What on earth will I wear? That old wool shirt smells, and the pants aren't mine and don't fit anyway."

"Come with me." He led her down the hall to the next bedroom and threw open the doors to the closet. "Let's see what's here."

There were several dresses hanging there from a few years ago, when he and Beth came to the cottage more often. "There are probably more things in the dresser." He pulled open drawers and found pantalets, folded short pants, light shirts and casual robes.

"I just pray you don't wear that Sanctuary robe."

She leaned against him and giggled happily. "Well, what's my incentive to leave it here?"

"If you promise to burn it …" He whispered something in her ear and watched her cheeks go even brighter.

"Abe!" She slapped his shoulder as her eyes grew round.

"What?" He tightened his arm around her. "I'm your husband. It's legal." His voice dropped. "And you know you like it."

Her face flushed darker as he led her back to bed.

By the time the doorbell rang, they were both dressed and had just polished off another meat pie between them.

"I'll get it." Abe stood and straightened his clean shirt. He'd found it here in the closet and it was too big on him. He'd lost weight since he was last at the cottage.

When he opened the door, Beth stood on the threshold, a tentative smile on her face. His heart contracted painfully under his ribs. He reached an arm for her and stepped forward as she fell against his chest. Her weeping was wrenching. He managed to drag her into the entry and close the door, then stood with both arms clasped around her, the tears running down his own cheeks.

"Beth." He ran his hand down her length of pale wavy hair. "I'm here."

She sobbed harder, her fingers tangled in the front of his shirt. "Abe, I almost gave up. I never heard and never heard. I couldn't bear it. Why didn't you let me know?" She thumped his chest with her fist and then wrapped her arms around his waist.

"I couldn't," he said simply. "I'll tell you everything, but I couldn't get in contact when it wasn't safe."

"I figured that. I'm not a dim wit."

He laughed and wiped at his face with the sleeve of his shirt. "Listen, we're both here now. I want to introduce you."

She laughed up at him. "I know Kerr, you silly." She turned, a sunny smile on her face and he watched it falter as she set eyes on Julianne. Then her face went blank. "You're wearing my dress."

Julianne went an embarrassed shade of red and moved toward the stairs to the lower floor. "I'll just change."

"No." Abe's arm shot out and grabbed her wrist before she could run. "Wait. Beth, this is Julianne Adjudicator. This is my wife."

Beth's mouth fell open and she took a couple of steps backward, coming to rest against the door. "Your wife?" Her gaze shot back to him. "You're married?"

"Yah, I am." He couldn't stop the self-satisfied grin from spreading across his face.

"You're married?" It was a screech this time. "You bastard." Beth launched herself at him, pounding her fists into his chest and kicking his shins. "I've waited all this time without knowing anything, and you take the time to court someone and marry them? I hate you!"

Abe gave a quick nudge to Julianne to get her out of harm's way and concentrated on subduing his sister. "Beth, cut it out. Come on. Grow up, why don't you?"

"Grow up? I've been left here taking care of Holdings and fighting off takeovers, getting married to protect it and you waltz in here …"

Abe covered her mouth with his fingers and muffled the rest of her words. He figured that was best. Who knew what she'd say that might hurt Julianne's feelings even if she didn't intend it that way? He held her off him with the other hand until she sagged in his grip. "Will you calm down?"

"I'm calm." Her voice was muffled under his fingers.

"Okay." He let go of her and put both hands on his hips, preparing to explain what had happened.

Beth reared back and slugged him right in the jaw. His teeth slammed together with a sharp click.

CHAPTER FIFTY ONE

By the time Abe was seated on a stool in the kitchen with an ice pack on his jaw, and Beth one on her hand, Julianne had put the kettle on the heatsurface to make tea.

"Can I introduce you to my wife now?" he growled, "Or are you going to attack her as well?"

Beth's mouth turned down. "I'm sorry. Things have been a bit tense."

Julianne was the one who laughed at that. "Tell me about it. We haven't had exactly an easy time either. It's nice to meet you, Beth. I'm wary but open to liking you."

Beth chuckled and Abe wrapped his arm around his wife's hips and hugged her up against his side. "She even likes me," he said happily, "and you know how difficult that can be." He laid his head against the side of her breast and took a deep breath.

"We just got married yesterday. Treeline did it on the boat."

"Oh." Beth got tears in her eyes and smiled up at her new sister. "I'm really glad to meet you, Julianne. Let me give you a hug."

"Okay, as long as you promise not to get violent." They were all laughing by the time the water boiled. Over tea, Abe told what had happened to him and Kerr while travelling with Uncle Jade. Beth seemed so sad and frightened by the news, he did his best to gloss over his injuries.

"So you see, I couldn't phone you, we lost everything. There was no one with a voicelink anywhere nearby, and even if they'd had one there's no coverage. When we started travelling along the northern frontier, same problem. I finally called you when we met the army east of Wymark. I borrowed some fellow's gadget and left you a message. You got that, right?"

Beth beamed as she nodded. "It was such a relief to hear from you. We'd been getting reports of sightings but nothing specific. The waiting was killing me. What about Kerr? Where did you leave him?"

He hoped she didn't notice the moment of hesitation before he leaned forward and took her hands, using his fingers to smooth the red spot on her knuckles where she'd belted him in the jaw. "I have some bad news for you, Bethlehem."

That look of alarm was back in her eyes. "Don't tell me …"

"Your husband had gone into the north, right?"

She nodded cautiously.

He glanced at Julianne, then back at his sister before continuing. "We had an encounter with him on the road. And in the midst of it, Kerr was killed. And your husband died as well."

"He died?" Her face was pale, her voice had gone faint. "What do you mean? That's not true. I just spoke to him last night on the voicelink."

Abe reared back and eyed her carefully. "You spoke to him last night?"

As she nodded, he narrowed his eyes. "I don't think so, Beth. It must have been someone else, one of his men. He's dead. I didn't kill him, but I would have if the mountain lion didn't get him first."

Beth's fingers went white as she gripped the edge of the table. "The mountain lion?"

"It attacked out of the bush. Maude shot Kerr and I was going to take him down, but the lion got him first."

"Maude?"

Abe stopped and stared at her for a moment. "Are we speaking two different languages here? Your husband, Sable Maude. He attacked us, Kerr and I. Luckily Julianne wasn't there, she'd taken the mules to water."

"Maude? Sable Maude isn't my husband."

"You were marrying him." Julianne leaned forward across the table. "Beth, I heard the conversation between Sable Maude and my father. Sable was getting married to you the next day."

"Just as father arranged," Abe added.

Beth's head swivelled back and forth between them. She put up her hands to stop the flow of conversation. "Listen to me." She took a deep breath and held it for a minute. "Just listen. I was supposed to marry Sable. I talked to his father, the Governor, and the wedding was arranged. The night before we were to marry, Sable Maude was arrested on charges of woman smuggling. He was put in jail. I married Dante Regiment instead."

Abe leaped to his feet. "What? You married Dante Regiment, the General's son? When? *Why?* You were betrothed to Maude by our father. By the graves, Beth, what were you thinking?" He paced in a fury, emotion rolling like a storm through his chest. "The Governor must be furious. How are we going to manage with a Territory Governor who's out to get us?"

"Abe. Let me finish!"

"What more is there to say?" He was teetering on an abyss, alarm pulling him in a dozen different directions. "How did you meet this Dante Regiment?"

She just stared at him until he took a couple of turns around the kitchen and threw himself back onto the stool at the counter.

"When did you marry him?" he demanded.

"The same day I was to marry Sable Maude."

He gave her a narrow eyed stare and she hastened to add, "Governor Maude withdrew the betrothal and supported my marriage to Dante."

Abe just shook his head.

"He did, Abe. Dante explained to him just before the wedding was to take place that his son had been caught smuggling women and young boys."

"By the dogs of hell! And this was your fiancé."

"Yes. Dante stepped in and married me instead."

Abe sat silent for a moment. "So this is your husband now. Dante Regiment, second son to the General of Khandarken."

"First son."

"Virgil is the first son." Abe clamped his jaw shut.

"Virgil is dead." Both women spoke at the same time.

Abe ground his teeth and stared at the wall. "I guess I don't know much about anything at the moment."

Julianne added quietly. "I knew Virgil was sick. He caught mangohrea from my stepmother. She had a liaison with him."

Beth turned to her with an expression of distress. "Oh, Julianne. I'm so sorry."

"She made my father sick as well, and I've not been able to find out where he is."

"We'll find him, honey." Abe took her hand and squeezed it gently. "Now that we're back, we'll find out where he is." He stared at his sister, frustration warring with fatigue in his brain. "If Sable Maude was in prison, how did he show up in the Northern Territory?"

"There was a prison break. Someone planted an explosion, hundreds of criminals escaped. Some died. It's been chaos, the constables working round the clock trying to round them up. Maude had appealed his death sentence, and they denied his appeal the day after the prison break."

"What a mess." Abe shook head. "Maude was like a wild man when we saw him. We met him on the trail. He recognized me and stopped to greet us. And when I asked him how the wedding went ..." Abe halted and pinched the bridge of his nose. "He hesitated before he answered. That's why he hesitated, because he didn't marry you. I should have known."

"How could you know?" Beth laid her hand on his shoulder. "Everything has been in such turmoil, I didn't even know until the morning the wedding was to take place."

"Poor Beth. Marrying a different man at the last minute, one you barely knew." He watched the colour flood her cheeks. "Not quite, eh? Well, is it happy, your marriage?"

"Yes. We're happy. He's not here on the farm very often, and I haven't been able to leave because I was the only Farmer left. So we haven't spent a lot of time together."

Abe stared through the large windows out to where the waves lapped against the sand. "There are two Farmers here now. What did you do about transportation back to the manorhouse?"

"Bowcott and Samuels are waiting for us. We brought two trykes."

"Bowcott is Faden's nephew right? And who's Samuels?"

"Samuels is army. Dante left him here as my bodyguard."

Abe grunted and rose. "Well, at least he's looking after you. We might as well go."

"What's a tryke?" Julianne whispered as they gathered what few items they had to bring with them.

"You'll see. It has three wheels and can accommodate the driver and two passengers. We can go together." He tucked her in against his body and kissed her softly. "Holdings isn't like the City, honey. I hope you like it. The manorhouse is comfortable and we grow a lot of our own food. We do have help so you won't have to cook for me."

"I can cook." Her mouth turned firm and he kissed the corner of it to soften her.

"If you want to cook, that's fine with me. Anything you want." He had an unruly feeling in his chest, like the flutter of wings. Was it nerves? They'd married under pretty unusual circumstances. She didn't really know anything about him.

Well, today she'd begin to find out.

CHAPTER FIFTY TWO

Julianne bumped along on the seat of the tryke. It was an odd looking vehicle with three seats. The driver sat in the front over the wheel and the passengers were seated behind. Abe said it was battery powered, but she didn't see a battery anywhere, and how would they charge a battery out in the wilderness where they hadn't had power since before the end of the Last War?

She was a little alarmed at her situation, but thrilled. Abe turned his gaze on her and reached to take her hand. His pale blue eyes always electrified her. She felt like she melted when he looked at her and smiled. She filled with joy.

She turned her head, embarrassed that his sister might see how she felt. They had travelled up the steep hill out of the village of Coronation and were trundling along a dirt track heading west. There were vast fields in every direction, some with plants growing in row upon row, some that appeared totally wild. She'd seen a flock of sheep grazing and several herders moved in the long grass nearby. Abe had waved to them.

Bowcott drove their tryke. Her husband had been pleased to see him, and they shook hands and slapped each other on the back. The driver had gone red as a beet when Abe introduced her as his wife.

She was getting tired by the time they approached a wooded area with a small lake below it. A herd of strange animals was watering there. A wider dusty road wound past that spot, leading away to the south.

"That's the mine road," Abe said. "It comes from the talc mine in the hills, see there." He pointed to some low mountains in the distance. "The talc movers come through here and out the gate to Romeo Road and the Southern Highway." He turned to his sister. "How is production now?" he called. "Have we solved the rumour problems?"

Julianne watched a giant vehicle move ponderously past them toward the gate across the fields. A band of dust rose behind its wheels. The driver waved, so she waved back. Abe was still talking to Beth, but he turned his head and gave her a quick grin.

She glanced at her new sister by marriage. She was a beautiful woman with Abe's distinctive colouring. Her eyes were the same piercing pale blue, her hair just as light platinum. The difference was her hair had a soft wave, whereas Abe's curled tightly on his head. His beard was a darker shade of his hair.

She wondered what the parents had looked like. Which did they take after with the light colouring?

She was very tired. "How much farther?"

Abe glanced over at her. "Not far, another half hour." He took her hand and tugged her to lean on his shoulder. She gratefully dropped her head against him but couldn't sleep. Now she was hungry.

She heard a whoop reverberate through Abe's chest and looked up. The manorhouse had come into view. She sat back up to take a good look. It was huge. Abe had said it wasn't like City houses, but this house was monstrous. She counted three stories of windows, with a few panes of plexi winking to show storage areas below.

The trykes pulled into the yard, coming to a halt, and Abe helped her off. The drivers took the vehicles over to a power panel against what seemed to be a barn and plugged them in. So maybe they did have power out here now. It was surprising.

"Come on, Julianne." Beth took her arm and led her toward a porch at the back of the house. "When we're working around the farm we use the back entrance. The front is for visitors and guests, usually."

They climbed the steps together and Beth kicked off her shoes in the entry hall, so Julianne leaned down to unlace her boots. She felt so silly in these clothes, her old scuffed boots, worn out socks and

Beth's dress from a few years ago. She sighed and looked behind them. Abe was still talking to the men.

Beth took her through into the kitchen. "Hannan, this is Julianne Adjudicator. Julianne, this is Hannan, our chief cook and bottle washer." A plump woman was just removing a baking pan from the oven. She set it carefully on the pad to the side of the heatsurface and turned to smile at her

"Welcome, Ms. It's good to meet you."

"And Abe's here too, Hannan."

Hannan bustled to the door. "Well, as I live and breathe. You get yourself in here," she called. "I need to see if it's not some imposter."

Julianne heard Abe's deep laugh and his footsteps in the entry, then Hannan wrapped her arms around him. "There you are, after all. Welcome home, Mr Farmer. Welcome home. I've just got lunch ready for you."

"Thank you, Hannan. Let me wash up."

Beth showed Julianne to the bathrobe and then through to the family dining room. They took chairs at the table while Hannan swooped around depositing dishes of food. A young girl had set the table and ran to get proper drinking bowls and jugs of fresh juice under the cook's watchful eye.

"Do you usually eat in here?" Julianne gazed around the pretty room. The windows were tall and looked out to the west where she could see a cultivated rose garden that transformed beyond into more wild shrubs and flowering trees. In the distance there were vast vegetable gardens that seemed to stretch a long way across the land.

"Usually. When it's just family, or a few friends. If it's more formal we have a dining hall that suits a larger party."

She bent her head to adjust her napkin in confusion. How big was this house? Perhaps Abe would show her around. He entered the room then and sat beside her. "Let's say a grace. I'm so thankful to be home." They joined hands as he prayed.

Julianne did her best with the meal. The bread was fresh and light, the cream flavoured with parsley. There was a pale pureed soup tasting of leeks followed by roasted duck with sage dressing, spiced lentils and squash. She had some of each, trying to adjust to the rich cooking. It all tasted delicious, but she was more tired than hungry. The dessert suited her, a frozen fruit compote with thin sweet biscuits.

"That was lovely." She wiped her mouth with her napkin. "Really delicious. Hannan is a talented cook. I won't try to do much cooking."

Abe laughed. "You can if you want."

"What I'd like is to see the rest of the house and then find my room. I need a rest."

"Of course." Beth pushed her chair back and stood, but Abe reached for Julianne's hand. "I'll take her, Beth. But you come for the tour."

They started at the Great Hall in the front of the house and worked their way around the main floor. The women's solar was lovely with east windows and soft light, a fireheat for cool days. The office had several desks and sets of tall shelves packed with documents. The library caught her imagination. "I'll come back here later when I'm not so tired," she said.

Abe and Beth both laughed. "Yah, it's one of our favourite rooms as well. Come upstairs."

There were numerous bedrooms, each with its own bathrobe. "This was Father's room," said Beth, showing her into a large room with dark woodwork. "We haven't really changed anything because – well, probably because we haven't had to. We will soon, won't we, Abe? Our mother's things have all been put into storage and it's probably time to deal with Father's as well."

Abe waved to the third floor. "We can go up there later. Mostly guest rooms, staff quarters, some storage. This is Beth's room and this is mine. Ours, I mean."

She felt her face flush and Abe seemed caught momentarily by the idea.

"Well, I'll leave you two," said Beth as she wandered off down the hall.

Abe pulled Julianne through the bedroom door and closed it. "This is where I've lived my whole life."

She looked around the somewhat crowded space. His bed was pushed to the side wall, fairly small with a few pillows. He followed her gaze. "This might need some work. I need a bigger bed." His neck grew red. "I've never given it any thought. I've been the only one here, so…" He glanced back at her.

"Maybe I need a different room with more space for your things. I can do that." He hugged her against him and buried his face in her hair. "Anything at all, Julianne. I'll do whatever you need."

She felt the want bloom inside her, for him to make love to her, to fill her. She was captivated by him. "I'm very tired, Abe."

"Yah, I know." He seemed to have to force himself to let go. "Lie down here and pull this cover over you. We can call you for dinner if you're still sleeping. Otherwise, come back downstairs. I'll probably be in the office."

She crawled up on the high bed, and he bent to pull the spread higher. "There you are." He stared at her for a long moment as his face flushed. "I better go."

He finally turned and left, closing the door softly behind him.

Julianne relaxed back against the pillows. The bedding was clean, smelled fresh of some fragrant soap. She could see the tops of flowering trees from where she lay. They moved gently back and forth in a soft breeze.

Rolling over, she drifted off to sleep.

CHAPTER FIFTY THREE

Abe found Beth already in the office, going over some documents on her desk. "There you are."

She glanced up and smiled. "I like her, your wife. Where did you meet?"

Abe grinned. "I'll tell you, but first I need to know what has gone on with the talc rumours, the attacks, everything."

She nodded and launched into the tale. "So the attacks have stopped," she finished. "I think it has to do with my marriage. It might have been the best move I could have made. They didn't know if you were alive or dead, but with Dante here, who is going to take on the army?"

"And Dante seems very welcome."

She blushed under his gaze. "Yes, it was a relief not to be marrying someone I didn't know."

"I know. I'm teasing, Beth. I'm glad you married someone you care about."

Her face grew sober. "Tell me about the mountain lion."

"Strange, that's all I can say." Abe shook his head. "We'd heard a couple of times along the perimeter road as we stopped at different villages that there had been sightings. We were warned to keep an eye out. They said there was one cat in particular that was quite large, and to keep a watch on the mules.

"At any rate, we didn't see any sign of mountain lion. And when Sable Maude first appeared, he got down off his mule and immediately pulled his pistol, holding it to Kerr's head." He swallowed and narrowed his eyes, staring out the side window.

"I never even imagined he'd shoot. He'd seemed a bit edgy when we first met up, accusing us of betraying him to the army, but I didn't think he was crazy. I thought I could talk to him, persuade him that we hadn't even seen the army let alone told them where he was. But he smiled at me as he pulled the trigger. I've never seen anything like it."

Beth took his hand and he looked down at their joined fingers, his knuckles clenched white. "I was unarmed and I couldn't reach him with a kick or my fist, but there was a plasmagun on the ground where Kerr had dropped it before Maude rode up. I dove for it just as Maude swung around to shoot me. Before I could get hold of the gun, there was a sound like wind across the grass.

He took a shallow breath. "We both turned and there it was, a big mountain lion, rough tawny coat, small ears laid back against his head, eyes like fire. He leaped and grabbed Maude on the back of the head. Maude went down in a rush and the cat let go, prowled around for a better grip and grabbed the side of his face.

"I was stunned. I had the gun by then but just staggered backward. Then I heard more mules coming fast down the track and knew Maude's men would get there at any moment. Kerr was dead, there was nothing I could do for him. So I found Julianne with the mules in the trees down by the creek and we ran. I heard the mules milling around up there, some shouting and shots."

Beth's face remained grave as she waited. When Abe didn't say any more, she shifted in her chair. "I have something to tell you. It's about Uncle."

Abe's head came around slowly. His look must have been pretty hard because she hesitated. "I think I know what you're going to say," he said.

"What?"

"He led me into a trap."

Her lips firmed. "That's what it looks like. We never got the full story, but Dante spoke to Mr Laboucaine."

"From the rubber-plastics factory?"

"Yes. Laboucaine said he warned you not to travel at night, told you that it wasn't safe. He offered you a room."

Abe grunted and nodded his head. "Yah, that's all true. And Uncle insisted we leave. He got downright cranky in the stables, trying to wake everyone up and get the mules saddled. Kept going on about how we had to be on the road from Krimen to Krimenrih in the morning. Some commitment he had."

"Yes." She searched his face. "There's more."

"Oh, God." He covered his eyes with his hand. "I don't know, Beth. I'm pretty beat up." He took a shaky breath and slowly let it out. "Okay, tell me. Go ahead." He took his hand away and rested his gaze on her face.

Her expression became bleak and her hands shook as she clasped them in her lap. "He raped me, Abe."

"What?" He felt like he was hearing her words down a long tunnel, echoing as they went. "What?"

"He drugged me and then raped me. I didn't know it was him, but I lost most of one day, woke up alone in the evening with some tell-tale signs on the blankets."

He watched the silent tears track down her cheeks and reached to grip her shoulder with his hand.

"Then after my wedding, Dante had gone into the City on army business, and Uncle tried it again. This time he took me out into the fields."

"By the dogs of hell." Abe thought his heart was cracking open inside his chest. "Our uncle." He breathed heavily through his nostrils, as if he'd been running. "By the graves."

"He didn't rape me that time."

His gaze focussed on her face. "He didn't?"

"No. He died first."

Abe watched her closely. "Dante killed him."

"No." She put her hands up to stop his words. "No, I thought he had. I was unconscious so didn't see what happened. Dante came to get me, but Uncle was already dead."

"How?"

"A mountain lion."

Abe felt a blow to his chest and sat back helplessly in his chair. "A mountain lion."

"Yes, it killed him."

"What does that mean?"

"He walked right across me and attacked him."

"No, no. I heard you. What does it mean that a mountain cat rescued both of us from attack? Did it try to hurt you?"

"We don't know. When Dante arrived, I was asleep on a blanket on the ground. The lion had Jade by the throat, but he was already dead. They sent a warning shot over its head to scare it off."

Abe stared out the window for the longest time, trying to reconcile what he knew and what he'd just heard. Beth's voicelink buzzed and she turned to answer the call. It must have been her husband, Dante, because her cheeks flushed and she glanced sideways at him.

Rising, he went out through the entry hall and down the front verandah steps of the manorhouse. He wandered aimlessly into the grounds along the facade of his home. The gardens were clipped and groomed near the wall. They slowly changing to less cultivated plants the farther he went, until he reached the untamed shrubs and blooming wild locust trees of the outer yard. The birds were singing crazily in the upper branches amongst the riot of blossoms. As he walked, they quieted nearby and took up song again when he moved on.

A mountain lion had killed Uncle Jade, right beside Beth who was asleep on a blanket. The cat didn't touch her.

He grappled with the image, trying to get his mind around it. She hadn't been touched. Perhaps because she was asleep, the cat went after the one who was moving. Jade might have seen it and tried to fight it off, and that solidified its interest in him rather than Beth.

It was incongruous. Mountain lions didn't hunt humans as a rule, and with all the llama and sheep around their farms, not to mention the poultry that roamed the back field behind the village cottages, there was far easier prey for a mountain cat.

But up north, Abe had been there when the cat came out of the trees on the perimeter road. The lion had targeted Maude. Was it because Maude was closest as it emerged from the bush? It went straight for him, didn't pay any attention to Abe, although both men were standing within feet of each other. It had even seemed to hold Abe's gaze as it changed position to take a better grip on Maude's head.

He swiped at the long grass with his hand, striding down the path to the edge of the gardens and then back again. Had they both been spared a lion attack out of sheer happenstance? What else could it be? Were the mountain cats getting bolder, multiplying, hunting humans now instead of just animals and their young?

And Beth had been raped. By their own uncle. He breathed out heavily, feeling pressure build up behind his eyes. It felt like a migraine, a surge of compression that was growing and swelling in his head. It felt like a wall being built in chunks of rock, one chunk for each betrayal they'd suffered. The Constable attack with laser guns on the Southern Highway had been just the beginning of the oppression, followed by rumours of contamination in their talc, the trip north and the betrayal by his uncle. Then came the attack on those peaceful tribesmen who'd done nothing but help him, followed by the murder of Kerr.

At least he had Julianne, and she'd married him, for better or worse. He knew it was for better. She calmed him, teased and delighted him. He needed her.

He heard a scooter come down Farmer track and stop at the front of the house. Walking back toward the verandah, he was in time to see Chadwick alight and brush the dust off his uniform shirt. "Chad."

The young man turned and his face broke into a grin of delight at the sight of Abe coming toward him. "Mr Farmer!" He strode forward, his hand out.

Abe took it in a firm grip. "How are you? You look more grown up than when I left, what, two or three months ago?"

Chadwick laughed, his cheeks red. "It's good to see you, sir. We heard you were coming back. Didn't know you'd be here already."

"Just arrived. We landed in Coronation on Treeline's boat."

"Yah, Treeline. We heard already. The gossip lines have been working overtime." He patted his beltlink.

Abe laughed. "I guess there're no secrets on this farm."

"No, sir."

"Where have you been?"

"Down to Farmerville. Mr Renfrew had some documents he wanted to get up here for you as soon as possible. He heard you were back."

"Here, I'll take them. Are you still in the guardhouse?"

"Yes sir. Major Regiment has talked to me about…" He hesitated, looking embarrassed. "He didn't try to change things, Mr Farmer," he hastened to reassure him. "But he gave me some training. It's been very helpful."

"Good." Abe gritted his teeth in frustration. He hadn't even met this new brother of his yet, and already he was changing things. "Thanks, Chadwick."

"Welcome home, sir."

CHAPTER FIFTY FOUR

Dante Regiment came home to Farmer Holdings two nights later. He arrived from the north in a military aircart, which landed in the llama grazing fields to the east of the manorhouse. Samuels went out and brought him in by tryke.

Abe was looking forward to meeting this man, the new heir of the General, and the one behind the machinations to marry Beth. He didn't believe for a minute that Sable Maude just happened to be arrested the night before his wedding was planned. Regiment must have had a strong drive to stop Maude before he married Beth. Then like a hero, he stepped in to take his place. Well organized, to say the least. He hoped he was also a good man.

Regiment was late, so they held dinner. Hannan was in a tizzy in the kitchen, pots slamming and low, urgent murmurs to her staff. The table was set in the family dining room, dessert warmed on the sideboard, some chocolate sauce delight with gingerbread.

In the family parlour, Abe was on his new voicelink with their steward Deloume Renfrew when Regiment entered the kitchen at the back of the house. He heard Hannan greet him and watched Beth dash through the doorway and down the hall. He said goodbye to Deloume and took Julianne's hand in his. "We'll be fine," he said, uncertain why he felt the need to reassure her.

He turned as Dante followed Beth into the dining room. He was tall and swarthy skinned, his black hair long at the nape of his neck, heavy sideburns down his cheeks. He wore an army uniform, a rank insignia on the jacket. He gave Abe a once over, and he realized he was probably doing the same thing to Regiment.

Distrust on both sides. But this was Abe's home, and Regiment had defended it. He stepped forward and pasted a smile on his face. "I'm Abe Farmer," he said, putting out his hand. "Pleased to meet you, Dante."

Dante's smile spread as he shook hands. Abe pulled Julianne forward. "And this is my wife, Julianne Adjudicator." His smile dimmed noticeably.

Abe immediately bristled. What was the man's problem? He wouldn't have any disrespect for his wife at Farmer Holdings, not from anyone, even Beth's husband.

He frowned to himself as they sat at the table and dinner was served, Hannan anxiously flapping in the background. Beth said a prayer over the meal, and the staff withdrew to leave them in peace.

He looked his brother by marriage in the eye. "What's happening in the north? Has Carlton been forced back into Legitamia? I'm sorry, I haven't had much time to watch the infolink, and the news is skimpy anyway."

Dante nodded and put his fork down. "Carlton is still in Discovery. And there's a second army approaching to the east of his camp through the Legitamian Mountains. We've asked for more men, and the General is considering calling up the reserves."

"The reserves?" He glanced at Julianne. "That would change things."

Dante shook his head. "You wouldn't be expected to go, Abe. You've just returned from a rather harrowing journey of your own."

Abe cracked a smile and tucked into his meal. "I don't see why I'd be exempt. Even some of the dispossessed at Farmerville are members of the reserves."

Dante raised his eyebrows but didn't reply.

When dinner was finished, they moved to the family parlour and Abe served a whiskey to Regiment. Beth preferred sherry, and Julianne shook her head when he glanced at her. He examined her face, she was still pale from fatigue. It had been a very rough journey. They wouldn't stay up late tonight.

As he turned to get his own whiskey, Dante said, "Julianne, have you heard from your father?"

"No. I'm hoping to get into the City soon to see if I can find him. I know he's been ill." Her mouth seemed pinched.

Abe sat beside her and took her hand. "We can go soon, within a day or two," he said. "I just have a few things here that need to be taken care of."

"Do you know where he is, Mr Regiment?" The hopeful expression on her face broke his heart, and his hand tightened on hers.

"No, if I did I'd have arrested him by now."

Abe choked on his whiskey. "You don't have to talk like that." He felt the blood rush to his face as he slowly rose to his feet. "Watch yourself."

"Abe." Beth leaped to her feet. "It's touchy."

"Damn right it's touchy. Watch your mouth, Regiment."

Dante stood as well, but kept his gaze on Julianne. "Your father has been attacking Farmer Holdings. We'd like to talk to him about that."

"Attacking Holdings?" Abe's head swung back again toward his wife. "What do you mean?"

"He and his cohorts organized two direct attacks on the farm and the mine after you left. There were shots fired, Faden was wounded, the mine was taken back after great effort and injury, and Bethlehem spent a night out in the bush by herself to evade

319

capture. He's in hiding because he's wanted for instigating an attack on a fellow citizen and inciting civil unrest, among other things."

Abe didn't even look at him, just watched his wife's face as her eyes glanced down and away, the hectic colour climbing her cheeks. "Did you know this?"

She didn't look at him.

"Did you know this?" he bellowed. "By the graves!"

"I told you." She glanced up and her eyes implored him to understand.

But he understood all too well. He'd been betrayed again, this time by his own wife. "You didn't tell me anything about it."

"I told you I listened to his conversations. That's how I knew about Sable Maude getting married to Beth. I told you."

Abe gritted his teeth. "You told me he was wanted by the General, perhaps for complicity in spreading his wife's disease to Virgil Regiment."

She gave him a sorrowful look, then burst into tears and ran from the room.

Abe stared at the empty place on the divan where she'd been sitting. The rage inside him built until it was ready to burst forth in something ugly, something totally monstrous. He turned and left the room with long strides before he acted in a way he could never take back. As he moved silently down the hallway to the back door, he heard Beth calling his name.

It was too late for that, too late to reason with him. Reason had put him in the position he found himself in now. It allowed him to continue doing what he'd always done while he was assaulted on all sides, while he allowed his trust to be betrayed by those around him, his uncle, the law, his wife.

He was finished with reason.

CHAPTER FIFTY FIVE

Abe reached the mine by midnight, then slept in the office till dawn when Faden found him hunched over in the office chair, his feet propped on the desk.

"Welcome home, Abe." Faden tapped one boot to wake him.

Abe mumbled a reply and sat up. "Faden." He stood and stretched. "Good to see you, man. How have you been? I heard there was some excitement up here at the mine shortly after I left. An attack, Beth said."

"Sure was. Not that we lost anyone, which was the good news."

"You were wounded. Show me."

Faden pulled his pants leg higher and showed him the red scar in his calf. "All healed now."

"It looks good and healthy. I'm glad."

"Yah. Now let's see what yours looks like. Your sister said there were two wounds."

Abe tugged his shirt out of the waistband of his pants and lifted it to show his side. "This one was the worst, it's almost healed."

Faden's face paled at the sight. "By the graves. That one could have finished you."

"Nearly did." He tucked his shirt back in. "Kerr got me out of there and kept me alive until he found the tribesmen. They nursed me back to health." There was a renewed stab of pain in his chest at the loss of his guard and friend. "Which reminds me," he added gruffly, "I have to find young Ventuzzo here at Holdings. His father sends his greetings, and he needs to be informed that his mother has died."

"I heard about Kerr." Faden's voice was sympathetic.

Abe gave a short nod.

"I'm sorry about it, Abe."

"Yah." He squeezed his eyes shut and pinched the bridge of his nose. "He's the only one who didn't betray me, Faden. The only one. Everyone else used me and then discarded me."

Faden studied his face for a moment, then sent a message on his beltlink. "I'm just ordering our breakfast," he commented, his eyes on the now empty bourbon bottle on his desk. Then he sat across from his boss and settled in.

"Your sister didn't turn her back on you. She stayed here and fought her heart out. And she's still here."

Abe turned away to stare out the open door as one of the men brought in two bowls of oat porridge and someone followed with toast and tea.

By noon he had caught up on the activities at the mine. Faden had everything under control, as usual. Mr Kneebone, their talc agent, was back in good health and said the false rumours about contamination in the talc had died a natural death. "Once Little Harry disappeared," he added. "The General's still searching for him, but there's been no activity against us since then."

Abe felt his gut clench at the mention of Little Harry Adjudicator. He imagined his wife down at the manorhouse pretending she hadn't seduced him into marrying her, when her father had Farmer Holdings under siege. He thought he'd be sick, the reaction was so violent. Deceived again, and by someone he'd fallen in love with. That's what caught in his throat.

He gagged and turned it into a rough cough. Faden gave him a strange look but went back to the papers on the desk as Kneebone nattered on.

He had to get out of here. He couldn't keep his mind on anything, his brain rattling around inside his head like a pea in an empty gourd. The thought processes had simply quit.

When he stood, Faden and Kneebone turned to look at him as if he'd interrupted a consultation, which maybe he had. But he didn't care. He couldn't handle this. "I have to go, Faden. I leave it in your capable hands, and I'll be in touch."

On his way down the mine road he placed a voicelink call to the Army Reserve Office in Deep Creek and put his name forward for duty. Then he steeled himself and stopped at the house, entering through the back door. Hannan was sitting with her feet up on another chair while she sipped a cup of tea.

"Mr Farmer." She set her cup down rather abruptly and pulled her feet off the chair.

"Hannan, don't let me interrupt you. I just need to get a few things."

"The ladies are out," she said. "They've gone to Farmerville to take some supplies to the barracks for Thames' men."

"I see." A kind of relief flooded through him. He wouldn't have to face them right now. "Well, I'll see them later then." He walked swiftly down the hall and bounded up the stairs. In his room he gathered his uniform and a few items he'd need. His heart beat erratically in his chest. Julianne's belongings, small feminine items, were set neatly on a corner of the shelf. He stopped and examined them, then lifted a hair clip in his fingers. She didn't have much. She'd lost everything, just like he had.

He hardened his heart. She'd go home. That had been her plan all along, she'd never intended to stay at Holdings. And she'd deceived him. She knew her father was behind the attacks on Holdings, but she'd kept that information to herself because she wanted to be rescued from the Sanctuary and taken back to the City. And she couldn't do that alone. She'd sucked him in and he'd fallen for her. He rubbed his fist against the ache in the centre of his chest.

He felt over-heated as if he had a high fever. He felt explosive, uncertain if he'd be able to hold his temper at the least provocation. He felt beaten, as if he'd sustained a steady assault and might yet succumb to the damage it had wrought.

CHAPTER FIFTY SIX

Julianne rapped on the table before her, and the children stopped chattering and gazed at her expectantly. They ranged in age from five to twelve years and attended classes in the young school at Farmer Holdings every morning except Sunday.

The single schoolroom was a bright space at the back of the barracks, with double desks facing the wall where a large noteboard had been attached. The teacher motioned to her to continue.

She held up a piece of origami, a single paper folded into a round flower shape with petals densely packed in the centre, slowly relaxing as they fluttered to the edges. "This is what we can make with one piece of paper." She smiled at the chatter as the children gaped at the object.

"It's called origami and it's an art. We start with the easy things and they slowly get harder. But if you persevere, you can make things like this." She held up a grasshopper, the back legs elongated and sharply defined. "Or this." She held up a little owl she'd made the night before.

The children erupted with excitement.

"We start with a single sheet of paper." She handed a small stack of paper to the nearest child, who stood and handed it out to the other students. "We're going to make an owl this morning. We start with one fold." She held up the paper and carefully demonstrated the first fold.

As she added folds to the design it grew more difficult and she moved around the room, helping the younger students make the folds with their pliable fingers.

Abe had left the day before. After dinner as she fled the room, she'd heard voices raised in conflict between him and his sister. She'd lain in bed, waiting for him to come so she could explain.

When she'd first learned his name at the Sanctuary, she'd been afraid to tell him who she was. Their families weren't on good terms. But then she gathered her courage, and she was convinced he'd recognized her name. There'd been something on his face that said he was angry but then softened toward her. She thought that whole issue was behind them.

For him to turn on her had been devastating. How could he treat her like that? And now he was gone. Beth said their steward, Mr Renfrew, called to let her know that Abe had been by to see him to sort out any outstanding issues on his way to join the reserves. He was going off to fight the Emperor.

Does he hate me? Her heart was breaking. They'd been through so much together, surely he could forgive her for what her father had done. She'd had no part in it. She wasn't the one at fault.

She knelt beside a little girl's table and helped her do a difficult fold. "Well done," she said. The delighted expression on the child's face caused tears to form in her eyes. This was why she taught origami. The schoolhouse in the City where she volunteered twice a week was waiting for her. At least there she was appreciated, there the children noticed if she didn't come to teach.

When she got back to the manorhouse, lunch was being served in the family dining room. Julianne washed up in the bathrobe and smoothed her hair, examining herself in the mirror. *Does Abe mean to simply turn his back on me? Would he even return?* Perhaps he would refuse to come back as long as she was here, yet this was his home. If so, it would be very difficult for her to stay. Her tears dripped into the sink.

That evening after dinner, she and Beth sat in the family parlour over tea and biscuits. Julianne had felt all through dinner that she was in some kind of play, so polite and artificial on the surface while her feelings boiled up inside like lava. "Beth, you've been very kind. I'm sure it hasn't been easy for you. You must miss Abe terribly, he's been gone so long."

Beth nodded, her mouth turned down. "Yes, I miss him. It's such a relief to know he's alive and well, but he wasn't here long enough to catch up and see how he really is." Her gaze was kind and open.

Julianne looked down at her empty cup.

"It's not all your fault, Julianne." She glanced up again in surprise, as Beth continued, "Abe has changed. He was a really easy going guy, my brother. My friends would complain about their older brothers, how overbearing they were, demanding that things be done their way. But Abe was never like that. He laughed easily, joked with me, let me make decisions if it meant something to me. I used to think he was a pushover.

"But he's changed. I can see that. He doesn't smile, his laugh is forced. He's tough and judgmental, even bitter. I guess everything that's happened has contributed to that."

"When I first met him he frightened me," Julianne admitted. "He was so grim, and Kerr was very ill. He relaxed a bit after Kerr began to get better, and I thought that was the real Abe, the one that listened, heard what people said, and did his best to help."

Beth watched her face, and she knew her cheeks grew red. "There's something I've wondered about." When she saw Beth's encouraging nod, she carried on. "As we were leaving the Sanctuary, one of the guards came out of the trees and tried to stop us from going. And Abe didn't say a word, he just kicked the man in the chest and he fell like a log. Then he reached down and hit him once in the face, and he was unconscious. It was brutal. It frightened me."

Beth actually smiled.

"Why would you smile at something like that?" she said indignantly. "It was shocking to witness."

"Julianne, how many people died on your journey?"

She felt the blood leave her head and braced herself against the arm of the divan. "Kerr, as well as some others died. A few men were caught by the mud slide."

"Well, think of what Abe did this way. He could have killed the guard that was trying to stop you from leaving. But instead, he knocked him out. He made a choice to let that man live."

"He could have killed him? The guard had a plasmagun, Abe didn't have a weapon."

"Yes, he did. Abe's weapons are his hands and feet. He trains in the fighting arts and he's very good at what he does. He's a master and a teacher. He can kill a man with one blow of his fist."

"Oh." She had to think that through. She'd never heard of fighting arts. It was just one more aspect of her husband that she'd not been aware of, that Abe hadn't shared with her.

She looked back at Beth and felt determination solidify in her chest. "I'm going back to the City, Beth. I thought you should know. I have to see if I can find my father, he's very ill. And our house and the staff have all been abandoned. It's time I went home and took care of things."

Bath looked sorrowful. "I wondered if you would go. I'm sorry, I'd hoped you'd stay, at least for a while, to give Abe a chance to simmer down and me time to get to know you."

"I don't think Abe is going to simmer down." She choked on the words. "And he won't come back home if I'm here waiting for him. It's for the best that I go."

CHAPTER FIFTY SEVEN

A be stood in a light wind on the field east of Discovery in the Northern Territory and threw another kick with his army issue boot. He watched as the group of reserves lined up in front of him tried to mimic the movement. "Once more," he shouted. "The purpose is to put the opponent out of commission." They were in an army camp getting the reserves ready for deployment along the Legitamian border.

"Why not just use the plasma?" one fellow piped up. Laugher rippled down the line of recruits.

Abe grinned determinedly. "When you use a gun, everyone knows you're there. These are skills that let you move into an area and disarm or disable your opponent without sending an alert to his comrades. It can be very useful. Go ahead and blast away with a plasmagun or your laser, but you make yourself a target. You can't sneak in and you can't sneak out."

The men began to nod in understanding as they lined up to practice the kick again. "Now remember this. Your legs are stronger than your arms. For sheer force, your foot is the best weapon. If you have to be sure you've disabled your opponent, use your heel. We'll work on hands later for times when you're doing a follow-up punch, or working in confined areas when there isn't room to throw a kick."

He noticed they were paying more attention now, beginning to understand what they were learning and the purpose behind it. He huffed out a frustrated breath. He'd volunteered to fight and immediately been shovelled into a training programme. He didn't want to train the men, didn't have the patience for it right now. He just wanted to get out there into the action. He'd been attacked too many times while unprepared. He was aching to fight back.

By lunch time they'd worked up quite a sweat, and he called a halt. "Okay, men. Enough for today. We start again first thing tomorrow morning. Be prepared." A few laughed but he noticed some respectful nods.

Picking up his shirt where it lay discarded on the ground, he mopped the sweat off his forehead and headed to the officers' quarters to shower. As he stepped inside the door to the common room, he caught a movement in the shadows. Halting abruptly, he watched Dante Regiment rise from a chair where he'd been waiting. The very last person he wanted to see.

"Regiment." His nod was brusque.

"Abe, I stopped by to see how it's going here."

"It's not what I signed up for."

"What do you mean? The training looked pretty darned good from where I stood."

Abe bared his teeth. "I signed up to fight. Not sit here and mark time."

Dante eyed him, but said nothing.

"I want to get out there!" He could feel the frustration in the back of his throat.

"Well, right now you can't. We put people where we need them. Stop acting like a jackass."

Something snapped inside Abe's head. It was as if a high tension wire suddenly broke, and he gave a huge leap forward. He did what he'd wanted to do since he found out about Julianne's betrayal. He fought. He spun sideways and nailed Regiment square in the chest with his foot. Dante flew backward and went down with a crash against the wall. He landed on the floor on his back, his gun suddenly gripped firmly in his hand and pointed right at Abe's heart.

Both men froze. Abe backed up a cautious step and stared at his brother by marriage in total alarm and defeat. Then he spread his arms wide, moved forward in grim resignation and said, "Go ahead and shoot. Just get it over with."

Silently, Dante got to his feet and replaced his gun in the holster under his arm, brushing his uniform off.

Abe eyed him angrily. "Why didn't you shoot? It would be so much simpler." He felt the rage burning hot in his gut. It wouldn't leave him, wouldn't cool.

Dante sat at a table and waved to another seat. "Because I think I'd be as angry as you are if I'd been through what you have."

Abe paced a few times around the room as the adrenaline rush reached his limbs, then threw himself into the chair and braced his forearms rigidly on the table. His hands shook. "I can't get rid of it. It keeps roaring up my throat."

"And how effective would you be on the battlefield, with men under your command and an uncontrollable temper?"

He pinched the bridge of his nose. "I don't want men under me. I just want to fight."

Dante nodded solemnly. "I understand. I felt that way after my brother died."

Abe watched the tight planes of his face. "Virgil?"

"Yah. Virgil was a good man and a smart one. And he was playing with it, wouldn't take his position seriously. Then that bitch Zanata gave him mangohrea and he died within weeks. I've never seen anything so aggressive. The doctor said …"

Abe watched him.

"Anyway." Dante shook himself. "I didn't have time to smash something or take someone out because I was in a different kind of fight."

"Marrying Beth."

Dante glanced at him and nodded, his face growing dark. "If you'd known what Sable Maude was like, you'd have done anything to ensure she didn't marry him."

"Listen. I won't fight you on that. I was surprised, okay. When I found out you'd married her, I was angry. I thought it meant we'd have the Governor against us."

"I took care of that."

Abe gave him a meaningful look. "You took care of a lot of things."

Dante gave a bark of laughter. "True."

"And I'm glad of it. I wasn't here, there was no one here to look after Beth. I thank you for your care of her."

Dante measured him with his gaze, then took the proffered hand in a hard shake. "You're welcome. I did it because it's my job." Then his lips moved upward at the corners. "But mostly I did it because of her. She's very precious to me."

Abe firmed his mouth. "I know. I'm glad." His gaze grew hard again. "I want to fight."

"I get that. But you're most useful here right now. These men need skills that they don't have and you do. And if you fight all day every day while you teach them, you'll find that your rage will begin to wear down. You'll burn it up. I know from personal experience."

Abe grimaced and gazed resentfully through the open door as a couple of officers came through, nodded to him and split off to their quarters. "It's not what I wanted."

"No. But it might keep you alive to fight another day with a cooler head."

He glanced back at Dante but didn't reply.

"And I don't think Julianne knew about her father."

Abe's face went blank. "Don't even go there."

"I'm just telling you what I saw. I was at several functions in the City right before all this erupted. Julianne thought she was going to marry Virgil."

His mouth fell open. "Virgil? Your brother?"

"Yah. It wasn't formal. However, there had been an understanding between the families since Virge was about fourteen. But he had other fish to fry, always aiming higher, for something more exciting. And Zanata caught his attention. It wasn't pretty."

His jaw snapped shut. "No, I don't suppose it was."

"She was hurt by that, both by Virgil's betrayal and her stepmother's. Then her father ran and left her at Zanata's mercy."

Abe stood. "I don't want to hear this."

Dante stood and stretched. "I can understand that. Just know this. Julianne is alone in the City, she's left Holdings and gone back. Bethlehem called me this morning. Apparently you aren't using your voicelink."

Abe's braced his hands on his hips as he stared Dante down, then turned to go. "I'm not surprised she went to the City. That's where she wanted to be all along."

As he walked away, he wondered if he felt a fissure begin to form in the sidewall of anger he'd sealed around his heart.

CHAPTER FIFTY EIGHT

The fighting along the border was ragged. General Elkon rode into the east camp with his crew, swung out of the saddle and handed his horse off to his adjutant. He was miles back inside the Legitamia border and it seemed they would stay here for the moment. There'd been no forward progress since the men first arrived.

He waved the major on duty over and approached the tent where he heard a low murmur of voices. "Ahoy, who's there?"

A head poked through the flap and then pulled back, and the Colonel stepped out, quickly buttoning his jacket. "General." He saluted and Elkon extended his hand.

"How's it going here?"

"Come inside, sir. We're just discussing our next approach."

Elkon ducked under the flap of the tent. The Colonel and Major were perhaps the only ones here from the regular army. The other men, four of them standing around a map table, were all dressed in rough civilian clothing, hats on and guns in slings on their backs. Even so, he liked what he saw. They all stood straighter and saluted with an ease and comfort that told him more about their military training than their clothing did.

The dispossessed in Khandarken and Jiran had all been in the army during the Last War, many of them fighting on first one side and then the other before the battles disintegrated into many local fights. Now most had no jobs, no position, and no real purpose. Emperor Carlton provided all three with his new battle. If only there was money to pay the men. But even without pay, they were flocking with determination toward the Emperor's cause.

"At ease, men. I wanted to drop in and find out how it's going and what the plan is. I suspect our communications are monitored out of Khandarken, and we might be able to use that to our advantage at some point. However, face to face this time is best."

"Yes, sir. We've just drawn the line here where we tried and failed to get across the border." The Colonel pointed to a spot on the map not far from the field where they stood. "They were ready for us and we were forced back pretty quickly, lost eighteen men. The good thing about our position is they don't want to cross the border into Legitamia and instigate Barrington to take any kind of action against them."

"No, but you must know there's intense diplomatic activity going on over this whole affair, and Barrington is under a lot of pressure from both Adar Silva and Khandarken to cooperate with them."

"Yes, sir. I understand. We can't stay here all year. We have to make progress. That's why we've come up with a different approach."

He pointed to the coastline about a hundred miles along the border to the east. "We wondered if we couldn't do two coordinated assaults, one through the border and the other by water. General Regiment of Khandarken has all his men between here and Discovery. And he has a fleet of aircarts, whereas we don't. But there hasn't been any activity along the coast. If we led a charge here, just as our ships left port in the east, they might land on the beaches while Regiment is tied up and diverted by a land battle."

Elkon pondered the map, knowing Emperor Carlton didn't like ships and wouldn't be too enthusiastic. But it was a plausible argument that just might work. "Who thought of this?" The major moved nervously beside his boss and the Colonel pointed to him.

"Major Nida, sir. His father's a fisherman and he said that a lot of the fishermen are supporters and don't do military manoeuvres, but they know the Catastrophic Ocean. As it is, we're kind of stuck. Khandarken has a lot more men than we do and we can't get through this pass. We could go back and try here or here." He pointed to other breaks in the mountains where cart trails and trading routes had been carved out over the years.

"This is good thinking, Major Nida. Okay, let's talk about this. What do the rest of you men say?"

CHAPTER FIFTY NINE

Julianne stepped out of the Farmer petrocar and slammed the armoured door. The driver took her pitifully small bag of belongings out of the cargo bay and carried it to the steps of her father's house.

She was back in the City. This was what she'd fled not so long ago, fled for her safety. But Zanata was under warrant from the Constables now, and Julianne was married. Everything was different, yet nothing was settled.

Now she had to find her father. Little Harry wasn't well, she was deathly afraid she'd find him in some hospital for the homeless outside the City walls. But she was determined to help him if she could. She went up the steps and knocked on the door. In a moment she heard a brisk step from within and the door opened.

"Julianne!" She found herself engulfed in a smothering hug.

"Beverly, how are you?"

Her housekeeper stood back and sniffed, patting Julianne's arm, then pulled her into another encompassing embrace. "Come in, Ms. Come in. We've been so worried." She frowned darkly at the driver and took the small bag with a swift grasp before she pulled Julianne inside with one hand and closed the door with the other.

"Just a moment, Beverly." Julianne tugged it open again and smiled at the driver. "Tell Beth thank you very much, Bowcott. And thanks to you as well for a safe journey here. Have a good trip back." Bowcott grinned and bowed before striding back to the somewhat shabby vehicle.

Beverly frowned out the door at the departing petrocar. "Did you travel far in that thing? It doesn't look safe or comfortable."

"Believe me, it was far safer and more comfortable than just about anything else I've travelled in since I left. Is Zanata here?"

Beverly's face grew cautious. "No. Were you expecting her?"

"I was hoping she wasn't."

"There's a warrant out for her with a reward attached to it."

"Good. I'm glad that's still in place. But she hasn't been caught?"

"Not that we've heard. Ed has been keeping an ear out." Ed was Beverly's husband and the house man. He took care of all manner of things. It was a small household for City dwellers of her class.

"Let me get my breath."

Beverly took her jacket and sniffed audibly. "Your clothes have suffered somewhat."

Julianne gave a grimace. "Kind of you to say."

"I'm sorry, my dear. I'm just so glad to see you. We've been worried, we didn't know ..." She shot an awkward look at the daughter of her employer, then drew her into the kitchen. "Let's do it this way. Sit here." She nudged Julianne into the rocking chair beside the cold fireheat and pulled a footstool up to rest her feet on, frowning at her worn and scuffed boots.

Muttering to herself, she filled the pot and set it on the heatsurface, then turned to pull out a loaf of fresh bread. "Here we go. I have some very good lamb paste with fresh greens from the garden and a bit of apple chili jelly. Just relax while I prepare it."

With food organized, Beverly moved to the back door. "Ed!" she called, peering into the yard. "You'd best come quick."

Ed appeared a few minutes later, and the joy on his face when he spotted Julianne in the chair made her smile warm and tears come to her eyes. She stood for his embrace as he rocked her in his arms. "There you are, Ms. We were that worried." He choked on his words and mumbled into her hair. "You'd been here your whole life and within days the family up and disappeared. It was ..." He wiped his eyes with his sleeve. "Well, enough of that."

"I'm just making an early supper, Ed. The kettle's boiling, you make the tea, spice caf just as she likes it, while I do the sandwiches. I'm sorry, Ms, it's pretty informal but I've done no baking or cooking, not knowing ..." She pressed her lips together and bent over her work, sawing thin slices of bread and arranging them on a tray.

Julianne rocked in the chair and closed her eyes. It was wonderful to be home. She could feel their curious gazes resting on her now and then, but she'd tell them everything soon. Right now she'd soak up the feeling of just being here.

As they ate, she told them about her travels, and soon realized she could never reveal the whole story. Who would believe it? And what would they think of her if they knew everything that had happened? When she'd eaten as much as she could, she leaned back in the chair and sighed. "That's all I can tell you."

Their faces wore identical expressions of amazement. "Well, that's plenty," said Ed. "You run off and come back married. It's more than I can take in. I thought you'd marry the Regiment boy or some City fella that caught your eye." Beverly poked him in the ribs with her elbow, and he shut his mouth.

"It's okay," Julianne murmured. "I was disappointed when Virgil chose Zanata." Her voice betrayed her with a little catch in it. "But it wasn't

Virgil I wanted, just the arrangement. It made everything safe for me. I didn't really know him. I wasn't heartbroken. I was just angry at my stepmother." *And at father for choosing her in the first place.* She kept that sentiment to herself.

"But things happened in the north and it was frightening out there. Abe Farmer came with his friend and they took me out of the danger." She nearly bit her tongue on that remark but had to admit it was true. She couldn't present him as a knave if she'd married him willingly. It would make her look foolish, she thought wryly. She may be very angry at him, but she'd present him in a good light for her own sake. Not his.

"At any rate, he's gone to fight with the reserves against the Emperor in the north. Neither of us knew Aqatain had died and Carlton was the new Emperor until we got near the village of Discovery and were captured by his men."

Beverly patted her arm. "I can't imagine what you've gone through. The Emperor's death caused quite a stir, you know. Apparently he was ranting against our Leader and the Khandarken government at the time, and just keeled over in the middle of it."

Ed gazed at his wife with obvious affection. "We can't believe those stories, Beverly. We don't know how reliable the tales are that come out of Legitamia, or who is telling them. But he certainly died quickly. Probably a heart attack. And young Carlton is their Emperor now."

"Well, they've started a small war up there. I hope it doesn't spread. There are a lot of dispossessed who live near the borderlands and don't have any affiliation. They may decide they'd rather go back to fighting. It's what they did before the Emperor was defeated. I imagine it becomes a way of life."

"There are a lot?"

She looked at the surprised faces before her. "We saw a lot of them. They live in camps in the bush near the villages or up in the hills along the border. Some of them work for whatever they can get, but jobs are scarce around there. Things are a little wild compared to here or even in the other Territories."

It felt odd being able to tell them things like this. Till now she'd never been out in the territories and had no knowledge of what it was like in the hinterlands. Farmer Holdings in the south had amazed her, the vast swathes of planted fields and pasture leading all the way up into the hills. She hadn't seen the mine or been into the mountains to the far south, but knew the estate reached the borders of Adar Silva. They even had two towns on their land. She was humbled by the size and breadth of what Farmer Holdings encompassed and how she'd first viewed Abe as a tribesman with his high boots and wild clothing.

"I'd love to go to bed."

"Come along, dear. Your maid's not here."

"Has she quit?"

Beverly chuckled. "No. But we didn't know what to do exactly. Zanata's maid went with Zanata, so that was solved for us. Your father's valet left for another job. We didn't know if Harry was coming home or not."

Beverly looked at her questioningly but she shook her head. "I don't know where he is, Beverly. That's the first thing I want to do, find him."

"Yes, dear. But not today. Your maid was here with no work, so she went to visit her family. Said she'd take some time and let us know when she was ready to return. We weren't able to pay her wages, you see."

"Yes, of course. I knew it would be a mess. How have you two managed? It's very kind of you to stay in the hopes that things would normalize again."

Beverly put her arms around her and hugged tight. "We wouldn't abandon you, child. We just worried about where you were and if you were safe. Come along."

CHAPTER SIXTY

J ulianne began to relax as she settled into her family home once more. Zanata was gone. It didn't seem likely she'd come back, although there was no word of a capture or arrest by the authorities. She set her mind to finding her father.

Going through the things in Little Harry's office at the courthouse had been heart wrenching. All the familiar belongings, his pipe in a bowl waiting to be filled at the end of the day, a small sealed bag of tobacco beside it and a firelight nearby. His judicial robes that hung on a hanger behind the door, the wig on its stand on the desk. His favourite pen that he insisted be refilled every morning so it flowed freely whenever he wished to use it. He'd always refused to use a tomo, although a lot of the adjudicators swore by them. These were things she'd grown up with, that now stood abandoned in Little Harry's empty office.

His assistant had asked her if she knew where he was, as some personal mail had arrived. She agreed to take it home for when he returned and tucked it into her bag. Not that she expected his return. She'd given up that hope a long time ago. It was just a matter of finding where he hid.

Closeted in her room that night, she pulled the package of mail out and examined it. There were a few greeting cards from colleagues, an invitation to a reception for the appointment of a new adjudicator. There was a banking envelope with Adar Silva postage. The document inside detailed a deposit account and requested instructions on the investment of the funds. It didn't give a value. Julianne stared at it. They weren't poor, Little Harry earned a very respectable income as a superior court judge. But investment funds?

Everyone she spoke to at his work denied any knowledge of where Harry might have gone. Most looked at her askance when she asked, their expressions skeptical given that it was common knowledge the Constables were searching for him. But she thought it was at least worth a try. Would father come home if he became seriously ill? How would she be able to care for him if she couldn't find him?

She attended the young school on the outskirts of the City and conducted her first origami class with her students since she had left home. The children were excited to see her and the bubbly jubilation lifted her spirits. Several of the little people were becoming very adept at the designs and she toyed with the idea of forming a club for those most interested which would meet after class in the afternoon and attempt more difficult patterns.

When she arrived home at noon she was pleasantly tired and ready for lunch. She used her key to enter the great hall. Beverly must have heard the door. She rushed out from the kitchens, then stopped uncertainly at the sight of her.

"I'm home," she said, smiling. "You're not used to having anyone here."

"No, Ms. That is … There's someone to see you. They're waiting in the parlour." She gestured toward the more formal room off the hall. Julianne felt her heart stutter in her chest. *Abe. He's come to see me!* Was he after a divorce? The blood must have left her head because she was suddenly dizzy and had to reach for the back of a chair to steady herself.

"It's all right Ms." Beverly took her arm, helping her to sit. "Just catch your breath and I'll stay right by your side."

"I'm fine, Beverly. Who is here?"

"It's a Constable."

Oh, no. Not Abe. What did it mean? *Am I in trouble?* Perhaps they'd found Zanata and been kind enough to come notify her.

"I think I need a drink of water." She could hardly get the words out between dry lips.

Beverly disappeared down the hall and reappeared at her side with a cold bowl in her hand. "Do you want me to stay with you?"

"Yes, please." She blinked back her tears and stood. "I can do this."

The young Constable leaped to his feet as she entered and showed his ident. "I have information, Ms Adjudicator. The Chief Constable sent me round to talk to you. Please have a seat."

"I'd rather stand," she said. Beverly fluttered at her side.

"Very well." He looked at her rather desperately for a moment. "I have information."

"Yes. What does it regard?"

"Ah." He went to sit and then stopped himself and stood again, his hands clasped tightly at his waist. "The Chief wanted you to know first, before the news got out. A body has been found."

Julianne felt the dizziness return in a wave that washed over her. She swayed. He leaped forward and grabbed her arm.

"Please sit, Ms. Then I can sit. Perhaps some tea?" He glanced past her at Beverly, who nodded and quickly left the room.

"There, that's better." He seated her on the divan and took a chair nearby. "It's not good news. I've not done this before, but it's hard to pass on such news."

"Please tell me." *Was Abe dead?* She prayed not, her heart squeezing in her chest.

"Your father's body has been found."

"Father?" She felt herself fall.

When she became aware again, she was lying on the divan, a light throw covering her shoulders. She turned her head. The Constable stood by the door talking low with Ed as Beverly entered the room with a tray.

What had happened? Oh yes. Father was …

In total denial, she turned her face into the pillow. He was supposed to be sick, not dead. He was supposed to let her help him, look after him in his illness. She was going to see him when she got back to the City, talk to him and find out what she could do.

Beverly set the tray down on a side table and took her arm, helping her to sit up. "Just drink this," she said.

It smelled awful, medicinal. "Just drink it." That was the tone Beverly used to use when she was a child and didn't eat her meal. "Just have five bites," she'd say in a tone that brooked no nonsense.

She drank. It tasted bitter and made her gasp for breath. The Constable turned back to her and moved across the room. He sat down and took her hand. "I'm very sorry, Ms. I didn't mean to cause such distress. But the Chief insisted you be told before the news got out and you heard it elsewhere."

"Where was he found?" Her voice barely eased out around the tightness in her throat.

He hesitated and her heart clenched at all the horrible possibilities. "In Old Towne, at the end of Bookseller Lane. The death diviner thinks he had a heart attack. Someone found him this morning."

She covered her mouth with her hand. *He was lying in the gutter of a lane in Old Towne?* Father had been so proud, and that was no way for a proud man to die. Tears flowed down her cheeks and she choked back a sob. "Did he suffer?"

"I'm sure not, Ms. They said he died suddenly, with little pain."

She watched the young Constable's earnest face and the eyes that wouldn't quite meet her own and wanted to believe him. She wanted to think that what he said was true.

After he left, Ed sat beside her and held her hand. He didn't speak, just gave her the comfort of his presence. It was a familiar feeling, to know Ed was beside her. "What do you think?" she finally asked.

He looked at her kindly. "I think it was coming, and now it's arrived."

She studied his open gaze. "Yes. I knew he was ill, that he wouldn't recover."

"Yah. It's sad, girl. Very sad."

"What do I do now?"

Ed glared at the floor between his boots. "I suppose you carry on. We have a funeral to arrange, a house to run. You have a husband to wait for." He glanced at her. "That's a lot for now, isn't it?"

She nodded mournfully. "Yes. It's a lot."

CHAPTER SIXTY ONE

Her cousin Roland dropped by to see her one afternoon. It was a beautiful summer day, and she took him out into the sunny garden for tea.

"It's good to see you, cuz. Did you know there's a reward out on you?"

She smiled wryly. "There was. I've had it cancelled by the court. Zanata put that out with an agent, not with the Constables."

"What a witch." Roland emptied his tea bowl and set it on the low table in front of him. He leaned forward to prop his elbows on his thighs. "I know you've had a rough time, Julie, but it's time to start to move past that. Why not come out with me and a few of the lads? There's a dance at the Learmonth tomorrow night. Nothing fancy, just a social for a young fellow finishing university. You'd have fun and see some of our old crowd."

"Maybe." She narrowed her eyes against the glare of the sun. "I don't know if I want to get back with the crowd. My father is newly dead."

He looked at her soberly. "I know, cuz. I'm sorry, I really am. The funeral was small but grand, even if a lot of his faint-hearted friends stayed away. The ones who counted came, didn't they? You've been through a very hard time. But you don't want to hibernate. Your dear departed husband may never show up again. You can't just quit living."

That prompted a small smile. "Perhaps."

"Good. I'll pick you up."

She laughed. It felt foreign, as if she'd suddenly remembered she knew another language.

~ * * * ~

Roland escorted her into the crowded lobby of the Learmonth Resort Hotel a few evenings later. She'd dug through her closet and pulled out a dress from last season that would be acceptable for the event. She'd loved that dress when she first bought it, the green and blue jewel tones matched her eyes and the design had been perfect with its small, off the shoulder sleeves and deep neckline.

Now she didn't care. It was hard to care when everything had gone off the rails. Her father was dead. She was literally an orphan. And her husband had deserted her. Although others would say he was brave for joining the reserves and going off to fight the Emperor, it made her angry that he found it so easy to dump her and sign up to fight. She decided not to think about it tonight.

Jack Learmonth himself stood at the bottom of the stairs greeting guests as they moved through the hotel entry and up the steps to the ballroom on the second floor. He was a medium height, stocky man with long greying hair swept back from a high forehead and closely trimmed sideburns down his jaw. He wore his trademark outfit of tailored suit and custom made shoes.

The lobby of the hotel was astounding in its luxury and detailed decoration. Every corner of the ceiling had been finished in plaster cornices and framing, most of it painted with gold leaf. The walls sagged with paintings of Khandarken masters of early years and Old Empire works. The staircase swept upward in a grand curve, each stair carpeted with fine wool matting in shades of rose to wine, the banister so heavy and luxurious it had been carved in place, it was said, by master craftsmen many years ago.

Jack Learmonth was the elder now in the Learmonth family distillery empire, his son a friend of the young man celebrating graduation tonight. He laughed and joked as acquaintances moved by. When Julianne appeared, the young assistant at Learmonth's side touched his arm and spoke quietly in his ear. He nodded and moved toward her through the crowd.

"Ms Adjudicator, Julianne," he said. "I met you a long time ago, and knew your father. Let me extend my sympathies." His expression looked sincere.

"It's a little awkward, I know," he continued. "The Constables were hunting for him at the end."

She felt her face redden.

"But that doesn't change how many of us felt about him. It's a sad loss." He bowed over her hand. "It's good that you've come out tonight. A little enjoyment in the midst of your sorrow."

As she moved on with her cousin and his friends, she glanced back to see his eyes following her. "Roland, what was that about?"

"It was about how beautiful you look in that dress. And he's damned smooth, always has been."

"Do people know I'm married?" she asked worriedly.

"No. I haven't heard a word spoken about it."

"Maybe I should start spreading the news."

Her cousin stopped on the stair and turned to her. "Why? We don't know if he's ever going to show up again." He patted her hand, lying in the crook of his elbow. "Give it time. You don't have to decide tonight. We don't even have to stay long, just see some old friends, have a drink and a bit of conversation. We can leave whenever you want."

The ballroom was crowded with young people, more men than women. Roland glanced around. "Females have the advantage at these things, don't they? With so many boys born compared to girls, the girls hold all the cards at events like this. That's why I bring my cousin with me."

She had to laugh. It must be one of the few times when women held the upper hand. Even though the genetic tampering had resulted in an overabundance of male children, they still dominated society. Although that hadn't slowed Maa down. She tried not to think of Maa and whether Zanata was still at the Sanctuary. If she was there, it was a good place for her.

A band began to tune up on the corner stand, and the crowd around the bars at each end of the room grew thicker. Roland grabbed one of the last small tables available and turned to his friends. "You two get the drinks, Julianne and I will hold the table." He seated her and stood at her side, scanning the room.

The noise of conversation was exhilarating, the music starting slowly over the hum of many voices. She felt a hand on her shoulder and glanced up. Bethlehem's pale blue eyes looked down into hers.

"Beth!" She leaped to her feet and hugged her. "You're here. Oh, you look beautiful."

"Thank you. You, too. What a great dress. Are you with friends?"

Her cousin had turned around and she put her hand on his arm. "This is my cousin, Roland. Roland, this is Beth Farmer, my sister by marriage."

Roland laughed and shook hands. "Your sister by marriage. So the husband does exist."

She watched Beth's mouth firm. "Don't tease, Rollie," Julianne murmured.

Beth turned back to her. "Come over to say hello during the break. Dante and I are over there." Beth pointed across the room and moved off into the crowd.

Roland watched her leave. "Does he look like her?"

"Kind of. The same pale blue eyes and light coloured hair."

"Hmm."

She poked him. "What does that mean?"

"Nothing." The drinks arrived and the dancing started. "Do you want to dance now?"

"Give me a bit, Rollie. I need to get used to this again." They talked and watched the crowd. Roland moved off to greet a friend, and within moments Julianne felt a firm hand on her shoulder. "May I have this dance?"

She gazed up into fierce pale blue eyes. He seemed different, healthier, as if he'd been sleeping better. The sideburns were clipped and the beard was gone. She stared at his face with the square jaw and full lips compressed now in a straight line. He wore a charcoal grey suit that fit him well, showing off broad shoulders and a deep chest that tapered to a lean waist.

She blinked. *Have this dance?* He was her husband. Normally, of course she would dance with him. But this wasn't normal. She felt her eyes narrow and his mouth immediately grew hard.

Reluctantly she put her hand in his and he tugged her to her feet. The dance had just changed to a waltz when he led her onto the polished floor. The hand he laid at the small of her back seemed to burn through her dress. *Was there smoke rising from that spot?* She looked into his eyes and felt an overwhelming rush of heat. He was so attractive, so powerful, like a magnet that drew her in. He stared moodily at her mouth.

She licked her lips, and he jerked as if he'd been shot. Ah, so it wasn't just her. At least that was some comfort.

"Hello, Abe."

"Julianne," he said.

"I thought you were in the Northern Territories."

"I just got back to the City for a few days. I'll be leaving again soon."

"Yet, you come to a dance, but don't come to see me." Her chest felt too tight to breathe beneath her dress.

His gaze bore into hers. "I called at your house as soon as I arrived and managed to bathe and change my clothes. You weren't at home."

"Oh." She dropped her gaze and examined the buttons on his jacket.

"You were here," he ground out.

She glanced up. "I see."

"Who are you with?" His mouth was even tighter, if that were possible.

"I'm with Roland and a couple of his friends," she said airily. *Let him think what he would.*

His jaw bulged. "Roland, your cousin."

So he already knew. Beth must have told him. She nodded and glanced away. The music stopped, and he held her still in the middle of the dance floor.

"We'll wait for the next one," he said when she glanced up at him. "If it's all right with you."

She couldn't help a little smile at his aggravated tone, and his mouth softened.

"It's all right with me."

He nodded, watching her face.

"Were you in the fighting up north?"

"No." That seemed to irritate him again, but she felt tension ease in her breast.

"That's good. I'm glad. We've been through enough fighting."

His mouth relaxed, and his eyes sought hers. "Yes, we have, haven't we? Let's just dance." And he moved them both in time to the music. Slowly he pulled her closer, gathering her into his arms as the tune flowed over them. She laid her head on his chest, and his chin rubbed in her hair, the strands catching on his whiskers. His hand tightened at her back.

When the music ended, they had danced through the open doors onto one of the balconies in the dim light. She lifted her head and he laid his mouth over hers. It was a soft kiss, not tentative but so tender that she felt like a flower opening to the sun. When he lifted his head, he was breathing as hard as she. Warm tendrils of desire unfurled in her belly.

"I've missed you." He stared at her mouth.

Tears sprang to her eyes. "Then why did you leave?"

"That's why I've come to apologize."

"Apology not accepted!" She wiped a tear from her cheek and angrily glanced away.

"I know. I'm okay with that. I'm still sorry. It's this rage in me. I couldn't …" He shook his head. "I couldn't control it sometimes and that scared me. I've always been in control, but not this time. Not with this."

"What have I done that's so wrong?" Her voice quavered, and she tried to steady it. Her back had gone ramrod straight.

He sighed. "It's not you, Julianne."

"Then what?"

"It's me. I felt betrayed, by the Constables, by my uncle, by your father. I thought my family supported me. I thought the law prevailed in the new regime in Khandarken. I trusted all that. And it turned on me."

"I didn't turn on you." She could hardly see him for the tears in her eyes and impatiently brushed them away. "I didn't know what my father had done. I knew he was meddling with your talc mine. I'd already told you that. But I had no idea he was attacking you, or sending armed men to …"

She choked and he tugged her up against him. "It doesn't even seem like something he'd do," she mumbled against his formal shirt front. "I've tried to imagine it. It's something Zanata would do."

"I think it was her idea."

"You do?" Her head came slowly around as she stared at him. "That almost makes sense. She's so savage, and father loved her." Her throat closed up.

"Don't cry, Julianne. I can't bear it. I don't mean to make you cry."

"My father died."

His hands stilled. "He did? When?"

"A week ago. They found him lying on the ground in a lane in Old Towne. He was abandoned there like an old worn-out shoe."

"Ahh." He held her close and rocked her against his chest. "I'm sorry, honey. I'm really sorry."

She wrapped her arms around his lean waist and absorbed the comfort he offered, letting it soak into her flesh until she felt almost whole again. Yes, she loved this man. She belonged in his arms, it felt so right. And he'd treated her badly, with no respect for her feelings. Reluctantly she pulled away.

"I'm going back in now," she said and turned to the doorway.

"Can I see you before I leave?"

She slowed her pace and glanced back at her husband. "Perhaps."

CHAPTER SIXTY TWO

Abe had sent word he would come by in the evening after meetings all day at the military compound. Julianne timed it just right and was relaxing in a freshly poured bath when he arrived at the house. She didn't hurry. Beverly reported that he was impatiently pacing the entry hall as she dressed and did her hair. *Let him wait.*

The sorrow rose again in her belly. Her father had run away and died alone in an alley, and her husband had left her. *Abe thought he was the only one who'd lost something?* He could think again.

When she eventually came down the stairs, he stood to greet her and froze, his eyes pinned to the flash of thigh through the slit up the side of her tight, short skirt. She smiled but he didn't seem to notice, his gaze rising only far enough to explore the cleavage exposed by the flexible sleeveless top.

She moved forward and held out her hand. "Hello, Mr Farmer." She finally had his attention. He took her hand and held it in his, kissing the backs of her fingers.

"I know you're going to make me pay. I don't blame you." His jaw flexed and his gaze darted down for another look at the tight top. "I'm here to apologize, Julianne. I don't know if you can forgive me. I hope so." He looked around the entry hall warily. "Can we talk somewhere a little more private?"

She led him to the parlour and went to the bar in the corner. "I have some whiskey," she offered. She found another bottle under the counter. "There's brandy, also wine."

"Just come and talk to me."

She turned but didn't approach. "I don't know if I want to." She knew she was pouting like a child, but felt childish. He'd injured her, not just her feelings but her deeper emotions. She felt tears gather and tried to hold them back. She'd promised herself she wouldn't cry when she saw him this time.

"Well, I'll come there." She watched him approach, this big tough man who made her feel unimaginable things when he touched her with his hard hands or just with his pale penetrating gaze. "Come and sit with me." She allowed him to lead her to the divan.

Settling beside her, he placed her hand on his thigh, holding the fingers there with his warm palm. His leg was hard under the dress pants he wore. She'd forgotten how his body felt, the hard muscles and taut planes of him. She couldn't look at him as he began to talk, his voice low, a little hoarse.

"Julianne, I'm sure you know why I was at the Sanctuary. We'd been in a firefight, several fights." His voice died off for a second and she looked up to see him gazing vacantly out the dark window.

"Beth told me. She told me about your uncle and how you were wounded."

"Oh." He looked at her hand on his leg. "Things had been going sideways even before the attack. That was sort of the culmination of events. Then we just had to fight to get back home."

"I know."

When he finally turned to her his eyes were wet and hot on her face. "I love you." His mouth was flat. "I love you, Julianne. And I think you love me. I'm hoping you do. I want you to come home."

She opened her mouth to reply, and he covered it with his own. His kiss was fierce and possessive, his tongue an invader against hers that lit a fire wherever he touched. She felt his hand on her breast, squeezing her through the stretch top of this silly dress she'd chosen just to tease him. She heard his heavy breathing in her ear.

She pulled back and he froze, slowly withdrawing his hand. Her belly ached at the loss. He sipped at her lips, then lifted his head to eye her warily. "I leave early tomorrow morning, well before sunup. We're going back north for an all-out assault. I won't be able to see you again before I go."

His voice cracked with desperation. "I want you, Julianne. I know I don't deserve you."

She reached to place her fingers over his mouth to stop the words. "Don't, Abe. Don't."

"Can we not get past this? I don't know what else to do or say." His eyes had become bleak, his mouth turned down. "When I get back, can I come to see you? Are you pregnant?" His voice was suddenly hopeful.

She wrapped her arms around his neck and stifled a giggle against his chest. "No."

"Oh, well, I thought ..."

"I know. You keep asking me that."

His arms tightened. "I love you so much." It was just a whisper but she heard and kissed his throat.

"I love you, too."

He stilled. "You do?"

She lifted her head. "Will you come upstairs with me?"

"Uh." His face turned bright red. "What about... I mean, you have staff here."

"They know we're married."

His gaze was desperate and wild. "Don't take me up there then refuse me, Julianne. I couldn't bear it."

"No," she took his hand. "I couldn't bear it either."

He grabbed her up in his arms and pulled her tight against him, breathing in her scent. "I need you."

"Then come upstairs."

He laughed and set her carefully on the floor. "I'll come."

Something foreign leapt in her belly, excitement, anticipation. She didn't deserve him either.

She darted through the door to find Beverly sitting over a cup of tea with Ed in the kitchen. "We're just going up for the night," she said airily, hoping they wouldn't notice her bright cheeks.

Her housekeeper gave her a wry smile. "Are you now? Well, have a good sleep."

Ed barked a laugh and Julianne had to grin. "We're married. You know that."

"Yes, my dear, we do. I'm glad he's come for you." Their kind smiles nearly started the tears all over again. She nodded and withdrew, closing the door softly behind her. When she turned to walk across the entry, Abe was already there, his gaze pinned to her face.

He raised his brows but she just took his hand and guided him toward the staircase. "This way."

Nodding, he took the steps lightly behind her as she led the way. How could such a big man move so quietly? It was one of the things she loved about him.

As they reached the second story landing, she heard Ed's heavy tread across the floor of the great hall to lock the front door. A sense of calm descended on her. She was finally home, and although Father was gone, she'd known before she left that he was ill and wouldn't be returning to her. But Zanata was banished to the northern wilds with a reward on her head, and Abe was here, with her.

"This is my room." A wave of shyness overcame her. Her room was almost the same as it had been when she was small. She had never allowed it be redecorated, clinging to anything that reminded her of when her mother was still alive. Now she examined it with suddenly critical eyes and saw it as a little girl's chamber.

Abe stepped inside and glanced around in the lamp's low light. What must he think? Yet when he looked back at her, his face was tender yet determined. Ah yes, he hadn't forgotten why they were here.

Nor had she. Something curled with longing in her belly, and she moved toward him, touching the front of his suit jacket, smoothing her hands under the material and up his solid chest as she slipped the garment off his shoulders.

CHAPTER SIXTY THREE

Abe stared out over the vast sodden plain, where a lonely tent stood in the distance, a bedraggled flag hanging from a pole on the roof and two mules grazing nearby. He shifted impatiently. He'd been waiting with his men for three days, fighting off the rain and clouds of biting insects. The tent had been erected last night, a day after the band of Emperor's men arrived at this lonely field.

He and his men had watched. They were wet and tired. They'd been sleeping in shifts, lying down wherever they could in the clothes they were wearing. Rest was hard to come by. But they'd waited.

Right on the border, their instructions were specifically to stay on Khandarken soil. Abe consulted his positioning monitor. They were well inside the boundary, and that tent was on the other side. He couldn't argue with that. Pressing the button to register their location, he put the device back in his pack.

Soon the Emperor's troops began organizing at the edge of the plain, something was about to happen. He scanned the field with his scope as they left in a single line heading west, still inside Legitamia. He heard the noise of their passage through the woods in the distance and sent two scouts to follow and report back.

Would this skirmish ever get underway? This was what he'd been after, a chance to fight. And now it was here. He wasn't so anxious to get going as he once had been. The time with Julianne had put him in a different place, given him a different perspective.

She softened him. She soothed him. She damn well excited him.

He had gazed around that cozy little bedroom and then down at his wife's face. Her expression had been eager but hesitant, as if she didn't trust what they had, what he would do. He couldn't blame her. Things had been rocky between them from the moment they first met. What chance did they have to court, to get to know each other, when they'd been running for safety at every turn or fighting for their lives?

She'd wrestled with the buttons hidden under the placket on his formal shirt as he glanced around. Her room gave up a lot of information that he'd not had before. The lace edging of the bed cover and bolster cases was pretty but worn. A line of objects along the top of her dresser included a small ribbon bow tattered on the ends, some rocks, one opal earring. He wondered how old she'd been when her mother died.

He helped her with the buttons, then took a handful of the low cut stretchy dress. "Does this come off over your head?"

She blushed. "It just pulls off."

He felt his ears get warm. "You mean, if I just tug on it …"

She laughed up at him impudently. "Why don't you try?"

"I'm afraid to." He gazed at it for a moment then took hold of the fabric over her breasts and pulled it down. The material slid to her waist and he looked his fill. His hands moved to cover her and feel the texture of her skin. Just as he remembered, small and firm, plump in his palms. Better than he remembered.

He glanced at the bed. It looked so proper and girlish with a prim headboard, three bolsters fluffed and stacked at the end. It was going to be a challenge to fit his long frame onto it. He'd grinned at the thought.

"What?" She gave him a curious look.

"That's a pretty small bed."

"Oh." She glanced doubtfully behind her. "I see."

"Don't worry. We'll be fine," he hastened to add, just in case she thought to change her mind. "I guarantee it."

Lifting her in his arms he laid her on the cover, then bent to pull his clothes off, hanging his suit on a nearby chair. "Let me help you with this." He took hold of the dress pooled at her waist and peeled it over her hips and down her legs.

She was beautiful, small and shapely, her body rounded to fit against him. Now she lay with only her smalls on, and he hooked a finger into the stretch linen around her hips. "We don't need these, do we?"

Her gaze shot up to his as she made a grab for them with her fingers.

"Come on, honey. I want to see you again. Let me," he'd coaxed and gave another tug. "Let me see you."

They'd made love on that little bed in her upstairs room. It had been magnificent. He moved restlessly as his body reacted to the vision in his head. Her stormy eyes had challenged him to a battle and he'd been up for a fight. Her soft pouty mouth drew him in the instant he kissed her.

His memory of that night faded as he heard the roar of a laser gun and jerked into awareness, glancing to his left. A group of the Emperor's dispossessed were advancing toward their position, flashing the undergrowth with fire to clear the brush and kill anything in their path. At the same time he got a beltlink message from his scouts, the army was inside the borders of Khandarken.

He motioned to his men and quickly adjusted their position. They had laser guns but were armed with old fashioned weapons as well. Abe took aim and fired. One of the Emperor's men in the lead of the column keeled over and lay still. The others froze as they probed the forest with their gaze, trying to pinpoint the enemy's position. Then the dispossessed let go with another laser rush and Abe and his troop took aim. Three more men fell, another staggered before tumbling to his knees.

The dispossessed were nervous now, glancing this way and that, not sure where the firing was coming from or what kind of weapons they were up against. Every time they let loose a laser blast, more of their men died.

Abe chambered another bullet and waited.

It had been Dante's idea. When fighting lasers, it was hard to fight back effectively without leaving his men open to disastrous injury. He had snipers with plasmas to cover them during any battle, of course.

But with old weaponry and metal shells, they could fire whenever the roar of the laser sounded, and the gunshots were almost inaudible in the din. Laser fire was deadly but didn't have the range of the old rifles with their jacketed rounds. Especially if the men using them had skill and accurate aim.

The Emperor's troops fell back and huddled for a consultation. Their leader soon barked an order, and they turned and advanced in a V shaped formation, firing a ferocious assault over a wide range. They slowly gained ground and marched with more confidence.

As they advanced, Abe ordered his men to divide and retreat, holding fire on two fronts. They were soon organized deep in the trees, ready for the next assault.

The enemy approached and the laser flashed through the undergrowth, getting closer all the time to their location. When they were so close it seemed too nerve-wracking to wait, Abe finally gave his signal.

At the next blast of laser from the Emperor's troops, his men opened fire right behind it. Men fell, their weapons flying from lifeless fingers to scatter on the ground.

There was sudden silence. Then the dispossessed moved slowly to the rear through the burnt landscape, finally fading back through the trees. They could be seen marching fast along the trail, returning across the border from where they came.

As the noise retreated in the distance, Abe turned to look across the wet plain. The colonel's camp was struck, the gear loaded onto mules. They would be travelling north as well, following the ragged line of troops heading into Legitamia. They would walk away without paying for the assault on Khandarken sovereignty.

Abe made a sudden decision, leaving his soldiers in position and taking two men with him, Slim who'd been involved in his fighting arts training, and a second man. Moving swiftly, they ran across the edge of the plain under the cover of brush. They were almost at the camp when the last boxes were loaded onto mules and tied down. They ran harder.

The dispossessed had broken ranks and were going fast for the mountain track, leaving the colonel vulnerable. The flag was the last thing down, the colonel waited beside his mule while his attendant folded it carefully for storage in the satchel. That decision was his undoing.

Abe took a leap and dove low, catching the man behind the knees and knocking him down before placing his hand at the neck and squeezing until the colonel was unconscious. Slim was right behind. He hit the enlisted man in the back with his full weight behind an outstretched fist, knocking the wind out of him. Then he twisted and kicked him in the jaw. The man sagged to the ground, out cold.

They hadn't made a sound. Unaware, the dispossessed continued onward to disappear around a bend in the trail. Quickly they tied the men up, threw them over the backs of the mules and traipsed south through the trees to Abe's waiting troop.

Abe and his men delayed until dusk, looking for any further action before abandoning their position and heading toward camp, carrying their wounded. It was early morning when they finally arrived. He escorted his two injured men to the medic's tent. One man was in a bad way, the laser fire had hit his face and caught his tunic on fire. They'd managed to put the fire out but the damage was extensive. The second soldier had a scorch mark on his leg.

Ooievaar greeted them and waved them to the cook's tent for a meal before they bedded down. He caught Abe back. "Who is this Colonel of the Emperor?"

Abe shrugged. "We don't know. He isn't talking other than to give his name, Major Nida, but his men left him there, didn't wait to see if he was coming. Nor did they come back for him once they found he wasn't with them. Not sure what that says about him or the army in general."

Ooievaar grinned. "Doesn't say anything good, does it? We'll see what we can get out of him. By the way, there's been some action near Eight Mile."

Abe's ears perked up. "I was just there a month ago."

Ooievaar paused as he moved off toward his tent. "You were? Tell me about it."

He described his observations of the small fishing village. "What kind of action? It's damned hard to get through the mountains there along the coast."

"Yah. Our scout says they're coming by boat, using the fish boats and crews to land inside the borders."

Abe moved his jaw sideways. "It would be easy enough to do. The town used to be Legitamian, they speak a hybrid language and I'm sure sympathies go in both directions."

Ooievaar thought that over. "I would have guessed it was in Adar Silva that sympathies go in both directions. That's where the Emperor lived, and his father and grandfather before him."

"Yah. But they've seen the oppression first hand and fought hard to get rid of them. Legitamia has taken these men in, and anyone who still follows Carlton has gone there with him."

Ooievaar nodded. "Get some sleep. We'll talk later."

He followed his men to the cook tent. The lentils and smoked pork were hot and welcome, the toast crisp and the tea steaming.

When he finally lay down on his pallet, he felt his spine click as the muscles relaxed. That's what he got for three days in the bush, sleeping in his coat on rocky ground. He sighed and rolled to his side. Just as he drifted off to sleep a vision of Julianne rose in his mind, the top of her dress tugged to her waist, her pink nipples jutting up for his attention.

He had pulled that dress right off her and placed his hands on those beautiful round hips. When he put his mouth… He smiled in his sleep.

~ * * * ~

The following days were mind numbing. March to the marshalling area, board an air transport, debark in another cleared patch. March to a new field of battle, engage in another skirmish.

The village of Eight Mile was awash with fish boats, most of them Khandarken but many from farther north. Everyone proclaimed their lack of allegiance to the Empire. Abe thought he'd laugh out loud if he heard one more fisherman who was adamantly loyal to their country. Whatever plan Carlton may have had for a fish boat invasion, it had come to nothing in the final execution.

His beltlink beeped and he glanced down. He had been summoned to the army depot which was set up in the carter's stables at the end of the main street. The same stables where he and Julianne had left their mules when they'd arrived in this little town weeks ago. He turned and headed in that direction. Ooievaar was still with the army headquarters near Wymark, where the main action was continuing as they tried to pry the village of Discovery out of the grip of the Emperor's troops. A new fellow, a young lieutenant, was in charge here at Eight Mile.

Abe ducked into the stables and waited as a flurry of messages was passed out to runners. The lieutenant waved him forward, but was interrupted again when his voicelink barked. His assistant grabbed it and both men leaned forward to listen and watch the message unfold. The sound emitted was garbled confusion, but the lieutenant nodded as if he understood, then nodded again as the decoded instructions flashed on the screen.

"Okay." He waved Abe to a chair. "That's just been confirmed. They're sending you home first thing tomorrow. It has calmed down here, and we're leaving a body of men to keep an eye on it. But there is no invasion in Eight Mile or along the coast. Dante Regiment sent word specifically. You're to go out on the first aircart back to Wymark. Then south from there."

Saluting Abe, he added, "Thank you for your help here, sir. It's been much appreciated. Hope to see you again." The lieutenant grinned. "But not in these exact circumstances."

Abe had to laugh and shook the man's hand. "You've been a great commander. But I'm glad to be going home."

Next morning the aircart took him as far as Wymark station. The platform was swarming with reservists heading home, all wearing camo outfits and carrying packs.

The pass Abe held was valid for forty-eight hours and would take him on transit anywhere in Khandarken. He laughed to himself. He lived in the absolute opposite end of the country and couldn't get there in forty-eight hours if he tried.

But it didn't matter. He was heading for the City and would start there to rebuild his life.

CHAPTER SIXTY FOUR

When Julianne opened the front entry, Abe was standing impatiently on the threshold wearing an army uniform and carrying a pack and a small square parcel.

Abe? She couldn't believe he was here. She'd received a couple of voicelink messages from him, but she'd never actually talked to him. She just knew he was coming soon but not when.

She stepped forward and he swooped her up with one arm to hold her tight to his chest. She buried her face against his shoulder and felt his jaw pressed to the side of her head. He inhaled deeply and his chest expanded. She clung to him, her heart racing.

"You didn't say when you'd get here." She tried to appear annoyed but was too excited to see him. "It would have been nice to know."

He laughed and swatted her on the bum. "I told you what I could. Besides, I didn't know exactly when I'd get here." His hair had grown again, a riot of pale blond curls. But his cheeks were shaven leaving the long sideburns trimmed against the planes of his jaw.

She placed her hand at the back of his neck to anchor herself to him. "I've missed you." Tears welled in her eyes. She had been a bit melancholy lately and found she cried easily. Beverly consoled her that it wasn't unusual, she'd just lost her father and her husband was off to fight the Emperor.

Abe's face softened, and he laid his lips carefully over hers. "I missed you, too. Don't cry," he said. "It breaks my heart when you cry." He backed her through the doorway. "You might want to let me in. Your neighbours will be gawking if you stand here kissing me all afternoon."

She laughed. "Yes, you'd better come in."

He put his pack on the floor by the door and put the parcel in her arms. "This is for you. It's delicate, be careful."

She hefted the parcel and carried it into the dining room to lay it on the long table. She glanced back at his face to see his pale eyes gleaming and a faint smile on his mouth. "What is it?"

"You'll have to open it to find out." His mouth quirked in a little smile.

She found a pair of scissors in a side drawer and snipped the wrapping along the seam, folding the bark cloth back to reveal a stack of paper in various colours neatly aligned and bound with flat ribbon. "Oh, is it really …?" Excitement bubbled up at the sight.

"As you see," he said. "It's origami paper."

"Did you get it in the north?

"Yes."

She knew her eyes were shining. "You got it at Wymark?"

"Right."

"It's the only place they make this." She felt a little breathless as she ran her fingers lovingly over the top sheets. "No one else in all of Khandarken makes this cotton paper. It's the best for intricate designs, and when I'm working with damp sheets it holds the folds better than any other kind."

"So I've heard."

"Oh, Abe." She threw herself at him and he caught her up in his arms. "Thank you so much. I haven't been able to get any for the longest time."

"Ah, honey. You're more than welcome." He rocked her gently against him and took a deep breath.

"Abe. You must want a bath and a chance to clean up after your long journey. Let me show you upstairs."

"Okay." He watched her eyes. "I've already seen upstairs."

She felt herself blush. "I know, but … Anyway, come on." She led him into her father's chamber. "I've cleaned this up and put away some things. So we can use this room. There's more space and … it's just better."

The look he gave her was so gentle, she felt the tears gather again. Impatiently she brushed them away. "You get cleaned up and then come to the dining room. I'll tell Beverly you're here so she can get dinner on the table."

When he came downstairs a half hour later, he was wearing a clean camo uniform. He gestured at his pants. "I don't have any civilian clothing with me. Sorry."

"You look fine." Julianne felt herself warm as she took him in, all long length and muscled breadth of him. She remembered what he looked like, what he felt like under that army issue cloth. A tingle rippled down her spine.

They had a lot to talk about. She didn't know if she would move to Farmer Holdings or he would come here, but for now they were together.

"Dinner's ready. Beverley just waited to serve until you came down."

Abe smiled at Beverly, and she watched her housekeeper smile back as her cheeks went bright pink. *Well, for heaven's sake. My own housekeeper?* She looked back at Abe. Yes, even Beverly was susceptible to his charm.

She felt herself relax as the young maid removed the soup bowls and put plates of sablefish pasta in front of them. The aroma was enough to make her mouth water, and Abe leaned forward to take a deep appreciative breath.

"This smells absolutely mouth-watering. I can't wait to try it. If you knew what we ate up there ..." His smile was lazy and satisfied as he took his first bite. "It's very nice to be here."

He ate all his meal, but Julianne could only manage a few bites from her plate. All she wanted to do was get her husband upstairs and undressed, but dinner dragged on. She made a moue with her mouth. *What is my problem?*

Next came the salad. Beverly had out done herself, adding summer greens and small nuts along with astro fruit and a mustard dressing. It was delicious, and Abe cleaned his plate. The maid returned with dainty bowls and saucers for tea. Julianne stared. Beverly had dug out the good china, square shaped with rounded corners, gold leaf trim and design. They never used this stuff. It was from the old Legitamia, irreplaceable and washed by hand with great care.

Abe sipped his tea as if he had all the time in the world and graciously accepted the glass of brandy placed in front of him. Then came chocolate cinnamon rounds and small dishes of fruit compote and gingerbreads. Julianne huffed to herself. Now her housekeeper had gone too far. *What was Beverly thinking?*

Her tea had cooled and she took a few more swallows before replacing her bowl carefully on the square saucer. "Well," she began as she finally saw the end of dinner in sight. "That's …"

She never finished her sentence. A heavy banging thundered at the front door. Beverly appeared from the hallway, staring with apprehension at the panel, Ed following close behind. He straightened his cuffs and reached a hand to open it just as the door jolted open. Ed was knocked backward, his head smashing against the wall as he fell. He lay silent on the tile floor of the entry hall.

Julianne turned to see Abe rising slowly from his chair as two men burst in, the burly one with thick shoulders and deep chest standing over Ed as the second taller man stood back to let a woman enter before him.

CHAPTER SIXTY FIVE

Zanata! Julianne couldn't believe her eyes. *Her stepmother, back in the City?* There was a Constable's warrant for her arrest and a fair-sized price on her head! She gazed wide-eyed as the woman swept regally into the entry and the fellow behind her closed the door with a decisive thud.

Abe moved forward, but Julianne stopped him with a hand to his chest. "This is my stepmother," she said low. "And these must be her bodyguards."

She turned back to have another look. Zanata hadn't changed, a person would never know she was ill. Her skin was clear and smooth, her large eyes dark, the lids at half-mast seeming to issue an invitation to any man she encountered. She'd painted her mouth a dark red, and the sultry expression was like a magnet to most males. Julianne whipped around to see Abe's reaction. He was staring at Zanata, his eyes narrowed.

Not him too! Is my own husband attracted to this deadly woman?

Abe stepped around her, one hand motioning Julianne back while he reached to help Ed. He grabbed his arm as her houseman rose awkwardly and stood swaying in the entry.

Zanata smiled like a predator in sight of fresh prey. "Who's this?" Her teeth were white, gleaming. *Like a shark.* But that's not what men thought when they saw her. Julianne examined her husband's expression again.

Abe assured himself Ed was steady on his feet and turned to the two men. "Well, boys. Are you here for a visit, or is this business?" Julianne blanched. Would the men take that as a challenge?

Zanata raised her eyebrow provocatively as the burly bodyguard turned to Abe. "Who are you?" His voice was deep, rough, but Abe just smiled.

"I'm Abe Farmer, Julianne's husband." She felt a wonderful sense of satisfaction unfurl in her breast. *Yes.* She wasn't alone any more when she dealt with Zanata. She was married and had her husband beside her.

"Her husband?" Zanata moved sinuously across the floor. *Like a snake.* She slid her pointed red fingernail up the placket of Abe's shirt to his throat and smiled up at him. "Glad to meet you. I didn't know she was married."

Julianne watched in horror as Abe smiled back. He gently seized her hand and held it in his. "Nice to meet you, too. Julianne has told me all about you."

"Has she?" Zanata's face turned toward her stepdaughter in surprise. "What has she said?"

"That you're charming and lovely to look at."

Julianne thought she'd gag on the spot.

"Come in and have a comfortable seat," he added, motioning to Beverly. The housekeeper quickly gathered together some bowls on the tea tray.

Zanata waved her hand languidly. "Not tea, Beverly. I think the occasion calls for something stronger. Perhaps the brandy. We should sit in the parlour."

Abe's smile would have blinded the sun. "Excellent notion. We can toast our marriage. Julianne, help your stepmama into the parlour."

Julianne tried to suppress her dismay, but Zanata's face showed satisfaction as she stalked ahead of her toward the parlour door.

Abe turned and a sudden a flurry of action erupted behind her. Feet and fists flew, bodies thudded into walls. The door smashed open and the burly bodyguard flew through, landing on the stone threshold. As he tried to rise, Abe's heel kicked to his throat and his head flew sharply back. He banged into the door frame and lay still.

Zanata whirled around. "What …"

Before she could take a step, Abe's fist shot out to nail the second man in the centre of his chest. The bodyguard's arms sailed up and out to the sides from the impact, and he gasped raggedly for breath. He staggered sideways but didn't go down. One more kick, landing right between the legs, and he fell to his knees. Abe stepped forward and pressed a spot in his neck until his eyes rolled back in his head and he slumped over, lying motionless.

Zanata stood with her dark red mouth open, staring at her men prostrate on the floor. The heavy one stirred and Abe leaned to silence him again with a slashing motion of his hand to the side of the neck.

"Now, madam." Abe's face was stern, his lips a straight line. "That will be all for tonight. Sit right there in that chair and don't move or say another word. Beverly, could you please call the Constables?"

Abe glanced at Beverly's husband. "Ed, you sit down here. You're going to need a few minutes to recover. Julianne, where is my voicelink? I think a call to Dante Regiment would be in order."

Julianne's heart was still hammering from adrenaline, but she couldn't help smiling. She felt triumphant, victorious, as if she'd created this chaos herself.

Zanata shot out of the chair. "Don't you dare!"

Abe pushed her and she sat. "Not another word." He pressed at a spot at the side of her throat and she began to sway in the chair. "I'll knock you out if I have to."

His face was tight, his mouth grim.

Julianne felt like clapping, but she was too unsteady. It had been like a rollercoaster ride since the moment her stepmother entered the house. She didn't know what they were here for, but the two bodyguards seemed as dangerous as wild creatures and Zanata was always unpredictable. She'd never seen her defeated. Was she finally going to be rid of that wicked woman? It didn't seem possible. But there was the warrant on her and the Constables would have to respond.

They were quick to arrive. The entry way was suddenly crowded with men wearing heavy gear and exuding more testosterone. They arrested Zanata and the two bodyguards, although one of them was still not moving. Julianne feared Abe might have killed him.

"We'll post one of our men outside your door for the rest of the night, sir."

"Is that necessary?" Abe asked.

"Just a precaution," the Constable replied. "We've been hunting her for some time. She must have had help evading us. And to get into the City without detection is pretty difficult."

Julianne headed up the stairs, herded closely by Beverly, as the men dealt with the officials. Abe was still on his voicelink when she left.

CHAPTER SIXTY SIX

Thanks for letting me know, Abe. I'll tell Father. He'll be pleased." Dante Regiment's voice was gravelly, as if he'd just been wakened.

"Not sure how she got into the City without alerting the authorities."

"Hmm. There are several ways that I know about. And there are probably more that I'm not aware of. But I'll send out an alert to try to tighten up security."

"Okay. Give my love to Beth. We'll talk soon." Abe clicked his voicelink off and tucked it in his pocket. The adrenaline was still running high and his hands shook.

Catching Zanata satisfied a huge obligation he owed to his new brother. Dante Regiment had married his sister and protected Farmer Holdings while Abe was injured and out of communication. He was indebted to him for that.

Paulo Regiment, the General, had suffered a serious loss in the death of his eldest son Virgil. And that death lay at the feet of Julianne's step mother. He'd paid that debt.

He rubbed his hands over his face and took a deep breath. By the graves, he was glad it was over. He just needed to see his wife right now, but he didn't want to frighten her. The adrenaline rush was still waxing strong.

By the time he appeared upstairs in the bedroom doorway, Beverly had finished getting her ready for the night. Her dark hair was brushed till it shone, and her pretty night dress with the little ruffled pocket covered all the parts of her that he longed to see.

Startled, she jumped up from her dressing table at the sight of him. "Oh, you're here." She fumbled with the lace on her gown and smiled tentatively. "What happened down there?"

"How do you mean?" His eyebrows rose in a quizzical expression as his gaze followed her fingers round and round that little breast pocket.

"What did the Constables say?"

He glanced up at her worried expression. "They arrested her, put restraints on her wrists and ankles and took her away. The bodyguards also. The big fellow was under warrant for suspected murder, so she really picks her sidekicks."

Her smile wobbled. "Yes, she does."

Abe's gaze sharpened. "You don't have to worry, not now. She'll be put in jail. But you'll have to testify at her trial. That might be difficult for you."

At her nod, he took her hands and pressed them gently between his. "I'm glad to be here with you."

"Oh." She pressed her forehead against his chest. "I'm glad too. I was afraid they were going to arrest you."

"Me?" Confusion stirred in his chest.

"I don't think that bodyguard is going to live."

Abe stilled and watched her eyes. "He might not," he admitted guardedly.

"Oh, no. What will they do to you?"

"Nothing. They took the fellow away. If he survives the night, they'll charge him." He waited, knowing there would be more she had to say, things he didn't want to hear. How she couldn't be associated with someone as violent as that, someone who had killed a man right in her own home.

"That's good," she breathed against his throat.

He paused for a moment. "It is?" He could hardly believe it.

"Yes. You saved me again. And I've been waiting for you."

"Yah. Waiting." His arms folded hungrily around her.

She felt wonderful pressed against him, the shape of her body exciting him, making him uncomfortably warm. She smelled like soap, sunshine and her own captivating perfume. He breathed her in. *When did I become addicted to how she smells?* On that long run to freedom, that's when. And he was hooked, he couldn't get enough of her.

"Come to bed," he said urgently, his voice hoarse. His erection pushed against her belly. "It's been a long time since I was here last."

"I know," she murmured.

He moved forward with his body till the backs of her thighs pressed against the mattress. Then his mouth descended to cover hers, the pressure firm, her taste temptation itself. She opened her mouth and he sank into the depths, his tongue caressing hers and running along the edges of her even teeth. "Open up for me," he whispered.

A long time later, he lifted his mouth and began to undo his shirt, easing each button free one by one. Her gaze followed his fingers. When she glanced up at him, her mouth curved in a slow smile. "Are you teasing me?"

He laughed softly as his gut clenched with need. "Maybe. I'm hoping I've got your attention."

"Oh, you've got my attention." When she began work on his belt buckle, his fingers moved faster. By the time she started on the fastener of his pants, he was tugging her night dress up, lifting it slowly above her hips to bunch at her waist. He looked his fill while she stood with hands arrested at his waist.

"You're beautiful," he breathed, taking in the pale, creamy skin of her belly and legs, the triangle of black curls at the top of her thighs. "Just beautiful. I thought of you every night that I was away." His breath caught in his throat and he tumbled her onto the bed. "I can't wait."

His hands shook as he smoothed them up her skin, the adrenaline rush over and reaction setting in. He needed her now, right now.

"Please don't make me wait." He urged the night dress higher, tugging it over her head, and there she was, naked and his. His fingers found her wet and ready between her legs and he shakily raised himself above her. Guiding his entrance, he tried to hold back yet had no will to wait. He pushed his way in, heard her gasp beneath him. Focussing on her mouth, those pouting lips, he pressed further, pressed home. She welcomed him, rising up to meet his thrust, moving faster and faster in answer to his movements until she gripped both hands at his lower back and held him tight inside as she contracted around him.

And then he came in a mighty rush.

Abe collapsed at her side, wrapped his fingers around her breast and fell asleep.

~ * * * ~

"Did I sleep very long?"

Julianne turned her head to gaze straight into those pale blue eyes. "Not long. About ten minutes." The lamp was turned low but she still saw the rush of blood that turned his cheeks red.

"I'm sorry." The sheets rustled as he rolled toward her. "It always gets me like that. When the fight is over, the adrenaline rush wipes me out."

She leaned up to him and laid her lips against his mouth. "Does that mean you might want to do this again?"

"Oh, honey. Do I ever." He bound her in his arms and laughed, rolling her against his chest. "I've missed you so much. Even when times were bad on the trail, you made me laugh."

"I don't remember it that way."

He glanced at her sideways. "No?"

"You got really grumpy along the trail, as I recall."

His ears went pink. "Well, yah. That's because..."

"Because what?"

He lay back and glared at the ceiling. "Because I was horny and I couldn't have you."

"That makes you grumpy?"

He gazed cautiously over at her. "Are you teasing me?"

She giggled into his shoulder. "Maybe."

He swatted her bum. "Just for that, I'm going to make love to you again. "

"Oh, good."

He put back his head and bellowed a laugh. When he finally stopped chuckling, he kissed her, such a tender kiss. "I love you Julianne. Don't ever forget."

CHAPTER SIXTY SEVEN

Abe threw one more kick, and Loyal Hawker went reeling across the mat. Chest heaving, Abe held up his hands in a signal they were finished. "That's it. You're getting so much better. You must have been working pretty hard on your training while I was away."

The facility where Abe trained with his cohorts was located on the outskirts of Deep Creek near the transit station. He was in town with Julianne at the moment, staying at their townhouse near the downtown core.

His cousin grinned and heaved himself off the floor. His pale curly hair and light blue eyes were an almost exact replica of Abe's. They could have been twins. "I admit I've been trying to get better. It's humiliating to get thrown to the ground by a younger man."

Abe laughed. He'd been unaware he had a cousin until his return from the north with Julianne in tow a few months back. That's when Beth informed him their Uncle Jade had been married and his son Loyal had been in touch at Holdings. Upon comparing notes one night they'd discovered, among other things, that Loyal was the elder by four months. He was also an only child, so seemed very taken with the idea of having cousins.

Now he wiped his face with a towel and slung it across his shoulder. "I have to be on the road, so I'd better get moving. Thank you for the workout, and I'm flattered you think I've improved."

Abe nodded. "You're getting good. You could compete soon, maybe this winter. But think of it as an insurance policy in your back pocket. You spend a lot of time out in the territories, you need some way to defend yourself. This is as good as any."

He thumped his cousin on the shoulder and watched Loyal head off to the showers. He was starting to like this man, although he still felt cautious around him. He hated that he was so distrustful, but that's who he'd become over the last year – a hard, untrusting, suspicious man. He shook his head and glanced toward the doorway at a sound in the street. A hydro truck or maybe a military transport.

Sure enough, within minutes the Chief Constable walked through the door. Abe smiled. Here was someone he did trust.

"Cownden, good to see you. I've been waiting, just got warmed up."

Lanser laughed and hitched his duffel higher on his shoulder. "Great to see you, Abe. You're looking well, better than the last time we got together."

Abe nodded. "Feeling better too."

"I'm glad. Those were some tough times. We're just lucky you survived. Anyway …" He examined the workout room. "This looks like a good facility. I've been here before but …"

"It's changed. I know. I bought it and moved a few things around."

Cownden's gaze flashed back to his face. "You bought it. Good idea. Are you going to run a school here? Fighting arts training?"

Abe shrugged. "I don't know if I'll go that far. But someone will. We need to train more men, and we need to be organized about it. I do quite a bit at Farmerville, the dispossessed are always keen to learn more."

"You and your dispossessed. They're a good source of help for you, aren't they? More people should look at them that way. So, I'll get changed. I've been looking forward to this. It's been a while."

Three hours later the men were sitting at lunch in a nearby restaurant. It was full of businessmen and shopkeepers talking over their meat and lentils, many of whom had greeted Abe when they entered. One of them had obviously recognized Lanser and was eyeing him cautiously as he ate, making comments to his table partner.

"He's recognized the Chief Constable," Abe observed and took a bite of llama steak. "It's causing him some discomfort to find you here."

Cownden laughed. "And well it might. He's probably got a guilty conscience. It's something I've noticed over time. The more extreme the reaction, the more likely they have something to hide."

Abe grinned. "Makes sense. Thus my obvious ease in spending time with you."

Cownden's eye's twinkled. "But only lately, so I'd guess that marriage has straightened you up and sorted out your difficulties with the law."

Abe threw back his head and gave a guffaw of laughter. "Good one. I'll remember that. Although speaking of difficulties with the law ..."

Cownden's face was suddenly cold sober, his neck a dull red. "I know, Abe. And I'm working on it. It causes me no end of embarrassment. I don't have much more information than I did when you were first attacked along the Southern Highway.

"The look of that scorch mark on your scooter and the thought of what might have happened makes my blood run cold. I've got an official version, of course. I've set up a commission that is doing a thorough investigation, going through all the channels to glean as much information as we can. You already know that, you've been part of it. Assistant Chief

Constable Duncan, as you know, is the head of that exercise.

"We're also doing an audit on the Constabulary as a whole. That's going to be a lot of work and will some take months. But it has to be done. Yours is not the only instance we're working with, there's trouble somewhere in the ranks and we have to find it."

"Is that what brings you to Deep Creek today?" Abe's gaze was keen.

"You mean other than to have a go at you on the mats? I'm here to meet with Governor Maude. I'm travelling to all the territories. With the Emperor at work in the north, General Regiment tells me there are stirrings across the Jirani border to the west as well, not necessarily to support the Emperor's claim but just to cause trouble.

"The Constables are under more pressure than ever to keep order, and the Governors need help. We have to work something out to support the military. It's going to be a busy time." His smile was no more than a baring of teeth.

~ * * * ~

Abe watched his wife take another bite of salad. Her mouth closed over the fork and he felt a sudden jolt in his belly. He glanced back at his plate, but his appetite had suddenly disappeared. He didn't want his meal right now. He wanted his wife.

Putting his utensils down, he braced his elbows on the table and steepled his fingers, trying to bring his attention to other things. "How did it go with the artist group today?"

Her face flushed lightly, and her smile came and went. The jolt to his belly intensified. "It went really well. I met with the head artist, Mr Cobb-Jones. He's a master origamist and he's been wanting to set up a school programme, he told me. We'd work on it together as partners.

Abe nodded encouragingly. "You must be pleased, to be asked to work as his partner." He struggled to keep his attention on the topic as her smile widened. Her mouth drove him crazy, those beautiful pouting rosy lips. He wanted to devour her right here on the dining room table.

"… so we'll meet once a week."

That yanked his attention back to the conversation. "Who will meet once a week?"

She blinked. "Mr Cobb-Jones and I, plus his assistant."

"How will you meet once a week, if you're living at Farmer Holdings?"

"Pardon?" She seemed taken aback by his sharp tone.

"I just mean, are you planning to live here in Deep Creek for this project? Then you'll visit Holdings, but stay here?"

"No." She gave him a sideways look. "Did you want me to stay here?"

"No." He rose and moved around the table, taking her hand. "I want you with me. If I'm here, I want you here. If I'm at Holdings, I want you there."

She smiled, so sunny he caught his breath. "Perfect," she breathed. "Because that's what I want too."

"Thank God." The pressure in his chest eased and he crushed her lips under his. A long time later he lifted his head because he had stopped breathing entirely. "I've had enough dinner."

She giggled. "I thought you liked my cooking."

"I do! I do. I'll have more of it later. Right now I'm suddenly very tired and need my bed. With you in it."

CHAPTER SIXTY EIGHT

Bookseller Lane was quiet this time of night in Old Towne. Assistant Chief Constable Duncan was home late as usual, his days were long. The investigation into the attack on Abram Farmer was taking up a lot of his time. He resented having been thrust into this mess by Little Harry Adjudicator.

Now Harry was gone, with Duncan left holding the bag. But he'd get through it. He knew procedure and if he played this by the book, things should turn out fine.

Wearily, he climbed the stairs and unlocked the door to his third floor flat. It wasn't much, but it was home and he could afford it. He liked the quietness and old world gentility of Old Towne. It was a bit shabby and run down, but the buildings were beautiful, if faded. The riff raff weren't here because the action was all downtown. Here he could relax.

He shoved the door open and fumbled for the light. Extreme quiet greeted him, and his hand stalled on the switch. Hadn't he left the fan on? He always left the fan on this time of year, otherwise it got too stuffy in the room.

He waited, half expecting to be assaulted, but nothing happened. When he flicked the light, the room sprang into focus. A man sat on his sofa, his arms crossed, feet propped on Duncan's footstool.

He was dressed in an expensive suit and tie, his long brown hair carefully groomed. He was handsome in a hard boned way, his features bold and even, expression guarded.

When he had Duncan's attention, he straightened and casually shot his cuffs. "You must be Duncan. I'm DuSatoy, Sable Maude's business partner. Good to finally meet you."

Duncan was speechless. Maude's business partner? Maude was dead. He'd heard all about it from Cownden Lanser, who'd gotten the story straight from Abe Farmer. And Abe Farmer had been there when the mountain lion attacked.

Duncan stepped inside and closed the door. Carefully he laid his bag on the counter and turned to face his visitor, a sardonic expression on his face. "I don't imagine you're his business partner now. Maude is dead."

"Dead?" DuSatoy snickered. "Is that what's been reported? Well, not so, sir. Sable Maude is very much alive and business is booming. We need your help."

From the Author -

I love to write and my readers are the life blood of why I write. If you enjoyed this book, please consider giving a review.

You can contact me at my website
www.sylviegrayson.com,
leave a review at Amazon
or email me at sylviegraysonauthor@gmail.com.
All comments are appreciated.

Sylvie Grayson

THE LAST WAR: BOOK THREE

Emperor Carlton has been backed into a corner. He may hold some land in Legitamia where he marshalls his troops and plans his expansion, but the skirmishes they've launched haven't been successful. However, he has bigger ideas aimed at overthrowing everything Khandarken has cobbled together since the final days of the Last War.

Cownden Lanser, Chief Constable of Khandarken, is a very private man who has a close connection to the Old Empire that he doesn't divulge to just anyone. Although he's dedicated to his position in Khandarken, things are not what they seem in the rank and file of the police. Something has to be done.

Selanna Nettles is a sookie, trained in Legitamia but working near her family home in the Western Territory. She treats the dispossessed and the injured mine workers, helping them heal. When she meets Cownden Lanser, her life takes a startling turn. He hires her to accompany him to a set of meetings in Legitamia, and she leaps at the chance.

Yet when the Emperor makes Cownden an offer, can he refuse? It might be everything he's secretly imagined for himself.

...a whole new world with a lot of the same old problems - sci/fi fantasy at its best created with a sure hand and enormous immagination...

Khandarken Rising,
The Last War: Book One

The Emperor has been defeated. New countries have arisen from the ashes of the old Empire. The citizens swear they will never need to fight again after that long and painful war.

Bethlehem Farmer is helping her brother Abram run Farmer Holdings in south Khandarken after their father died in the final battles. She is looking after the dispossessed, keeping the farm productive and the talc mine working in the hills behind their land. But when Abram takes a trip with Uncle Jade into the northern territory and disappears without a trace, she's left on her own. Suddenly things are not what they seem and no one can be trusted.

Major Dante Regiment is sent by his father, the General of Khandarken, to find out what the situation is at Farmer Holdings. What he sees shakes him to the core and fuels his grim determination to protect Bethlehem at all cost, even with his life.

Other books by Sylvie Grayson

...Contemporary suspense, romance and attempted murder...

When Chloe Bowman's husband disappears, never did she imagine that in the midst of the search to find him, she'd discover she didn't really know this man at all. She's left alone with her young son and a time bomb on her hands. Lurking in the shadows is the mysterious Rainman.

Police Detective Ross Cullen was already investigating Chloe's husband when he disappeared. But the deeper Ross digs the less he knows, and the more he's attracted to the young wife as she struggles to put her life back together. Can Ross break through the Rainman's disguises to solve the case so he can be with Chloe?

... I loved this book. I've found my new favourite author...

Katy Dalton worked hard to save her money. But then her job disappears and she needs it back, everything Bruno has loaned to Rome Trucking. Then Bruno stops answering his phone and bad things start to happen.

Brett Rome is frustrated. The last thing he wants is to leave a promising career in hockey to come home and run his ailing father's trucking business. What he discovers is a company teetering on the very edge of bankruptcy and a young woman demanding the return of her money.

But danger lurks in the form of Bruno's dubious associates. What secret are they hiding and why are they willing to kill Katy? Can Brett put this broken picture back together, and is Katy part of the solution or the problem?

Interesting characters, family conflicts and divided loyalties make this a book that kept me up half the night...

When Emily Drury takes a job as legal counsel for an import-export company, she does it because she needs to get away to safety.

Joe Tanner counts himself lucky. He's charmed a successful big city lawyer into heading up the legal department of his rapidly expanding business. But why would a beautiful woman who could easily make partner in a high profile legal firm give it all up to come to Bonnie? As Joe realizes she has become essential to his happiness, his first reaction is to protect her. But he doesn't know the whole story.

Can Emily trust him enough to divulge her secret? Will he learn what he needs to know in time to stop the avalanche that's gaining speed as it races down the hill toward her?

... a fiercely professional young woman, a solitary guy who finds her very attractive and a wildcard assistant - throw in a few unsavory characters, and I couldn't put it down ...

ABOUT THE AUTHOR

Sylvie Grayson loves to write about suspense, romance and attempted murder, in both contemporary and science fiction/fantasy. She has lived most of her life in British Columbia, Canada in spots ranging from Vancouver Island on the west coast to the North Peace River country and the Kootenays in the beautiful interior. She spent a one year sojourn in Tokyo, Japan.

She has been an English language instructor, a nightclub manager, an auto shop bookkeeper and a lawyer. Now she works part time as the owner of a small company, and writes when she finds the time.

She is a wife and mother and still loves to travel. She lives on the coast of the Pacific Ocean with her husband on a small patch of land near the sea that they call home.

If you enjoyed this book, please consider giving a review.

Sylvie loves to hear from her readers, you can visit her at her website – **www.sylviegrayson.com** or find her on Facebook.